Praise for Donna Grant's Sons of Texas novels

"This first-class thrill ride will leave readers eager for more." —*Publishers Weekly* (starred review) on *The Hero*

"Dangerous, steamy, and full of intrigue." —*Booklist* on *The Hero*

"Grant's dizzying mix of danger and romance dazzles . . . off-the-charts chemistry and a breath-stealing plot." —*Publishers Weekly* (starred review) on *The Protector*

"Non-stop thrills and hot romance drive this story at a breakneck speed." —*BookPage* on *The Protector*

"Grant really packs on the intrigue and non-stop thrills, while the romance is steamy hot." —*RT Book Reviews* on *The Protector*

The Dark Kings series

"Loaded with subtle emotions, sizzling chemistry, and some provocative thoughts on the real choices [Grant's] characters are forced to make as they choose their loves for eternity." —*RT Book Reviews* (4 stars)

"Vivid images, intense details, and enchanting characters grab the reader's attention and [don't] let go." —*Night Owl Reviews* (Top Pick)

The Dark Warrior series

"The world of the Immortal Warriors is a thoroughly engaging one, blending powerful ancient gods, fiery desire, and touchingly human love, which readers will surely want to revisit."   —*RT Book Reviews*

"[Grant] blends ancient gods, love, desire, and evil-doers into a world you will want to revisit over and over again."
    —*Night Owl Reviews*

"Sizzling love scenes and engaging characters."
    —*Publishers Weekly*

"Ms. Grant mixes adventure, magic, and sweet love to create the perfect romance[s]."   —*Single Title Reviews*

The Dark Sword series

"Grant creates a vivid picture of Britain centuries after the Celts and Druids tried to expel the Romans, deftly merging magic and history. The result is a wonderfully dark, delightfully well-written [series]. Readers will eagerly await the next Dark Sword book."
    —*RT Book Reviews*

"Another fantastic series that melds the paranormal with the historical life of the Scottish highlander in this arousing and exciting adventure."   —*Bitten By Books*

"These are some of the hottest brothers around in paranormal fiction."   —*Nocturne Romance Reads*

"Will keep readers spellbound."
    —*Romance Reviews Today*

ALSO BY DONNA GRANT

A
COWBOY
LIKE YOU

DONNA GRANT

St. Martin's Paperbacks

This is a work of fiction. All of the characters, organizations, and events portrayed in this novel are either products of the author's imagination or are used fictitiously.

First published in the United States by St. Martin's Paperbacks, an imprint of St. Martin's Publishing Group.

A COWBOY LIKE YOU

For information, address St. Martin's Publishing Group, 120 Broadway, New York, NY 10271.

www.stmartins.com

ISBN: 978-1-250-25004-9

Our books may be purchased in bulk for promotional, educational, or business use. Please contact your local bookseller or the Macmillan Corporate and Premium Sales Department at 1-800-221-7945, ext. 5442, or by email at MacmillanSpecialMarkets@macmillan.com.

Printed in the United States of America

St. Martin's Paperbacks edition / December 2019

10 9 8 7 6 5 4 3 2 1

To all the men and women who protect our
streets and cities—Thank You!
This book is for all of you, for protecting us,
for putting your lives on the line each
and every day.

Acknowledgments

A very special thanks to everyone at SMP for this book—from the art department, to marketing, to publicity, to production. I'd also like to thank Mara Delgado-Sanchez for being such a big help for so many things. It goes without saying that a shout-out is directed to my editor, Monique Patterson.

More thanks to my agent, Natanya Wheeler, who is always so supportive in whatever direction I happen to be headed in.

A special thanks to Scott Silveri for answering my many questions regarding sheriffs and their roles.

As always, thanks to my children. And to G.

Hats off to my incredible readers who have fallen for my cowboys!

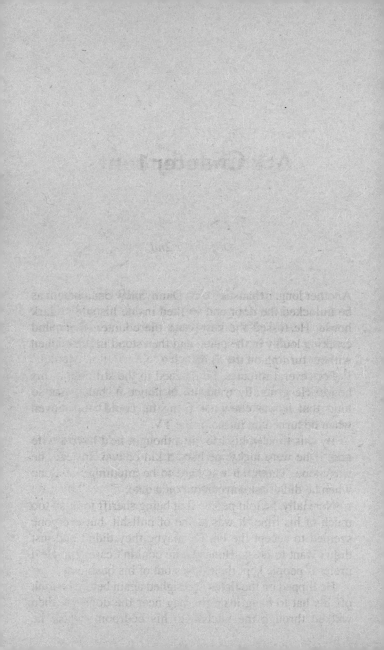

Chapter 1

December 2nd

Another long, exhausting day. Danny blew out a breath as he unlocked the door and walked inside his silent, dark house. He tossed the keys onto the counter, the sound cracking loudly in the quiet, and then stood in the kitchen without turning on the lights.

For several minutes, he listened to the stillness of his house. He generally tried not to notice it, but it was so loud that it was the only thing he could hear—even when he turned on music or the TV.

By this time in his life, he'd thought he'd have a wife and, if he were lucky, perhaps a kid or two. Instead, he was alone. Though it was hard to be anything but alone when he didn't ask anyone out on a date.

Normally, he told people that being sheriff took up too much of his time. It was a line of bullshit, but everyone seemed to accept the lie. Or maybe they didn't and just didn't want to press. Honestly, he couldn't care less. He'd prefer if people kept their noses out of his business.

He flipped on the lights and sighed again before he took off his hat to hang it on the peg near the door. He then walked through the kitchen to his bedroom, where he stopped beside his nightstand and removed his gun along with the shield that designated him as sheriff. Only then did he remove his jeans and the tan shirt with the county insignia on it.

Once he was in a pair of well-worn sweatpants that probably needed to be tossed in the garbage and a black tee, he returned to the kitchen and opened the fridge. He'd hoped to find something edible, but he soon realized that it had been over a week since he had bought groceries.

The only thing fit for consumption were the eggs. It would be easier to just jump in his truck and go get something, but he was so tired of eating out.

"Makes my decision on dinner easy," Danny mumbled to himself as he pulled out the carton.

He turned on some music to try to fill the void as he prepared to cook. He didn't want the eggs. In fact, he didn't want anything, but he needed food in his stomach before he reached for the bourbon sitting just to his left.

The funny thing was that he'd never been much of a drinker in high school or college. He'd had a beer or two here and there, but that was it. It wasn't until years later, working as a sheriff's deputy, that he found solace in alcohol and used it to help him cope—first, with the horrific crimes he saw, and secondly, the loneliness.

Danny didn't bother to sit. He ate the eggs standing up while listening to the radio. As soon as a Christmas song came on, he reached over and flicked off the device.

Christmas used to be his favorite time of year. Then he went into law enforcement. The worst crimes seemed to happen from Thanksgiving through New Year's, and each year it grew more and more difficult to deal with.

It was the first week of December, and already he'd had to deal with a suicide, a half-dozen domestic calls, and issue an Amber Alert for a one-year-old who had been kidnapped by her father because it wasn't the dad's year to have custody of her at Thanksgiving.

As soon as the meal was finished, he washed and dried his plate, fork, and pan, and then poured his first shot of bourbon. He used to try to take notice of how much he drank each night, but then he stopped caring.

He never got drunk. Just had enough to help him get to sleep without seeing the horrors of his job. The only problem was, it took more liquor to accomplish that each month. It was a good thing he lived alone, because if he didn't, he was sure that someone would step in and call him on just how much alcohol he consumed each night.

Danny kept his blinds closed so no one could see in. As an elected official, there was always someone out there trying to get dirt on him. Another reason he didn't date. It was just too damned complicated.

He downed his shot and decided to fill the glass with a double. Then he pushed the nearly empty bottle away and walked into the living area.

It was a sad room. The TV was rarely on. The leather sofa was six years old but looked brand new since he never sat in it. The only reason the place wasn't coated with inches of dust was because his aunt cleaned the house every other week. She was getting on in years, though, and he didn't feel right having her clean for him. She claimed she loved it and didn't need compensation, but after several fights, she'd finally relented to letting him pay her.

She always brought food over for him, too. She was a great cook, so he wasn't going to turn down anything she made. Danny was grateful that she never mentioned his bare fridge or pantry. The fact that she brought him meals said it all.

He walked to the window and separated two slats of

the blinds to peer into the darkness. The houses were lit up with various colored lights and yard decorations. But not his. Not one Christmas decoration could be found anywhere—inside or out.

In fact, he couldn't remember the last time he'd put up a tree. Why should he, when he was rarely home to enjoy it? It was just more work to put something up, only to take it down. It was easier to skip it altogether.

Danny looked down at the glass in his hand and the double shot he'd poured. He set the tumbler aside and walked to his bedroom. But once there, he didn't know what to do. It was too early to sleep, and lying in bed staring at the ceiling was something he saved for when he woke in the middle of the night. No use doing that now.

"Well, fuck," he murmured.

His stomach grumbled then. He winced because he knew he needed more food. Danny thought back over the day. He had stopped at the bakery to get breakfast but never managed to order anything because he had to intervene in a fight between two women who were arguing over the last blueberry donut.

Then, when he tried to leave to get some lunch, he'd ended up in a meeting with the local police chief, Ryan Wells, about a joint task force. By the time that was over, Danny hadn't been able to get away to get anything to eat. No wonder he was hungry.

But the thought of more eggs made his stomach turn.

He changed out of his sweats into another pair of jeans before slipping on his boots. After grabbing his coat, he slid his gun into the holster on his belt and put on his hat before he walked out of the house.

Just as he was shifting his truck into reverse, his phone rang. He was going to ignore it, but he glanced at the caller ID and saw his friend's name.

There was a genuine smile on his face when he answered. "Hey, Clayton."

Clayton East was one of the richest people in the county and owned a massive cattle ranch, but he was also one of the nicest men you could ever meet. Then Clayton went and married Abby Harper, who Danny had graduated with.

The moment Danny thought of his younger years, his memories turned to the girl he'd had a crush on. The one he'd never asked out. The one he still, to this day, thought about.

Was it still a crush all these years later? Maybe Danny should move on. Holding onto something that could never be wasn't healthy.

"Wanted to see what you were up to," Clayton said, the noise from others in the background coming through the phone. "Abby's been baking all day with the kids, and we're drowning in Christmas cookies. Brice, Naomi, Caleb, and Audrey are here, as well. Me and the boys have been on the grill cooking dinner. Thought you might want to join us."

The fact that Clayton invited him meant a lot to Danny. It was an invitation he got about once a month, and he usually accepted. There was something great about sitting at that huge table with Clayton and Abby, along with Abby's two younger brothers and their wives.

But Danny wasn't up for it tonight. He couldn't explain it, but he wanted to be alone. Which was stupid, because it was the loneliness that caused him to drink. This was different, though. He was in a funky mood, and the others would likely see and comment. Danny didn't want to lie, and he certainly didn't want to explain. It was better if he remained by himself.

"Sounds like a feast," Danny said with a chuckle.

Clayton laughed. "You know us. We can't fix a small meal, not when there are so many mouths to feed. My children are healthy eaters as well, so if there isn't enough, I'll have a mutiny on my hands. And I'm pretty sure Jace and Cooper will find their way over soon."

Danny shook his head and grinned because he knew that Caleb and Brice's friends would definitely be there. While not blood-related, Jace and Cooper were part of the East/Harper family simply because they were always around.

"I need to take a raincheck," Danny told him.

There was a beat of silence. "You good?"

It was Clayton's way of asking if he needed to be concerned. Many answers filled Danny's head, but in the end, he decided to go with honesty. "I'm making it."

The noise faded, and Danny knew Clayton most likely went into his office for some privacy. Then Clayton said, "I realize this time of year is hard. You know we're here for you, right?"

"I know."

"You can come over anytime. You don't need an invitation. You're family, Danny."

"I know, and I appreciate that. Truly."

Clayton went on as if Danny hadn't spoken. "You can take one of the horses for a ride. Hell, no doubt my kiddos will tackle you as soon as they see you. They adore you. And then there's Abby. She'll talk your ear off. And if none of that suits you, come out with me while I work. You can sit and do nothing."

"Thank you. I'll be sure and do that."

"You better," Clayton stated in a soft voice.

"I will," Danny promised.

They hung up, and Danny pulled out of his driveway and onto the road to head into town. He didn't intend to dine in anywhere, just swing by and get something. He wasn't in the mood to talk. It's what he did all day. But then again, his only other choice was to go back to an empty house.

After grabbing some grilled fish from a favorite restaurant, Danny decided to eat in his truck. He drove to the rest stop just outside of town, which also happened to have one of the best views around, and parked.

He turned on his favorite station and pulled out his food. It wasn't the first time he'd used the destination as a place to eat, and it wouldn't be his last. At least here, he wasn't at home, but he also wasn't in a restaurant with people who constantly wanted to talk to him about some issue or another.

It really was a conundrum. He loved his job, and that meant dealing with all the nuances that came with it.

He was nearly finished with his meal when a sleek red sports car pulled into a parking space four spots down. Danny craned his head to see the badge of the car since there wasn't another like it around.

"Alfa Romeo," he said to himself.

Curious, he looked it up on his phone and discovered that it was a 4C Spider. After perusing the details on the website, his attention turned back to the car.

The vehicle was still running but parked. No one had exited yet. The cop in him looked for signs of any movement inside, in case there was an argument that might escalate to physical violence, but he saw nothing.

Just a few minutes later, another set of headlights brightened the area as someone else pulled into the rest stop. Danny frowned. While the highway was nearly always busy, the rest stop didn't usually get a lot of attention.

The moment the headlights appeared, the driver of the sports car shut off the engine. It could all be just a coincidence, but Danny knew from experience that that was rarely the case.

He closed the food container and set it on the passenger seat. Then he made sure to have the station number ready to call as the new arrival—a white Audi—parked next to the Alfa Romeo, blocking Danny's view of the sports car.

The driver's side door of the Audi opened, and a man exited. He glanced over at Danny, but since his car was turned off and his windows were tinted, the man could see nothing in the dark of night. The stranger shifted his attention to the sports car, staring at it for a long minute.

Danny thought the man might be admiring it since it was a nice-looking car. But that thought shattered the moment the man slammed his hand on the hood of the vehicle before slowly walking to stand in front of it.

"You know better than to run from me," the man said in a cold, violent voice.

Danny had seen enough physical disputes to know what was about to happen. He dialed the station and let them know where he was, what was happening, and to send a deputy immediately. Then he withdrew the weapon he always wore on his hip and slowly opened his door to slip out.

Chapter 2

She had the worst taste in men.

Skylar's heart pounded as she stared through the windshield at Matt, the guy she'd made the mistake of not only dating but also living with for the past three months.

"I said, get out."

He didn't yell. He didn't need to. Skylar knew what that tone meant—and it wasn't good. When she didn't move, he slammed his fist onto her hood. She saw the dent, but she didn't care. That could be hammered out. Another broken bone wouldn't be fixed so easily.

She'd dated Matt for nine months before moving in with him, trying to make sure she knew everything about him. Not once had he shown such aggression. Not until she was in his house, that is. Once she was there, he seemingly changed overnight.

Sadly, this wasn't the first time she'd tried to leave. But this had been the one time that she actually thought she might get away.

"Skylar," Matt said through clenched teeth, his anger palpable.

She briefly thought about starting the car and running

him over, but despite the pain he'd inflicted on her, she would never be able to live with herself if she killed him.

But what other option did she have? If she got out of the car, he'd take her back to their house. No doubt he'd dole out his particular brand of emotional and verbal abuse here, but when they were behind the walls of his house, he would level his fists on her.

He never hit her in the face. Never left a mark that could be seen unless she was naked. He kept his blows to spots that could be hidden by her clothes. He was smart that way.

"You know better than to get me this angry," Matt said as he walked around to her door. "You know what happens next."

Yes, she did. She tried to reach for her purse where she kept her gun, but the window broke, glass raining down all around her. She screamed in surprise, even as she valiantly tried to get her weapon, only to wince as Matt's hands tangled in her hair and yanked her backward.

"You're mine, Skylar," he whispered in her ear as he tried to drag her through the broken car window.

Her eyes locked on her purse as she reached back to try and relieve some of the pain of the pulled hair on her scalp. If only she'd managed to wrap her fingers around the pistol. She'd had her concealed carry license for years, but Matt had such an aversion to guns that he'd asked her to get rid of it before moving in with him. She'd stupidly acquiesced.

The first thing she'd done on her way out of Houston was to stop by her friend's house and buy back the weapon. Skylar didn't want to shoot Matt any more than she wanted to run him over, but she wasn't going back with him.

Ever.

Suddenly, a booming voice broke the silence. "Freeze. Hands in the air."

Skylar's gaze jerked to the side to see a silhouette of a man with a gun pointed at Matt. She couldn't make out the man's face since his cowboy hat shadowed his features, even with the many lights in the rest area.

Matt released her and raised his hands, but his gaze never left Skylar. She sank back into her seat and rubbed her sore head while glaring at Matt.

"It's just a little disagreement between me and my girlfriend, officer," Matt said.

"Sheriff," the man corrected him. "I heard—and saw—enough to know it's much more than just a little disagreement. You threatened her, and you assaulted her."

Matt's lips turned up in a confident smile that he showed Skylar before he wiped it from his face as he turned to the sheriff. "You're right. This is much more than a disagreement. She stole something of mine."

"Is that so? And what might that be?" the sheriff asked, sarcasm in his voice.

Skylar contemplated turning over the ignition and getting the hell out of Dodge while she could, but that wouldn't put her in a favorable light with the sheriff. And no doubt there were deputies on the way.

"That's between me and her," Matt said, jerking his head in her direction.

The sheriff didn't look her way. Thankfully, he also didn't ask her to step from the vehicle. She wasn't sure her legs would hold her at this point. Fear and relief mixed together inside of her, and the potent mix made her nauseous.

"Put your hands on the hood of the car," the sheriff ordered Matt.

Skylar's heart hammered wildly against her ribs as her hand slid into her purse once more. The fear that had gripped her when she spotted the headlights following her was diminishing slowly, thanks to the arrival of the sheriff. Not that she believed the nightmare was over. It was far from it, but at least now, she had a chance of getting away. Could possibly even get a protective order against Matt.

Not that she believed a restraining order would keep someone like him away. She understood now why someone as handsome and successful as Matt had been single.

"I'm not going to repeat myself."

Her fingers tightened on the butt of her pistol at the sheriff's words. She knew Matt. He didn't like authority of any kind, especially cops. The only thing keeping him from lashing out was the weapon pointed at him.

Matt slowly turned and leaned over, placing his hands on the hood of her car. His blue eyes locked on her as he mouthed, *"You've made a big mistake, honey."*

Skylar was thinking of all the ways Matt could retaliate, but then she heard the sirens of approaching cruisers. The slight grin Matt directed at her slipped as he looked at the red and blue lights as two police cars raced into the rest area. One parked behind her, and the other pulled in behind Matt's vehicle.

In a blink, the deputies were out of the cars and approaching with guns drawn. One tossed the sheriff a set of handcuffs.

Skylar had to bite back a smile when they pushed Matt down onto his chest on the hood of her car as the sheriff read him his Miranda rights. Then Matt was put into one of the deputy's cars and driven away.

She hadn't said anything to anyone yet. Just watched as the sheriff spoke to the remaining deputy, pointing to

Matt's car. Skylar still couldn't see the sheriff's face. She wanted to thank him for helping and being so calm, but she wasn't sure her voice would work, so she remained inside her car.

She released her hold on her pistol and covered her face with her hands. After a few minutes, she took a deep breath and lowered her arms. Her gaze darted to the left, and she saw the sheriff staring at her.

He'd given her all the time he could. Now, it was her turn to talk. Skylar wished she could make the entire situation with Matt go away as if it had never happened, but that wasn't how life worked.

She opened the door and got out of the car into the cold. "Thank you, sheriff. I appreciate the assistance. I also want to let you know that I have a pistol in my purse, along with a concealed carry permit."

There was a beat of silence as the sheriff stared at her. She stood beneath one of the many lights. The glow illuminated her, even while he was still cloaked in shadow. She licked her lips nervously. Skylar wrapped her arms around herself, wishing that she'd grabbed a coat before she left Matt's, but then again, she hadn't been thinking about her things. She'd been more concerned with escaping with her life.

"Skylar?"

She frowned at the question in the sheriff's voice. Matt had said her name. Surely, he'd heard it. "Yes," she replied. "I'm Skylar Long."

He took a step toward her and removed his hat. "It's been a long time."

For an instant, she couldn't move. She knew those hazel eyes and that dark brown hair. It had been years since she'd last seen Danny, but he'd always been one to come to someone's rescue. His shoulders had widened, his cheekbones were sharper, the jaw more defined, but he still looked as fit as he had in high school—which was the last time she'd seen him.

"Danny," she said. To her horror, her face crumpled as relief surged through her. Because she knew that if anyone could protect her, it was Danny Oldman.

She turned her head away while trying to regain her composure. She wasn't the type to cry easily, but the emotions that welled up inside her when she realized it was Danny who had saved her were too much.

"Here," he said as he draped something across her shoulders.

She realized that it was his coat, and she gratefully slipped her arms into the sleeves. "Thank you."

They stared at each other for several seconds. He didn't seem fazed by the cold temperature, but then again, Danny had always been a stoic one. He made friends easily because everyone liked him, but he was very selective in who he allowed close.

Unfortunately, Skylar hadn't been in that select circle. Few were, actually. But she'd had friends who were close to Danny, and they always spoke highly of him. Danny had been nice to everyone. They'd shared many classes together in school, and there wasn't a day that went by that he didn't give her a smile and speak to her.

"Sheriff," the deputy said as he walked up.

Skylar moved back a step as the two men drew close to speak. She could still feel the warmth of Danny's body from his jacket as she huddled inside it. For the first time in months, her thoughts weren't on how she could get through a day without angering Matt. She was finally free. She lifted her face to the night sky and closed her eyes.

The sound of a car door drew her attention. She saw

the deputy drive away, and then Danny walked to her. He wasn't exactly frowning, but he wasn't smiling either.

"What is it?" she asked.

"Matt has been arrested for domestic assault."

Skylar pulled the coat tighter around her. "What does that mean?"

"Well, it depends. Has he been arrested before?"

She shrugged. "Not that I'm aware."

Danny pressed his lips together. "If he has no prior convictions, he could get off with just a fine."

Skylar nodded, the brief taste of freedom she had felt slipping away and dissipating into the night sky like smoke.

"Is this the first time he's been physical with you?"

It was hard to hold eye contact with Danny. Skylar felt like a fool for being in such a relationship. But she was trying to get away and start her life fresh. "No."

"Did you report it?"

She closed her eyes in shame and shook her head.

"Many don't," he said after a beat of silence. "It doesn't change anything. I saw what happened here tonight, and there are also CCTV cameras. They recorded everything."

Her eyes opened to meet Danny's. "That's good." She paused, swallowing. "I should have reported it. I always swore if anything like that happened to me, I would. I used to talk about how I didn't understand women who stayed in such relationships. I used to say that all they had to do was get away. I was so damn naïve."

"If you don't mind me asking, how long has this been going on?"

"Three months. This is my third time trying to leave."

"You've tried. That's something."

Leave it to Danny to make her feel better. She shot

him a grateful smile. "The first time, I made the mistake of telling him I was leaving. That was just three weeks after moving in with him. We dated for nine months, and he'd never exhibited any kind of violence with his fists or his words before that."

"I gather you didn't get far the first time."

"He hit me once and swore it was a one-time thing. That was the second week we lived together. Then it happened again because I brought home the wrong brand of beer. I picked myself up off the floor and stepped over the smashed six-pack of bottles. I was angry and told him that he'd never lay a hand on me again, that it was over. I got my purse and headed to the door. Except I never made it. I woke up in the hospital."

Skylar saw Danny's lips part, and she shook her head. "No, I didn't tell anyone what really happened. He doted on me, and with the pain in my head and the medication they had me on, he convinced me that I'd slipped on the beer and fallen and hit my head. It wasn't until I was back home, and the pain meds wore off that I remembered what'd happened. I packed a bag and got to my car. He followed me, crying and telling me that he'd made a mistake, that the nine months before was who he really was."

"He asked for another chance," Danny guessed.

Skylar nodded. "And I stupidly gave it to him."

"You weren't stupid. You wanted to believe him."

"He'd already hit me twice. I should've realized."

Danny gave her a reassuring grin. "It's okay to forgive yourself, you know. We aren't perfect, and you had a good relationship before. You had every right to think that those two incidents were out of the norm."

"Perhaps. But after that, he became obsessive and possessive, wanting to know where I was at any given moment."

"He was worried you'd try to leave."

"That was another red flag that I ignored. I'd had obsessive boyfriends before. I thought I could handle him, reassure him that I was his. I was wrong. We got through nearly two weeks before he hit me again."

Danny folded his arms over his chest. "What was it this time?"

"My boss called me. Matt immediately believed that we were having an affair."

Chapter 3

Of all the people Danny had thought he might run into, he'd never in a million years expected to see Skylar Long again. If he believed in destiny, he'd almost accept that his thinking of her earlier had brought her straight to him.

One of the things he remembered about her was how she'd wanted to get out of their town and move to a big city. Her sights had been set on Houston or even Dallas. She had wanted to get lost in all the people.

Many of his classmates had spoken about leaving their little town, but few did. And many who left eventually returned. Not Skylar. She'd gotten out, and he'd figured she would stay gone forever. After all, her parents had moved about ten years ago, which meant there was no reason for her to return.

Yet, here she was. And more stunning than ever.

She had been Danny's crush from the time they were in grade school. Skylar had always been a free spirit. She had confidence that most girls her age lacked. It wasn't arrogance, simply a belief in herself that came through in everything she did.

While beautiful, she had been a little reserved. She had run with the popular crowd, but she didn't wield that social level to degrade anyone or use it to her benefit like others had. She had been kind, and she wore her heart on her sleeve.

He and Skylar had been able to talk about anything. She was always open and engaging, but Danny had never pursued her as his girlfriend. He'd never thought he was good enough for her, not when so many of his other friends had wooed her.

Danny looked at her. The harsh light of the streetlamp above them couldn't diminish her beauty. Her golden blond hair was pulled up haphazardly with strands falling around her face and neck. But her large, azure eyes still held more shock and fear than he liked.

She was on the petite side with curves in all the right places. Her lips were full, pouty even, and they made his blood heat just looking at them. Her skin had the dewy glow of a healthy lifestyle that made him want to reach out and run the pads of his fingers down her cheek to see if her skin was as velvety as it appeared.

Hearing her story earlier made him want to go find Matt and punch him a few times. Danny had never been so happy to be in the right place at the right time. He gave himself an inward shake to get back to the matter at hand.

"And what happened tonight?" Danny asked to get the final piece of the puzzle.

Skylar shrugged. "It was Matt's night out with friends. I made sure to keep to my same schedule, not doing anything that would alert him that I planned to leave. I waited an hour after he left before I grabbed an overnight bag and threw a few things in. I just wanted to get out. I didn't care about the rest of my stuff. I figured I could get it back later or replace it."

"It was a good decision. Things can be replaced. Your life can't. So, how did he figure out that you left?"

"I honestly don't know." Concern clouded her face. "He was gone, I know it. I even drove by the bar to make sure his car was there. Then I headed straight out of town."

This wasn't the first time Danny had dealt with a domestic situation like this, but he didn't like that he knew one of the parties involved. Mainly because he knew the odds of how such circumstances turned out.

Danny ran a hand down his face, his gut churning. "If he was gone from the house and at the bar, then he had to know you left somehow. Are there cameras in the residence?"

Her eyes widened, and her lips parted in shock. "I . . . I don't know. There could be. It sounds like something he'd do. He was adamant about me moving into his place. It was bigger than mine, even though mine was in a better location, so I agreed."

"What about tracking your car?"

She shook her head and shrugged her shoulders at the same time. "I wouldn't put anything past him."

"Does he always know what's going on in your life? People you've talked to, places you've been?"

"Yes."

"What about phone calls and texts? Does he ask you specifics about them?"

She frowned as she thought about his question. "He used to, but not anymore."

Danny figured as much.

Skylar's gaze sharpened on him. "Why? Do you think he installed some kind of spyware on my phone? Oh, God. He installed spyware on my phone."

"We'll get you a new one, and I'll have my guys look over your car to see if there's any kind of device."

Her eyes filled with tears that she hastily blinked away. "How did I get into such a situation?"

"It doesn't matter. What counts is that you're getting out of it. *If* that's what you want."

Her head bobbed up and down rapidly. "Yes. I knew I was getting away from him tonight, one way or another."

Danny recalled that she had said she had a handgun in her car. Not that he could blame her for having it, but he was happy she hadn't had to use it. "I'm glad you pulled in here."

"I wasn't going to. As soon as I thought the headlights were from a car like his, I thought it was just my imagination, that I was just scared and seeing things. Then something told me to pull in here and see if the vehicle followed. As soon as it did, I knew it was Matt. Why were you here?"

Danny lifted one shoulder and twisted his lips. "Eating dinner."

She blinked and looked around. "At a rest stop?"

"Yeah. Where were you headed?" he asked to change the subject. He didn't want to discuss his lack of a life, not when her situation was more important.

Skylar blew out a breath. "I don't know. I just got on the road and drove. I didn't even realize I was here until I saw the county sign five miles back."

"Is there anyone in town you can stay with?"

Her gaze dropped to the ground. "I didn't keep up with anyone here. I can stay at a hotel."

"That's the first place Matt will look for you when he gets out of jail. I could post a deputy to keep watch, but that's a temporary fix."

"I understand." Her gaze lifted to his, and she forced a smile that didn't reach her blue eyes. "You've been a great help tonight, but you've done enough. I'll figure something out."

Danny took a step toward her. "If you think I'm going to walk away, then you don't remember me at all."

"Oh, I remember you," she said. This time, the smile was the one he remembered from years earlier.

"Then let me help."

Worry crossed her face once more. "Matt is the kind that won't give up, isn't he?"

"Let's just say that I don't want to take any chances with him. I know the perfect place you can stay. It's a fortress unto itself. There's no way Matt can get anywhere near you there."

"Really?"

"Really."

Her relief was so great that her shoulders drooped with it. "I can follow you there."

"Your car is staying here. I'll have it towed to the station to be looked over. Get whatever you need. I'll drive you."

She clearly didn't need to be told twice. Skylar immediately opened the door and got her purse before popping the trunk and taking out an overnight bag. Danny took the bag from her and walked her to the passenger side of his truck, where he opened the door for her.

Once she was inside, he stowed her bag in the seat behind her and then walked around and got behind the wheel. That's when he realized that she was holding his dinner.

"Sorry about that," he said and tried to take it.

She pulled it out of his grasp, a smile on her face. "I think I can manage to hold this fine, sheriff."

He laughed and relented before starting the engine. He backed out, still unable to believe that the events of the night had led him to Skylar. If he hadn't believed in Fate before, he certainly did now. Especially since he had been thinking about her a lot these past few months.

"How long have you been sheriff?" she asked.

He glanced over to see her gaze on him. "About seven years."

"It suits you."

"Does it?" he asked with a chuckle.

She nodded. "Definitely. You were forever helping others. Did you always know you wanted to be a cop?"

"Actually, no. I kinda fell into it, but once I went through the academy, I knew this was where I belonged."

"And sheriff? Did you always want to be in this position?"

He scratched his chin and considered her question. "I knew it was something I'd eventually try for, but I didn't expect it so soon. Again, I fell into it. I didn't anticipate winning. I don't think anyone was as surprised as I was when the results came in."

"Oh, Danny, you can't honestly believe that," she said with a laugh.

He frowned as he looked her way. "Why do you say that?"

"Because you have a way about you that makes people feel safe. You're not only likable, but you also have a strong personality that works well for your job. The criminals know not to mess with you, and the victims know they can trust you."

"Thank you," he murmured, unsettled by her praise.

She tsked. "Always so humble. Is it any wonder you were voted the most likable in our class? Everyone wanted to be your friend, and every girl wanted to be your girlfriend."

He didn't believe that for a second, because if that

were true, Skylar would've been his. Or maybe that was his fault since he hadn't tried to win her.

Danny couldn't believe how much he was enjoying being with Skylar, and when the East Ranch came into view, he actually considered driving past it just to be with her a little longer. It was a stupid thought, especially after everything she'd been through.

"Holy shit," she said as they drove along the road and the miles of fence. "The East Ranch is still going strong, huh?"

He briefly cut his eyes to her as he slowed the truck and turned into the drive. "Yep."

Her head snapped to him. "You're taking me here?"

"Clayton and his wife are my closest friends. You can trust them."

"Are you sure I won't be putting them out?"

"I'll give you thirty seconds with them for you to come to that conclusion on your own," he said as he parked behind the other vehicles.

"There are a lot of trucks here."

He turned off the ignition as he looked at her. "Do you remember Abby Harper?"

"I can't place the face, but the name sounds familiar. Did she graduate with us?"

"She did. She raised her two younger brothers, Brice and Caleb. When she married Clayton, her brothers came to live here with them. They've since started a horse ranch of their own and found their partners. Brice is with a photographer named Naomi, and Caleb married an equine vet, Audrey. Jace and Cooper, two of Caleb and Brice's friends, are also inside, so their trucks are here, as well."

Skylar pressed her lips together as she looked toward the huge mansion. "I've always wanted to see the inside of this house."

"They're good people," he assured her.

Her head swung back to him, and she smiled. "If you say they are, then I'll trust that."

"Good. You ready to meet them?"

She took a deep breath and released it. "Yes, but let's leave my bag until we have time to tell them what's going on. I don't want to assume anything."

Danny chuckled but relented. "You've been in the big city too long if you've forgotten the hospitality out here."

"That's for certain."

"Where did you go, anyway?"

She lifted one shoulder. "Houston."

"Is it all you hoped it would be?"

"That and more," she replied with a wide grin.

Danny didn't know why her words soured him. Skylar wasn't meant for small towns. She was meant to shine brightly in the city where she obviously had created a good life.

He opened the door and walked around the truck to help her out. Together, they made their way up to the back of the house, but before he could get to the porch, the door opened and Brody, Clayton and Abby's middle child, came running out. He launched himself at Danny.

He managed to catch the seven-year-old, and swung him up into his arms. "Oomph. I think you're getting too big for this."

Brody grinned at him. "Never, Uncle Danny. Momma said you'd come, even after Pop said you declined. Momma's always right."

"Be sure to go tell your father that," Abby said from the doorway. She wore a bright smile, showering both him and Skylar with it.

Brody wiggled free and rushed into the house, telling everyone that Danny was there. Danny cleared his throat and put his hand on Skylar's back. He didn't get a chance to say anything.

Abby held out her hand to Skylar and said, "I'm Abby. Come on inside. Would you like something to eat or drink? I've got plenty."

Abby turned and walked into the house, waving them inside. Danny looked at Skylar, who glanced his way and said, "I see what you mean."

Chapter 4

To have gone from a nightmare to being surrounded by laughter, good food, and people Skylar would have no problem calling friends seemed too good to be true. But she knew she was in the right place.

Skylar wrapped her hands around the warm mug of chai and slid her eyes to Danny. On either side of him were two of Clayton and Abby's children—Brody and Wynter. Hope, their youngest, was only three years old and already tucked into bed for the night.

Skylar liked how relaxed Danny was. He seemed at home with the Easts and Harpers, and the easy way they all talked with each other proved how close they were.

"You knew Momma when she was a little girl?" Wynter asked Skylar when there was a break in the conversation.

Skylar glanced at Abby before she smiled at the little girl, who had the blond hair of her father and eyes that often shifted from blue to green. "I remember your mother, yes."

Abby took pity on Skylar and told Wynter, "You know how you have all the different groups in your school?"

Wynter nodded.

"Well, it was the same in ours. Skylar and I weren't in the same group. I knew her, and she was always friendly."

Skylar was relieved to hear that she hadn't been rude to Abby. That would've been really awkward. She smiled at Abby, wishing that she had known her back in school. Abby seemed the type of person to always have her friends' backs.

Loyalty wasn't something Skylar had with those she called *friends*. Not since she'd left and moved to Houston, that is.

Brody leaned forward slightly and caught Danny's attention. "Did you know Miss Skylar?"

"I sure did," Danny said with a smile.

Wynter's face furrowed in a frown. "But you knew Momma, too."

"That's because Danny was friends with everyone," Skylar told the children. "He was part of all the groups."

Brody nodded slowly and turned his head to his father. "That's what you told us to do."

"That's right," Clayton said as he and Abby shared a smile.

"Can we hear some stories about Uncle Danny?" Wynter asked Skylar.

Suddenly, Caleb and Brice got to their feet, each grabbing one of the kids and hauling them over their shoulders. The children squealed with laughter and held still as their parents kissed them goodnight.

Skylar was so intent on watching Abby's brothers lovingly take the kids up the stairs to put them to bed that she didn't realize Danny was in deep conversation with Jace and Cooper until she looked his way. The two men's faces were set as they gave him a nod and rose to their feet.

Cooper was the first to shoot her a brief smile. "It was nice to meet you, ma'am. I'm sure we'll talk again soon."

"Ma'am," Jace told her, touching the brim of his cowboy hat that he'd settled on top of his head.

Clayton pushed off the sofa. "I'll walk you two out."

Skylar caught Danny's gaze. One side of his lips turned up in a grin that made her smile in response. "Everything all right?"

"It sure is."

She couldn't help but wonder if his conversation with Jace and Cooper had something to do with Matt. Neither of the men was a deputy, but they were close friends with Danny, so it stood to reason that they would be willing to help. Was Danny that worried?

Or was she that wound up after everything that she was reading too much into things? For all she knew, the three of them had been setting up a poker night.

"Get used to it."

Skylar turned her head to look at Audrey. The equine vet, with her golden brown skin and hair and eyes, was a beauty to be sure. "What do you mean?"

Naomi chuckled and tucked a strand of her wheat-colored hair behind her ear. "The men always band together when there's an issue."

None of this was said in a hushed tone, and with Danny the only male left in the room, Skylar looked to him. He shrugged but didn't give her a reply.

It was Abby who said, "Danny has a lot of power as sheriff, but there are other things that those of us who don't wear a badge can do."

"I see." Skylar swallowed and took a drink of the tea as she went suddenly cold from the inside out.

"No one can get to you here," Abby continued. "With the security system Clayton set up, and our employees, you're safe, Skylar. I promise."

She slid her gaze to Abby. "And I'm eternally grateful to you and Clayton for that, but I can't stay here forever."

"Why not?" Abby asked with a smile. "Have you seen the size of this house? You could be on one end, and I'd never see you."

Everyone laughed, but Skylar was already thinking about the future and what she was going to do.

"Why don't Naomi and I go get your things in Houston?" Audrey offered.

Abby sat forward, her eyes wide as she said, "I'll be going, as well."

Danny blew out a breath. "All three of you are insane if you think your men will let you go without them."

Abby quirked a brow as she shot Danny a quelling look. "I don't need my husband's permission to help a friend."

"Depends on if your life will be put in danger," Clayton said as he walked up and resumed his seat beside Abby.

"We offered to get Skylar's things in Houston," Audrey told Clayton.

He twisted his lips as he put his hand on Abby's leg. "I think it's a good idea, though I'd feel better if I, Brice, or Caleb went with you three."

"I can't ask any of y'all to do that," Skylar said.

Naomi shot her a wide smile. "That's the great thing about it. You didn't ask. We offered."

"Don't worry, Skylar. We got you on this," Audrey said.

Skylar wasn't sure what to say. She hadn't wanted to involve her parents in any of this, and she didn't trust any of her friends in Houston to actually get her things from Matt. But those in the room with her now . . . she wholeheartedly believed they would come through for her.

"Thank you," she said, her throat tightening with emotion.

She found her gaze snagged by Danny's. The last thing she should do is latch on to him. He'd just been doing his job. Though she wasn't sure any other person in his position would've taken her to their friends' house to keep her safe.

And *that's* why she knew she couldn't allow herself to become attached to him. Now that she was safe—at least, relatively—Danny would go back to doing his job. She knew he'd check in on her, but that's all she expected him to do. He was the sheriff, after all. He had other responsibilities.

She was just some old friend from high school that had gotten herself into trouble.

But Skylar knew that had Danny not been there at that rest stop, there was a good chance she wouldn't be alive right now. She would've fought with everything she had to get to her gun, but it would've been a long shot.

Even if she had gotten hold of the weapon, she knew it would have sent Matt into a rage, and she would've had to fire it. She was an excellent shot, so she wasn't worried about hitting her target. Because if she aimed her weapon at someone, then it was because she was protecting herself.

But then she would've had to deal with the consequences. Not just Matt's death, but also the authorities and everything else. Given the fact that there was no paper trail of the many times Matt had beaten her, Skylar knew it would have taken a lot to prove that she'd only been protecting herself.

The many scenarios played out in her head, and none of them ended well for her. Sure, Matt would have been out of her life, but the repercussions would have rippled throughout her life.

At least now, she had a chance. Danny had given her that.

His brows briefly snapped together as he gave her a questioning look. She shook her head and tried to smile, but her lips wouldn't obey her.

The next thing she knew, the others rose and left the room. She watched them go before looking at Danny. "Did I say something?"

"They're giving you a few minutes. They realize you've had a trying night. There were a lot of people here, and everyone made sure to keep the conversation going."

For her, she realized. None of those people knew her. Sure, Danny and Abby might remember her from school, but none of them really knew her—or she, them. Yet they had gone out of their way to comfort her.

Emotions swarmed her again, and to her embarrassment, her eyes filled with tears. She hastily blinked them away and looked anywhere but at Danny.

"It's going to be okay now," he told her.

She nodded, but the more she fought the tears, the more they grew. One fell down her cheek. She hastily wiped it away, but another followed, and then another.

The mug of tea was taken from her, which allowed her to bury her face in her hands. She was so focused on trying to get herself under control that she didn't realize that Danny had moved to sit next to her until his arms came around her.

She immediately turned to him and wrapped her arms around him. He said nothing, merely held her. And that's all she needed.

Thankfully, the tears dried quickly. Yet she remained in his arms for a heartbeat or two longer, simply because it felt so good. Reluctantly, she drew back. His hands stayed on her, slowly moving down her arms until he stopped when their fingers touched.

"How long do I have until Matt is released?" she asked.

"He's already called an attorney, but I'm sure he'll be sitting in the jail, waiting to talk to the judge."

"You're sure he'll be in jail?" she asked.

Danny drew in a deep breath. "It depends on his lawyer. I've seen great lawyers get people off felonies, and I've seen bad lawyers get their clients the maximum sentence."

Skylar squeezed his hand. "I see. The time will allow Abby, Naomi, and Audrey to get to Houston and get my things. Most everything I have is in storage. Matt didn't like any of my furniture or pictures, so it's only clothes and such at his place. And, frankly, I couldn't care less about any of that."

"It's yours," Danny said. "The items should be returned. Will you go back to Houston?"

She'd been thinking about that since Matt had been arrested, but she didn't have an answer. "I don't know. My life is there. I've got a good job, but it isn't like I couldn't find another one. I need to find a new place to live anyway."

"You should get a protective order."

"I do want one, even though I know it's not much help if he shows up."

Worry filled Danny's hazel eyes. "I know men like Matt. He won't let you go easily. Especially now that he's been arrested."

"No, he won't." That fear is what kept her gut knotted so fiercely. "It doesn't seem fair that I should have to uproot my life because he won't let me go."

"There are few things in life that are fair, but I'd rather see you uprooted and alive than the alternative," Danny told her.

Skylar saw the gold flecks in his hazel eyes and discovered that she didn't want to look away. "I know how differently tonight could've turned out had you not been at that rest stop."

"Don't think about that. You're free of him. Think on that."

"Am I really free?" She shook her head. "We both know I've got a long road ahead of me. I've watched movies, Danny. I know the extent that some women have gone to with identity changes and moving across the country to escape their abusive partners. If the man really wants to find her, he always does."

Danny let out a long sigh. "I wish I could tell you that you're wrong."

"I don't want to be one of those women always looking over my shoulder, fearful that Matt will be there waiting to hurt me. I did this to myself, though. I should've reported him the first time he did it. If only I had gone to the police."

"You should've taken pictures."

Skylar couldn't believe she'd forgotten. She rose and looked through her purse. When she returned, she handed her cell phone to Danny with a file of various pictures and dates of when he'd hurt her.

Danny looked through them, then slowly raised his gaze to her. "This will definitely help your case."

Chapter 5

December 3rd

Sleep was always a testy mistress, but last night, the bitch had been nowhere to be seen. Not that Danny expected anything different after arresting Matt and discovering that it was Skylar he'd helped.

Danny strode into the police station, his nerves rubbed raw. Hearing Skylar's story was one thing. Seeing the photos was another animal altogether. After all the things he'd seen in his career, it shouldn't have bothered him so much.

But it did.

It was the only thing he saw each time he closed his eyes. Skylar's bruised ribs, arms, legs, and hips, and other injuries that didn't show. He had to give it to Matt for not hitting her where others could see.

Danny had encountered more domestic violence than he cared to admit. From shouting matches to those trying to kill each other and everything in between. In fact, domestic situations were some of the toughest cases a cop handled. There were always two sides—and sometimes, more—to every story, and it was the law's job to listen to everyone involved and piece together the truth.

Danny might be the county sheriff, but the small communities that made up the county, where everyone knew everyone, made it so *not* knowing someone involved with a call was a rarity.

"Sheriff."

He stopped when Deputy Glen Wilson halted in the middle of the hallway. "Morning, Wilson. What do you need?"

"It's about Matt Gaudet."

Danny's stomach tightened at the mere mention of the man. "What is it?"

"His lawyer is demanding we charge him or release him."

"I've got a few hours left before we have to do anything."

Glen's lips twisted, and his brown eyes looked away. "They're claiming the arrest was unwarranted."

Danny's eyes narrowed on Glen. "Is that so? On what grounds?"

"That Miss Long and you, having been friends back in the day, set up the entire encounter so you could have some reason to arrest him."

"You've got to be kidding." Danny should've seen this coming. "Have them check Miss Long's phone records and mine. They'll find we've never communicated. I didn't know it was her in that car, and she had no idea I was there."

Wilson shifted his feet. He was young, but a good deputy that could one day be sheriff. "Why were you there, sheriff?"

"I was eating dinner. I go there often because I like the view."

"Oh," the deputy said with a nod.

Danny moved a half-step closer. "How did Matt and his attorney learn that Skylar and I went to school together?"

Wilson shrugged, frowning. "I'm not sure."

"His attorney got here from Houston quick."

Glen nodded, his brows raised. "He flew in."

"Flew in?"

"A helicopter. He's been in with Mr. Gaudet since he arrived."

Danny looked at the clock on the wall that read seven in the morning. "And when did he arrive?"

"Two hours ago."

"Thanks, deputy."

Wilson hesitated. "I'm guessing you want me to wait until the last possible moment to charge Mr. Gaudet with domestic assault."

"I sure do."

The deputy blew out a breath. "These kinds of circumstances are never good, sir."

"No, they really aren't. I was in the right place at the right time last night. Things could've gone a lot differently."

Wilson looked down at the report in his hands and said, "Miss Long claims that he's beat her multiple times. Did she file any reports?"

"No, but we both know that isn't out of the ordinary. What she did do was take pictures after each occurrence."

Wilson's young face split into a wide grin. "That's good."

"It'll help. We just need a judge who will be compassionate and understanding of such scenarios. Luckily, Judge Harmon is just that. But first, we need Matt charged, and I also need you to get a statement from Miss Long as to what happened. I'll submit my report within the hour."

Whatever joy Danny had, evaporated at the wince on Wilson's face.

"Spit out whatever it is that has puckered your lips," Danny ordered.

The deputy lowered his voice and said, "I overheard the attorney talking to Matt. He mentioned Matt's family knowing Judge Harmon. Says their families go way back. I don't think it's going to be a slam dunk for Miss Long, sheriff."

No, it wasn't. Fuck! Why couldn't things be easy? After everything Skylar had endured, now this.

"Wilson, I want to know everything about Matt Gaudet. I'm also putting you in charge of this investigation. Since Matt claimed that I colluded with Skylar, it'll be better to hand this off to you from the start."

The deputy bobbed his head. "Yes, sir. I'll get it to you ASAP."

Danny continued on to his office in the back of the building. He shut the door and blew out a breath. Then he walked to his desk and tried to sort through the mound of paperwork he had, but his thoughts kept returning to the new information he had about Matt.

Finally, Danny gave in and called Clayton.

"Skylar is still sleeping," Clayton said in lieu of hello.

Danny glanced at his door and the closed blinds, verifying that no one could see into his office. "Good. She needs the rest, though she will have to give a statement later today. Deputy Wilson will come out to her."

"All right. Though it sounds like you need some rest, too."

"Sleep isn't always a friend for a cop."

Clayton grunted. "I can hear something in your voice. What's going on?"

"I had an ace up my sleeve."

"Yeah. Judge Harmon. She's hard on criminals, which is perfect for us. Abby and I spoke about it last night after Skylar went to bed. Has something changed?"

Danny ran a hand down his face. "It seems that Matt's family is close friends with the judge."

"Damn. That is a hiccup."

"Don't tell Skylar anything."

Clayton immediately said, "That's not a good idea. Trust me. Keep her in the loop. This is her life, and she's going to want to know everything."

"I don't want her to worry."

"Right," Clayton said with a short bark of laughter. "As if that's going to happen. Everyone is concerned, Danny. That's the nature of this particular beast."

Danny squeezed his eyes shut. "You didn't see the violence in his face last night, Clayton. He would've killed her. Because she was going to fight back. I saw it in her eyes."

"Then tell the judge that."

"That's the other wrinkle. Matt's attorney, who arrived by helicopter two hours ago, is claiming that Skylar and I colluded and set the whole thing up so I could arrest Matt."

"That's ludicrous."

"It certainly is. And while I jump through hoops to prove that, I'm waiting until the last minute to officially charge him."

It was Clayton's turn to sigh. "I'd do the same."

"His lawyer is going to keep fighting anything we do. I've got a bad feeling about this."

"What do you think about not charging him and letting him out?"

Danny's eyes flew open. "Have you lost your mind?"

"Jace and Cooper are already in place. The girls and Brice left an hour and a half ago for Houston. We both know that Matt isn't going anywhere. He's going to remain right here for a few days. It allows you to keep an eye on him while also proving your innocence."

Which was so fucked-up. Danny wasn't the one in the wrong, but as he'd told Skylar the night before, there wasn't much about life that was fair.

"Everything has to be by the book on this one," Danny said. "I don't want Matt getting off on some technicality, and I'm definitely charging his ass. I want this on his record."

"Skylar deserves to live a life without fear. Abby and I have already decided that we'll do whatever is needed to keep her here for however long this takes. No one needs to know where she is."

Danny leaned back in his chair and considered Clayton's words. "The attorney will try and find out where she is. That means that Skylar can't leave the ranch. No one can see her out in town."

"Agreed. I had a talk with the kids on the way to school. They won't mention her name or anything that happened."

"Good."

"You're great at your job, Danny. Remember that. Use the resources you have."

Danny scratched the back of his neck. "I've dealt with some high-profile lawyers from Dallas, but hearing from my deputy makes me think this one is even bigger."

"Who is Matt, anyway?"

"His last name's Gaudet."

"Oh, fuck."

Danny dropped his head back on the chair. "That doesn't make me feel better."

"Sorry. Yeah, this attorney is going to be the best in the state. You need to prepare. He's going to come at you with everything."

"Who is this guy?"

"The attorney? I don't know. Get me the name. As for Matt? Well, his family is loaded. They're in oil."

Just what Danny needed. "So they're swimming in money."

"Exactly. No doubt the lawyer is going to claim that Skylar went after Matt for his money."

"She never said anything about that when we spoke."

Clayton made a sound in the back of his throat. "Damn. Just when I thought this might be solved quickly. You're going to have your hands full. Don't worry about Skylar. We'll take care of her. Get here when you can, because I know she's going to want to talk to you. Besides, she needs to hear all of this from you anyway."

"Yeah." Danny sat up and rubbed his eyes. "It won't be until tonight."

"Dinner?"

"Sure. And make sure Skylar's phone remains off. I've got deputies searching her car for trackers, but I've got a suspicion that Matt cloned her phone without her knowledge."

"That's how he found her when she left," Clayton said.

"Matt Gaudet is crafty. No matter what precautions we take, he'll find her."

Clayton laughed, the sound anything but humorous. "Let the bastard try to come onto my land."

"Thanks, Clayton."

"Don't thank me. You've helped me, Abby, Brice, and Caleb more times than I can count. We owe you. Just tell us how we can help."

"I appreciate it."

"That's what friends do, right?"

Danny smiled when he heard the grin in Clayton's voice. "That's what we do."

They disconnected. Danny then rose and walked out of his office and through the building to the garage that was set up to search vehicles.

He made his way to Skylar's red sports car and the three men looking it over. "Any news?" he asked them.

Bobby, the lead technician, jerked his head to the table where two different tracking devices were laid out.

"Two?" Danny asked in shock.

Bobby lowered the clipboard. "That was our thought, as well."

"Did you find anything else?"

"Nope."

Danny rubbed the back of his neck. Two tracking devices. "Can you tell if both were installed at the same time?"

"One was in the car beneath the driver's seat. The other was under the car. From the looks of it, I'd say the same person installed them."

"You can tell that from wires?"

Bobby nodded. "Every installer has a certain method. Same was used on both. I don't know if they were done at the same time, but it was done by the same person."

"That's good to know."

But Danny knew if Matt had gone to these lengths, then there was no telling what was on Skylar's phone. They had to get it as far from the East Ranch as possible.

Chapter 6

December 4th

The relief that had filled her earlier disappeared during the night, and Skylar couldn't figure out why. She should feel less of a weight on her shoulders. Yet she felt anything but.

She was shocked to discover that she'd slept until one in the afternoon. Then again, she hadn't really slept in months. The fact that she knew Matt couldn't get to her because he was still in jail allowed her to get the rest she so desperately needed.

After she'd readied for the day, she walked down the stairs, her gaze immediately going to the various windows situated throughout the massive house that showcased the beauty of the East Ranch. There was a reason everyone wanted a glimpse of the ranch, and especially inside the grand house.

When she reached the bottom of the stairs, Skylar simply stood and looked out at the various barns, stables, and paddocks, taking in the horses grazing nearby. In the distance, she could see herds of cattle in the pastures.

"I'm pretty sure I wore that same expression my first time here," Abby said.

Skylar turned her head to find Abby standing in the doorway leading to the kitchen. "I used to wonder what this place looked like. I imagined all sorts of things, but it's more beautiful than I could have dreamed. And you get to see it every day."

"I know. I'm pretty lucky." Abby pushed away from the wall. "Hungry?"

"Starving, actually."

Abby chuckled. "I've got plenty. Come see if anything suits you. If not, I can run to the store or fix something else."

"Oh, I'm not picky. I'll eat whatever," Skylar said as she followed Abby into the kitchen.

"Between my kids, Clayton, my brothers, and Jace and Cooper, I have just about anything you could want. I swear my pantry and fridge is a mini-grocery store."

Skylar smiled, thinking that Abby was exaggerating until she looked inside the pantry.

"I told you," Abby said as she leaned close before walking to put a dirty cup in the dishwasher. "There's some leftover brisket from last night if you'd like that. I usually make sandwiches with it if I'm lucky enough to actually have leftovers."

That sounded amazing. Skylar got out what she needed and put together a brisket sandwich while Abby chased her youngest around, trying to get Hope to pick up her toys.

Skylar found the everyday life she was witnessing calming after everything she'd been through. Hope was nearly four and quite a handful by the looks of it. But Abby easily corralled her and got the child to do as she wanted. Then again, Abby had raised her brothers and two other children, so she was a pro at parenting.

Once Abby had Hope in her booster seat at the bar with a snack, she let out a long sigh, blowing a strand of brunette hair from her face. "She keeps me on my toes, that's for sure."

"She's beautiful. All your children are."

Abby brushed Hope's brown locks from her face while the toddler's green eyes focused on Skylar. "Thank you. I'm a little biased since I think they're absolutely perfect. Sometimes, I'm amazed that Clayton and I were able to make such amazing little humans."

Skylar took a bite of the sandwich and nearly sighed at the delicious taste of it. She'd eaten some last night, but she'd been so shaken up that she hadn't really tasted anything.

"Have you ever thought of having kids?" Abby asked.

Skylar shrugged as she swallowed. "I always thought I would one day. That's what I always said. *One day.* I'm running out of days."

"You've still got plenty of time. There's no rush."

"It's kinda hard to think about a family when my life is so messed up."

Abby's lips twisted. "Sorry. I shouldn't have brought it up."

"No, it's fine. Really. I guess if it's meant to happen, it will. If not, then it wasn't." She took another bite of the sandwich.

Abby put more Goldfish on the bar for Hope before "swimming" one of the snacks toward her daughter's mouth. Once Hope had gobbled the yellow-orange cracker, Abby turned her head to Skylar. "Clayton and I want you to know that you can stay here as long as you need."

"I appreciate all you've done, but my momma always told me to never overstay my welcome."

"You couldn't do that. I promise. Besides, this is more than just a friendly visit."

Skylar shifted her feet at the seriousness that filled

Abby's blue eyes. "I'm a planner. I always have been, but I don't know what to do next. I keep sorting through my options without being able to decide on anything. That isn't like me at all."

"Why not give yourself a few days to just relax? You've had a lot going on, and recharging your mind while allowing your soul to find some peace might help. Can you take some time off work?"

"You might be onto something. Taking time off won't be a problem. Especially when I tell my boss what happened. He never liked Matt."

Abby grinned. "Good. Then you don't have to make a decision about anything but what to eat and what places around the ranch you want to see. You can stay here because there is plenty to fill your time. Do you like to horseback ride?"

"I've never been," she admitted.

"If you want, that can be remedied."

Skylar knew Abby was being helpful, but she also wasn't a fool. "Danny told you to keep me here, didn't he?"

Abby wrinkled her nose, grimacing. "Yes. Was I that obvious?"

"It just makes sense. And it's exactly something Danny would do. I know Matt is getting charged, but I don't know what the next steps are, or if he'll get out anytime soon."

"Danny will be here later," Abby said. "He wants to fill you in on everything, and he can give you all the details on what will happen next."

Skylar finished another bite. "I was hoping he would come by, but I didn't expect it."

"He's very worried about you."

Skylar smiled as she thought about how kind Danny had always been. "I've been gone a long time, but he hasn't changed much. He was always helping others, even back in high school."

"Yep. That's Danny. He was there for me when I needed him."

"Is he married?" As soon as the words were out of her mouth, Skylar wished she could take them back.

Especially when Abby's smile filled with excitement. "As a matter of fact, he isn't. Nor is he dating anyone."

"Oh, I wasn't asking because I was interested," Skylar quickly said, though she couldn't help but wonder what it would be like to go on a date with him. Danny was handsome and a true gentleman.

"Yeah," Abby said with a knowing grin. "Of course, you weren't. It's okay, you know? Danny is a good guy, and you're single."

"He essentially saved me last night. That's . . . well, huge. I don't know if I'm transferring my gratitude for what happened onto that and making it into something else or what."

Abby wiped Hope's face and fingers after she'd finished with the snack and helped her down before the child ran off to play. "I say don't think about it too hard. It's not like you just met Danny. Maybe you're feeling things because of last night. Or perhaps it's something altogether different. Why not just set that aside for now?"

Abby was right, Skylar knew it. With Matt and everything going on there, Danny should be the last thing she was thinking about. She didn't want to get something started with him, only to realize that it was nothing more than gratitude she felt.

Skylar was left alone to finish her meal, but her thoughts returned to Danny. She should be thinking about Matt and what to do next, but it was the sheriff who filled her mind. The thoughts were a welcome reprieve from the turmoil she'd waded through the last few months.

After she was done with the sandwich, Skylar washed and put away her plate and cleaned the area while Abby carried Hope upstairs for a nap. Skylar then wandered around the downstairs, looking at the family photos that were displayed all around the house. Her mom had always been snapping pictures to put into albums or frames. Skylar couldn't remember the last time she'd put a photo into a frame, but it was something she should do instead of keeping them on her phone.

When she moved from the foyer to the living area with its arched windows, a fireplace that soared high to the ceiling, and comfortable sofas, she found even more pictures that she'd missed the night before. She hadn't been that observant the previous evening, but she was remedying that now.

She looked at every photo on the tables, mantel, and even the ones hung on the wall. When she finished, she turned to find Danny standing there with his cowboy hat in his hands.

He wore the black coat he'd let her borrow the night before, dark jeans, and his cowboy boots. She could just make out a white button-down shirt between the unzippered sides of the coat. She had no idea how long he'd been standing there, but there was no ignoring the jump of excitement that went through her when she saw him.

"Hi," she said with a smile.

His lips turned up at the corners. "Hi. You doing okay?"

"I slept until one," she said with a shake of her head as she walked toward him. "I haven't done that since college."

He moved to her, meeting her halfway. "I'm glad you were able to get some rest."

There was a stretch of silence, and Skylar clasped her hands behind her back as she cleared her throat, trying to think of something to say. "I know you don't want me to leave the ranch, and I don't intend to, so you don't need to worry about that."

"Thank you. I suspect Matt will stay in town for a bit."

"What's going to happen next?"

Danny took a breath and released it. "He's officially been charged. His lawyer arrived at five this morning."

"That's early," she replied with a frown.

"He took a helicopter in."

Unease slid down Skylar's spin. "Matt makes good money, but I don't think he has *that* kind of money."

Danny didn't respond to that. "I sent my report on the incident to the State Attorney's Family Violence Division last night with a request that Matt be prosecuted. An assistant district attorney has already gotten back to me and agreed that a crime was committed against you. Matt's arraignment happened an hour ago. He entered a plea of not guilty and is out on a five-hundred-dollar bond."

"What?" Skylar asked, shocked. "Not guilty? You can't be serious. You saw it. I saw it."

"I know. Unfortunately, it's his first offense. Reported, anyway. He also has one of the best attorneys in the state. One of my deputies overheard Matt's lawyer and the ADA scheduling to meet up later today to talk. No doubt Matt's attorney will put a deal on the table so this doesn't go to trial."

"Why such a small amount for bail?"

Danny shrugged. "Like I mentioned, it's his first offense. The amount is standard."

"So, he's out, walking around?"

Danny's hazel gaze lowered to the floor as he turned his hat in his hands. Then he swallowed and met her eyes once more. "Yes."

She'd known that Matt would be released, but that didn't make any of this better. "I see."

"Why didn't you tell me who he was?" Danny asked, a frown creasing his brow.

Skylar shook her head, not understanding. "I didn't know I needed to give you his last name. You were arresting him, so I thought you'd get that information from his driver's license."

"I mean, who his family is."

Now she was thoroughly confused. "His family? I met his younger brother once, but his parents are dead."

"No, they aren't."

As if her world weren't already upside down. She reached out to grab something to hold onto, but there was nothing. Until Danny took her hand.

"Easy," he told her.

She looked into his eyes, trying to calm her racing heart. "His parents aren't dead?"

"They're hale and hearty. And one of the richest families in Houston. They're in oil."

"Matt said he made his money from learning the stock market from his father." Her stomach churned. "Was everything a lie?"

"Have you ever heard of the Gaudets?"

Skylar shot him a flat look. "Of course. Everyone in Houston has. And I asked him about it, but Matt told me they were no relation to him whatsoever. I believed him."

What a fool she was.

Chapter 7

Each time Danny thought he had his anger at Matt under control, something new happened. "It's not your fault."

Skylar gripped his hand tightly, just as she had the night before. The ground kept tilting beneath her feet, but he would hold her steady. He liked that she kept reaching for him, seeking his comfort.

It might be nothing more than him being a cop, but he liked her touch too much to care. She had been all he'd thought about all night, and he had gone to the ranch as soon as he was able.

Just to see her.

Though he wished he had better news.

Danny drew in a deep breath before he released it. "You should also know that Matt claims you and I set all of it up last night so I would arrest him."

She rolled her eyes, anger replacing her shock. "That asshole. Any good detective will sort out that you and I haven't spoken in years."

"My deputies already have. However, it means that I have to stay clear of the case so it doesn't look as if I'm tampering with anything."

The worry was back in her blue eyes. "I see."

"It'll be fine, I promise. It's just a move they made to delay things, but it didn't do anything but make them look stupid. I've already been cleared, so there's no worry there."

She swallowed loudly. "But Matt has money, which means they can make all of this that much harder. Right?"

"It was never going to be easy." When she raised a brow, he twisted his lips and nodded. "But, yes, it's going to be even more difficult now."

She pulled her hand from his and walked to the sofa, where she sank onto the cushions with a frustrated sigh. "He's going to get away with all of this. I'm going to have to change my name, move, and do all those things I said I didn't want to do."

"No, you aren't," Danny said as he walked to stand before her. He perched on the edge of the square ottoman between the sofas. "You're safe here."

"Not forever. I don't mind hiding for a week or two, but I want my life back."

"And I'll make sure you get it."

She gave him a dejected look. "You can't watch me 24/7, and I don't expect you to."

The idea of being there to protect her appealed to Danny in a way that nothing else had in a very long time. He set his hat aside and leaned his forearms on his thighs. "You should start the paperwork for a restraining order against Matt."

"Yes, I agree. Anything else?"

"You need a lawyer."

Skylar gripped her hands together. "From here? Or Houston?"

"It depends on where you want to file the protective

order. I would suggest doing it in Baxter County since you're here now, and that's where he was arrested."

"Then that's what I'll do. Besides, I don't want to go back to Houston just yet."

That made Danny ridiculously happy to hear, but he didn't let it show. Skylar needed him as a sheriff and friend, nothing more. He had to remember that before he made a fool of himself.

"I know a few good ones," he told her. "Clayton does, as well. If you need money—"

She shook her head. "Thank you, but I've got that part covered. And it's my money, not Matt's."

"The offer is there if you change your mind."

"The car is mine, as well," she stated.

Danny glanced away as he gave a nod. He'd run the VIN on the car to check for himself that it belonged to Skylar. "I know."

"You checked, didn't you?"

"Yes."

She nodded, no anger in her gaze. "It's your job. I would've checked, too. Especially after learning that Matt comes from a wealthy family. But he didn't buy the car for me."

"I didn't mean to imply that he did."

"It's fine," Skylar said, holding up a hand to stop him from saying more. "Really, Danny."

He looked down at his hands and wished that was all he had to tell her, but unfortunately, there was more.

"You can tell me whatever it is."

Danny lifted his gaze and stared into her azure eyes. They reminded him of lake water reflecting a cloudless sky during the summer. Bright, open. Welcoming.

No one deserved to be in her situation, but Danny wished with all his might that he could take advantage of his position and ensure that she got the justice she deserved. But it wasn't in him to put her case in jeopardy just for peace of mind.

"Danny?" she asked, her eyes growing more troubled the longer he remained silent.

He cleared his throat, hating that he had to deliver such news. "Matt intends to remain in town until all of this is solved."

"What?" she asked, her voice a shocked whisper as she slowly sat back against the cushions.

"My guess is that he knows you're still here, which is why his attorney informed us of the decision."

She shook her head, no words coming forth.

Danny wanted to take her hand again, but he fisted his instead. "My techs found two tracking devices in your vehicle. One under the driver's seat, and another under the car. If Matt went to such lengths to keep track of you, then there's no doubt he put something on your phone."

"We shut it off last night."

"That doesn't always stop things. I had Clayton take it from the ranch. I have a friend who owns a mobile phone store. He's working with your company to get you a new mobile with your old number but free of any malware or anything that Matt could use to listen to your calls, read texts, or track you."

She inhaled, and her face settled into hard lines. "I'd rather have a new number, please. I know how to get in touch with anyone I need to contact. I don't want to chance anything."

"I'll make sure it's done. The phone will be delivered sometime today." Danny watched her, noting how she was grappling with everything. Regrettably, this was all just getting started. "You need to prepare yourself."

"For?"

"Anything. Matt and his attorney seem the type that'll

use anything they think they can to either make you look bad or turn the tables on you. If you know of anything that might come up, you need to tell the deputy in charge of your case. His name is Glen Wilson."

She wrapped her arms around her middle and nodded. "Is Glen good?"

"Very. He's young, but don't let that get in the way of trusting him. Wilson is smart and a natural at the job. He was on the scene the night Matt was arrested, so Wilson knows everything."

"If you trust him, then I will, as well." Skylar turned her head to the side, her gaze distant. "Matt is going to lose his mind if I'm able to get the restraining order."

Danny could no longer go without touching her. He put his hand on her knee. "He can't hurt you here."

Her head swung to him. "How long before he has you followed here? How long before he discovers that you and Clayton are good friends? How long until he threatens anyone who has helped me?"

"I feel sorry for him if he does." Danny smiled then. "Matt isn't from this area, so he wouldn't know how well-respected the Easts and Harpers are. Not to mention, Clayton was a Navy SEAL, Brice was a Marine, and Caleb a Green Beret in the Army. Cooper was a special operations Combat Control in the Air Force, and Jace was in the Marines and the MARSOC special-ops. All those men grew up shooting, and then they joined the military and were trained to kill. In other words, no one should fuck with them. Abby, Naomi, and Audrey can all shoot, as well. Matt isn't going to bother any of them."

Skylar put her hand over his. "I would never forgive myself if the children were harmed."

"Trust me, no one will ever get close enough to Clayton and Abby's children to do them any harm."

"Matt will discover I'm here."

Danny shrugged, his lips twisting. "Eventually. But he won't be able to bother you."

"You don't know him."

"Based on what you told me, he's skilled in spying on you. That means this isn't the first time he's done this. What we need to do is find a few of his past girlfriends and see if we can get them to talk."

For the first time since he'd walked in, Skylar gave him a smile. "I hadn't thought of that. Do you think they would stand against him?"

"It's certainly an option we should look into. The sooner, the better."

Her smile suddenly dimmed. "If Matt's family has the money you say they do, then they might have made sure those women don't talk."

"If that's the case, that will be uncovered, as well. I became a cop because I wanted to help people and deliver those who have broken the law to the justice system so they could pay their dues. Our system doesn't always work. I'll be the first to admit that. But I'm going to make damn sure we do everything we can."

Her fingers tightened on his hand. "I'd like to think I'm special, but the boy I knew in school never would have been unfair to anyone. And I can guarantee the man he's become wouldn't either. You tell everyone that you'll do everything you can because that's the kind of person you are, Danny Oldman. It's why I've always liked you."

"I *will* fight for you."

"I've never doubted that, and I never will. If anyone else but you had shown up last night, I wouldn't have told them anything."

He frowned, confused and worried. "Why? You obviously needed help."

"Because I've become a scared woman. I don't like it, but it's the truth." She glanced down at their hands.

"When I saw you, I remembered how you used to make me smile, how you always looked after others. It's been many years, and I had no idea how you might have changed, but I knew how you used to make me feel. That unlocked something inside me. As soon as I started telling you about Matt, I felt some of the fear recede. It was . . . amazing."

His lips curved in response to her shy smile. God, she had no idea what her words did to him. Despite what Skylar said, he knew she was strong enough to take care of herself. She had made the decision to leave Matt. That was a huge step in and of itself. But he liked that she saw him as someone who could—and would—help her.

"The more I'm with you, the more I see you are still very much like you were when we were younger. It's no surprise at all that you're sheriff," she said.

Danny chuckled and shook his head. "I'm just doing my job the best I can."

"And you're still humble." She laughed, her eyes brightening. "You are one in a million."

Danny's body heated, his blood pumping through him as hot as lava. The need, the rampant desire came over him so quickly, he was dizzy with it. His gaze dropped to Skylar's lips, and he desperately wanted a taste of them. It was worse than the crush he'd had on her in school.

He returned his gaze to her eyes and was unable to look away. No matter how much he wanted her, he couldn't do anything now, not while he was helping her with Matt. It would be a conflict of interest, and if—no, *when*—Matt and his attorney found out, they would use it against her.

Danny wouldn't be the reason she continued to fear for her life. He could maintain control of himself, keep the burning desire that consumed him in check. He had to. There was no other choice.

"Why didn't you ask me out when we were younger?"

Her sudden question took him aback, but it made him realize that he'd always wanted her. *Always*. "I saw all the other guys going after you, and you rejecting them. I didn't want to be like the others. And I liked being your friend."

When he saw the flash of disappointment in her blue eyes, he quickly said, "But if I'd thought I had a chance with you, I would've asked you out."

"I really wish you had." She slipped her hand beneath his so their palms touched.

"You were out of my league."

She smiled softly. "I think it's more that you were out of mine."

"Never."

"After all these years, we find ourselves together again, with you looking out for me."

He rubbed his thumb across hers. "You were always strong enough to take care of whatever came your way. You faced the future with your head held high and determination in your eyes. Something that I found remarkable. I saw that and tried to do the same."

Her eyes widened in surprise. "You mean, I did something you thought was remarkable?"

"Skylar, I thought everything you did was astounding. You had an outlook on life that none of those our age did. You were so open and accepting of everyone, no matter what. And you were kind."

"I followed your example," she replied.

He frowned, his head jerking back. "Mine?"

She laughed loudly. "I've surprised you. Good. But, yes, to answer your question, it was your example. You stopped to help a younger kid that had been pushed down by bullies. After you told the bullies off, you picked up the kid's books and chatted with him as you both walked down the hall. All the rest of us watched while this poor kid was being tormented by the older kids. You were the only one who had the guts to stand up to them."

Danny lifted one shoulder in a shrug. "I just did what I thought was right."

"I know," she said in a whisper.

Chapter 8

"Let's start from the beginning."

Skylar tried not to fidget, but sitting in the office at the East Ranch with the woman she'd hired as her attorney was anything but normal.

"Sure," Skylar said as she looked at Leslie, sitting in the chair opposite her. Neither had gone near the huge desk.

Leslie's soft brown eyes watched her like a hawk. She wore an olive green houndstooth plaid jacket that looked as if it had been custom-made. Beneath was a cream shirt, all paired with a black skirt and knee-high suede black boots with four-inch heels.

The attorney had come highly recommended by both Danny and Abby, and after a brief phone call with Leslie, Skylar had hired her. To her shock, Leslie had dropped everything and immediately came out to the ranch so she could get all the facts.

"I'm sorry," Skylar said and shook her head, realizing that she had just been sitting there. "It all started one night when I was out with friends. It was a Thursday. We met up after work for a drink at a bar in downtown Houston just a few blocks from my apartment."

Leslie nodded as she listened. She wasn't taking notes since the conversation was being recorded. "Did you drink?"

"Yes. I had two glasses of wine. Even though I wasn't driving, that was always my limit. I liked to be aware of my surroundings."

"That's good." Leslie crossed one leg over the other. "What happened next?"

Skylar picked at the chipped polish on her thumbnail. "One of my friends pointed out that we were being stared at. I looked over and saw three guys sitting together. Sure enough, all three were looking our way. I didn't pay much attention to them. There were five of us, and three of them, and to be frank, I wasn't looking for anything. I'd been single for six months, and I liked things just as they were.

"Then Matt walked up to the table. Once more, I ignored him since I assumed he was there for one of my friends. But it turned out he wanted me. He struck up a conversation. I don't even remember what he asked me, but we began talking. His two friends came over then. The table got crowded, so we moved off by ourselves and kept talking."

"So, he was nice?" Leslie asked.

Skylar bobbed her head. "Very. He was polite and attentive. He tried to buy me another drink. When I declined, he accepted that. I had two glasses of water while we talked."

"And what did he drink?"

Skylar had to think a moment. "Um . . . I believe it was bourbon, but I could be wrong. I know it was just a shot of something. He had two while we sat there."

"Do you know how many he had before that?"

Skylar shook her head. "I didn't ask. Why is that important?"

"It's the little things," Leslie replied. "Did he appear drunk?"

"Not at all. But I will tell you that he liked to drink. Sometimes more than others."

"Did he hit you when he drank?"

"No. When he got that drunk, he was too out of it. He'd yell and say all kinds of horrible things, but he couldn't stand up straight, much less hit me."

Leslie perked up at that information. "In other words, he was sober when he beat you."

"Absolutely."

The lawyer smiled gleefully. "Go on."

"There isn't much to say about that night. It got late, and I decided to head home. He asked if he could see me again and gave me his number. He didn't even ask for mine. All I knew was his first name, and all he knew was mine. I thought he was nice-looking, and he was certainly a gentleman. But I didn't call him on Friday. Or Saturday. I didn't contact him until Sunday afternoon.

"When I told him it was me, he said that he'd hoped I'd call. We talked for an hour on the phone before he asked if he could take me to dinner. I agreed but said I'd meet him at the restaurant. He was waiting for me when I got there at seven. We were the last to leave when they closed for the night, and honestly, I didn't want to go home. He was so easy to talk to."

Leslie folded her hands in her lap. "Did he tell you his surname at this point?"

"Yes. I asked him if he was related to the Gaudets I always hear about in Houston. He laughed and said it would be great if he was, but that they were no relation. I didn't think twice about it."

"Did you have sex that night?"

Skylar was a consenting adult who didn't have to answer to anyone, yet she knew that others would likely judge her for her actions. "We did, yes. He kissed me when we got to my car and then asked if I wanted to go to his place. It was close, and I ended up staying until about two in the morning."

"When did you see him after that?"

"He called the next day at lunch," Skylar said. "We met up for dinner that night and were with each other nearly every day after."

Leslie tilted her head to the side, causing her straight, jaw-length, dark brown hair to move with her. "Did he ever raise his voice at you?"

"I think we had a few disagreements, as all couples do, but no, he never raised his voice to me. He was always a gentleman. I never saw anything that would've led me to believe otherwise."

Leslie's lips pressed together. "Mr. Gaudet and his team will use that against you."

"Can't we use it against him, as well? He led me to believe he was one person, when he turned out to be another."

Leslie grinned in response. "That's exactly what I'm going to tell the judge. Now, I need you to think back. Did Mr. Gaudet ever get jealous of anyone you spoke with? Did he want to know your every move, etcetera . . . ?"

Skylar had to think through an entire year. She tried to search her memories, but she couldn't come up with anything. "I was very independent. Matt said he liked that about me, that I wasn't clingy or needy. When I met up with my friends to get pedicures or go shopping, he never seemed to mind. He used that time to hang out with his friends."

"Did he buy you expensive things?"

"He bought me a gold necklace with my initial on it for my birthday. We spent a long weekend in Napa Valley, California, to celebrate me moving in, but we split the cost of that trip. So, no, I wouldn't say that he spent any significant money on me."

Leslie's smile said she approved of what she was hearing. "No designer purses, shoes, or clothes?"

"I've always bought those things for myself. I never asked him for anything like that."

"Great. That proves you weren't after his money. Now, you said that you never met his parents."

"That's right. Just his brother," Skylar explained. "Matt told me his parents died in a car crash several years ago. It seemed to upset him, and he didn't like talking about it, so I didn't push."

Leslie uncrossed her legs. "I plan on speaking with Sheriff Oldman about last night, but before we get to that, I need you to tell me about the times Matt attacked you."

Skylar had only ever told one person about it—Danny. Now, she would have to tell Leslie, the judge, and probably others. She took a deep breath and went through each time with Leslie, just as she had done with Danny.

"I know it's tough, but thank you. You did good." Leslie reached over and squeezed Skylar's hand while giving her a reassuring smile.

"How many more times am I going to have to tell that story?"

"I don't know," Leslie said as she puckered her face. "I wish it was just once more in front of the judge, but you should be prepared for Matt and his family to fight this."

Skylar jerked back. "What does his family have to do with it?"

"Their name is important to them, and they will likely go after anyone who dares to try and besmirch it."

Skylar got to her feet and walked to the window overlooking the back of the ranch. She spotted Hope and Abby with a horse in a small paddock. Abby held Hope, who draped silver and red tinsel over the horse's neck.

Clayton came out then and took Hope from Abby. Once the toddler was out of sight, Abby quickly removed the tinsel from the animal.

"This is going to get ugly, isn't it?" Skylar asked Leslie.

"That's definitely a possibility. I like to tell my clients to prepare for the worst."

Skylar turned back to her attorney. "And the worst for me is?"

"They dig up every shred of dirt on you and sue you for defamation."

"All I want is my life back!" Skylar squeezed her eyes closed after her outburst. A few deep breaths later, she looked at Leslie. "I'm asking for a restraining order so Matt will leave me alone and I can get on with my life."

Leslie got to her feet. "From what I know of the Gaudet family and their lawyers, they aren't going to simply sit back and let that happen."

"Even if their son is at fault?"

"I'm betting they know exactly what Matt has done. But that isn't the point. Their oldest is in politics. Everyone in Houston knows he wants to be governor of Texas and then president."

Oh, for fuck's sake. How in the world had she stepped into such a pile of shit? "You're telling me that even if I drop the restraining order, they'll still come after me?"

"Probably. You had their son arrested."

"*I* didn't do anything. Matt did that all on his own, and I'm not the one pressing charges, the district attorney is."

Leslie shrugged. "Be that as it may, that's not how the Gaudets will view it. First things first, we need to get the order of protection paperwork filed immediately. You need to sign the petition for the order, along with the affidavit of everything you told me today.

"Everything?" Skylar asked.

"Just the facts about the case. The judge will read

what you told me. How you and Matt met, how you came to date, how he acted during those nine months, and how things changed once you moved in together. The affidavit will detail each incident of abuse, where he hit you, and why you didn't report it. I need you to email me every photo you took. Those will be printed out and used as evidence."

Skylar immediately got her phone and began emailing said pictures so she didn't forget. When she finished, she set her phone aside and met Leslie's brown gaze. "Have you taken many cases like this?"

"It's not my first, if that's what you're worried about. And just so you know, I often go up against attorneys in Houston, Dallas, and Austin, so they don't scare me. I'm a fifth-generation lawyer. There isn't anything someone in my family hasn't dealt with."

Skylar grinned at her. "Abby told me you were fierce. I didn't hire you simply because you're a woman or because they recommended you. I hired you because of how you spoke to me on the phone."

"You have to trust the attorney representing you, and I want you to know that I will fight whatever the Gaudets and their team throw at us. You were physically, emotionally, and verbally abused. You shouldn't be victimized more simply because of who Matt is."

But they both knew that's exactly what would likely happen.

"What about Danny?" Skylar asked. "Is he really cleared from Matt saying that we set all this up?"

Leslie rolled her eyes at the mention of it. "That's such a load of bullshit. Yes, Danny has been cleared."

That was a relief. "Which means that Danny is off the hook."

Leslie gave her a peculiar look, one Skylar couldn't read. "Yes, you could say that. Since he was the one who came upon you and Matt, and the fact that you and Danny were classmates, things could get interesting. Not that I'm telling you not to jump right into Danny's arms."

Skylar's eyes widened. "What? That's not what I mea—"

"Listen," Leslie interrupted her. "Just keep things quiet with Danny, okay? I'll be in touch in the morning."

Skylar watched the attorney walk from the office.

Chapter 9

"What the hell do you mean, I can't talk to her? She's my fucking girlfriend. I can do whatever I want."

Jace cut his gaze to Cooper, who sat in the booth opposite him. They had been following Matt Gaudet and his attorney ever since they left the sheriff's station that afternoon.

The smug look on Gaudet's face made Jace want to punch him, but since he and Cooper were supposed to keep their distance, he couldn't give in to such rage. Which was really too bad, because no one needed to have an attitude adjustment more than Matt Gaudet.

"And to think I voted for his brother," Cooper mumbled while dipping a fry into some ketchup before eating it.

Jace shook his head. "You know politicians. You can't believe anything they say."

"Yeah, but you have to vote for someone. It's always a toss-up, you know that."

"I just don't get why people can't be honest." But that was always Jace's problem.

He believed that people should do what they said, and

actually do the jobs they were supposed to. It never turned out that way. He should be used to it by now, but people still disappointed him.

His thoughts halted as their targets began talking again.

"Matt, keep your voice down," the attorney whispered urgently as he looked around to see if anyone was staring.

In response, Matt glared at the lawyer. "Rodney, if you tell me to calm down one more time, I'm going to throw this drink on your expensive suit."

"You may not want to hear it, but it's what you need to do," Rodney said. "This is a small town, not Houston. Things are different here."

Matt snorted. "Exactly. No one knows me."

"Not yet," the lawyer cautioned. "It won't be long before everyone knows you."

Cooper smiled at Jace and pulled out his phone. "That just gave me an idea."

Jace grinned, knowing exactly what his friend was doing. After the text had been sent, Cooper handed Jace the phone so he could read the message. Sure enough, Cooper had alerted Beverly Barnes of Matt's whereabouts so she could hopefully get a picture of him and print it in the county newspaper, along with an article.

Beverly replied immediately, saying she was on her way.

"Hot damn," Cooper said when he saw the text after Jace had handed him back the phone.

"Good idea."

Cooper's forest green eyes crinkled. "Say that again. I need to record it."

"Kiss my ass," Jace replied, but there was no heat in his words.

The two had been friends since the first day of kindergarten. They had been inseparable ever since. The duo had quickly hit it off with Brice and Caleb Harper, and the four of them did everything together—including joining the military.

Though they'd each joined different branches, they kept in touch weekly, if not daily. One by one, they finished out their tours and returned home. The same, but different.

And their friendships were just as strong as before. In fact, it was as if they hadn't spent years apart. None of them had actually said they would return to their hometown, but they all had. They had been watching each other's backs for years, and that wasn't going to change anytime soon.

"I can't hear what they're saying anymore," Cooper complained before he finished off his beer.

With the angle of their booth, Jace was able to see both Matt's and Rodney's faces. The two leaned in close to each other, their voices pitched low.

Jace looked back at Cooper and shrugged. "Me either."

"Do you think he'll be stupid enough to go after her?"

Jace didn't need to ask who *her* was. Skylar Long was safely ensconced at the East Ranch. It would take some creative and well-trained men to get onto the ranch without being detected. And he and Cooper should know since they often tested the system to see if they could beat it. They hadn't yet.

"He'd be a fool," Jace answered his friend.

Cooper's eyes burned with fury. "I kinda hope he tries. Any man who thinks it's okay to beat up on a woman deserves whatever is coming to him."

"That's not what we're doing." Jace waited until Cooper looked at him.

Finally, his friend nodded. "I get it, but I don't have to like it."

"I certainly don't," Jace said.

Cooper ran a hand down his face and sat back in the booth. "It all has to be done by the book. That's what Clayton told us. I'm not sure how Danny does it."

Jace didn't either. He was proud to call Danny a friend, but he'd seen on several occasions how the sheriff's hands were tied in certain situations. But that's how it had to be in order to keep the law running.

It was also one of the reasons Danny had enlisted Jace's and Cooper's aid. And they were always ready to help a friend in need.

Cooper blew out a breath and set his elbows on the table, clasping his hands as he sat forward. "Did you notice the way Danny was looking at her?"

"A blind person would've noticed that."

Though they kept their voices down, they wanted to make sure not to say Skylar's name. There was no sense in drawing attention their way, especially from Matt or his attorney.

"I call bullshit," Matt said loudly.

"Matt, please," the lawyer begged.

The abusive bastard shook his head of blond hair. "She has no grounds. How did you find out what she was doing anyway?"

"It pays to have friends," Rodney answered.

Jace flattened his lips. So much for Skylar and Leslie filing the restraining order before Matt found out. Before he could call Danny, Cooper beat him to the punch.

Unfortunately, it proved that Skylar would have to be extra careful. If Matt's lawyer could discover that she'd gotten the paperwork to file a restraining order, then they could find out almost anything. The problem was, had they learned it from someone there, or was it someone in Houston?

Matt's laugh went through Jace like a hot brand. He glanced to the side and found the asshole looking at him.

"You got a problem?" Matt demanded.

Jace saw Cooper tense, readying for a fight. But Jace wouldn't let it come to that. Not yet, at least.

Cooper shook his head. "Last I heard, I could look anywhere I wanted. If you don't want people to look your way, perhaps you shouldn't be so loud."

Matt started to get to his feet when his lawyer hastily reached out an arm and stopped him. Cooper relaxed, a grin now in place as the waitress brought over another beer.

For his part, Matt jerked his arm from his attorney's grip and stormed out, leaving over half his steak uneaten. Rodney sighed and waved over the waitress. He pulled cash from his wallet and shoved several bills at her before following Matt out of the restaurant.

It would be too obvious now for Jace and Cooper to get up and follow Matt. They had anticipated just such a situation. Jace dialed Brice and simply said, "Handing off."

"I got 'em," Brice replied before the phone went dead.

Cooper caught Jace's gaze and said, "This isn't going to go away easily."

"No, it isn't," Jace agreed.

"He's done this before. I know it."

"So does Danny. It's proving it that's going to be difficult."

Cooper just smiled.

Jace stared at his oldest friend. "What did you do?"

"When Abby mentioned that Danny suspected that Matt had done this before and they should find old girlfriends, I decided not to wait. I called Cash."

Jace thought about that a moment and nodded. "With Danny having to hand over the investigation and also clearing his name, and Skylar working on getting the restraining order, no one thought about that."

"They would have eventually. I just saved us a day or so." Cooper grinned as he chewed another fry.

Unable to help it, Jace laughed. "I gather that Cash was eager to take the job."

"You know it. He finished up the case he was on in San Antonio, then headed straight to Houston. Even before the military, he had a vast network of people. After his discharge from the Air Force, he used the skills he learned to help out his brother. That's how he got into the private investigating business."

Jace had only met Cash a handful of times, but he liked the guy. He was quiet, a loner. The exact opposite of Cooper, which made it odd that they'd developed such a tight friendship. Jace knew firsthand that combat could bring the unlikeliest of people together.

"If anyone can dig up dirt on Matt, it'll be Cash," Cooper said.

Jace knew very little about the private investigating business, but Cash always seemed to have clients who wanted and needed information. Jace had no idea if it was mostly people wanting to know if their spouse or significant other was cheating or not. The fact that Cash was in high demand spoke of how good a job he did.

"Did Cash say how long it would take?"

Cooper shook his head. "Each job is different. I've heard that line from Cash too many times to forget it. He knows we're on a time crunch, and he knows who we're up against. He'll work as fast as he can."

"I agree with Danny. There are other women out there," Jace said, drumming his fingers on the table. "They've probably been paid off so they won't ever talk.

Cooper grunted. "That would certainly be an issue."

"It seems like a legitimate one. There has never been any

type of abuse story involving Matt and a woman in the papers or on social media. That either means that it's never happened before, or they were paid to keep quiet."

"That won't stop Cash. He'll get what we need."

Jace looked down at his empty plate. He was tempted to order dessert, but then he remembered Abby's peanut butter cookies she'd been baking earlier.

Ten minutes later, they had paid and were on the way back to Cooper's truck when he said, "So, what do you think of Danny and Skylar?"

"This again?"

"You admitted to seeing how he looked at her."

Jace shrugged. "They knew each other in school. What's the big deal?"

They reached the vehicle, each on their own side. Cooper rested his arm on the edge of the bed of the truck. "It's Danny, Jace. You know. *Danny*?"

"Yeah. I get that it's *Danny*." Then it hit him. "Ohhhhh. You mean because he rarely looks at women like that."

Cooper rolled his eyes. "Took you long enough."

"Maybe the timing was off in school. Could be that something happens now."

"It won't."

Jace frowned as he got into the truck and waited for Cooper to get behind the wheel before he asked, "Why do you say that?"

"It's Danny. He won't do anything that might mess up Skylar's case, especially if it gets as big as everyone thinks it will."

"Oh, it will."

Cooper shot him a look that said *exactly*! "When it's all over, regardless of the outcome, Danny will then make a move."

"And you think it'll be too late by then," Jace guessed.

"It usually is. Danny is married to his job. Granted, he's a damn good sheriff, but he was eating alone at a rest stop."

Jace nodded slowly as he looked out the windshield. "Skylar was looking at Danny, too. There's something between them, that's for sure."

"I hope Danny doesn't let her go."

"It's not always up to the guy," Jace said, trying not to think of his own past.

Cooper cleared his throat. "Right," he said hastily and started the engine.

Chapter 10

It was everything Danny could do to stay away from Skylar when he finally called it a day. He'd been in contact with Clayton and Abby to ask about her, but it wasn't the same as talking to her himself.

Danny told himself it was for the best. Matt Gaudet and his lawyer had already tried to link him and Skylar together, and Danny wasn't just going to hand them something they could twist and turn in an ugly way, simply because Danny was trying to be a friend.

He snorted as he reached for the bottle of bourbon. A friend. That was a load of the deepest bullshit he'd ever tried to feed himself. He wanted more from Skylar. Hell, he always had.

The sad part was that he'd honestly believed she'd just been a high school crush. Right up until he saw her face again the other night. He'd immediately known that what he felt was much more than a crush.

"I'm so fucked," he murmured to himself.

He downed the alcohol in one swallow and set the empty glass on the counter without even attempting to look for something to eat.

How was it that the one woman who could grab hold of his heart in such a way was not available? Again. Sure, she might be single, but she wasn't free. Her future hinged on proving that Matt was abusive, which seemed simple enough.

But Danny knew more than most that nothing was that simple. Matt had the Gaudet fortune and connections at his disposal, as well as others willing to do whatever it took to keep the family name unblemished. That didn't bode well for Skylar.

Danny was just reaching for the bourbon again when his doorbell rang. He rarely had visitors, so he was immediately on edge. He cautiously walked to the front door and peered outside to see a red truck in the drive. He opened the door to Caleb Harper.

"Danny," Caleb said.

"Caleb."

"You going to let me in?" the youngest Harper sibling asked.

Danny stepped aside to allow him entry. Once Caleb had passed, Danny shut the door and locked it out of habit. "What brings you here?"

"Just thought I'd drop by and see how you're doing."

Danny wasn't buying that, not in the least. He quirked a brow. "Try again, son."

Caleb chuckled. "I told Clayton that shit wouldn't work on you."

"Clayton. Of course," Danny mumbled to himself. He should've known his friend would go to such lengths. "What's Clayton worried about now?"

"Isn't it obvious? You."

Danny ran a hand down his face. "It's been a long day. I told Clayton that. Every day until this entire Matt Gaudet thing is finished will be a long one."

Caleb walked into the kitchen and poured himself a

shot of bourbon. He sniffed it before taking a sip. "This isn't bad."

"There's better."

"And worse," Caleb said after taking another drink. "Danny, you've been a family friend for as long as I remember. You've helped Abby, Clayton, Brice, Naomi, me, and Audrey. You've always been there for whatever we need."

Danny crossed his arms over his chest while looking into Caleb's brown eyes. "And you don't think I'm accepting your aid now? Because I have."

"That's not it at all." Caleb shook his head and set aside the unfinished drink. "I came to tell you two things."

"Okay. And they are?"

"We got Skylar's things. Your suggestion to have a police officer there to watch over things was one I never would've thought of. Two showed up to stand guard and observe. And Audrey recorded everything from the time we pulled up until we left. So everything is documented from our end as well as the Houston police's."

Danny let out a breath. "That's good. Where are Skylar's things?"

"On the way back. Abby called her to see if there was somewhere Skylar wanted us to bring everything. Skylar asked if we could find a storage facility and put everything but her clothes there."

"She must have a reason for that," Danny said, though he was unsure what it could be.

"I'm just doing what she wanted. The storage place is about forty minutes away. Skylar asked that I keep the keys."

Danny nodded, waiting for the second thing Caleb had come to talk about.

Caleb looked around the kitchen before he met Danny's

gaze once more. "Skylar is holding up well, but she needs a friend."

"She has all of you."

"She needs you," Caleb insisted. "She's not said it because she knows you're in a difficult position, but you're the only one she really knows. We're poor substitutes."

Danny shook his head. "It's better like this."

"Because you're attracted to her?"

Danny blinked, his lips parting in surprise.

Caleb rolled his eyes. "Did you really think none of us noticed? Give us some credit. Look, I get it. You probably took her out in school or something. Y'all had a little fling. Those kinds of emotions will last until you face them."

Danny didn't bother to correct Caleb. It was better if he thought things just as he did.

"She's surrounded by strangers, and she's terrified that her life is over," Caleb continued. "In the thirty minutes I was with her, I saw her type a text six different times and erase it. And do you know who those texts were to?"

"Who?" Danny asked, but in his heart, he was screaming, *Let it be me!*

Caleb stared at him a beat. "You."

Elation erupted inside Danny, but just as swiftly, it diminished when he realized that her actions only meant that she was lonely and wanted a familiar face.

"Go see her," Caleb urged. "Or, at the very least, call her. She needs you."

Danny rubbed the back of his neck. "I've got Matt and his attorney followed. For all I know, someone could be trailing me."

"And all they'll see is the sheriff going to see a friend that he visits all the time."

That was true. Though Danny also realized that once

Matt locked in on Skylar's location, he would hound her continually. Until the protective order went into effect.

"All right," Danny relented.

Caleb grinned and slapped him on the back. "Great. Now, get cleaned up, because, dude, you look like hell. Did you sleep at all last night?"

Danny didn't bother answering. He changed clothes and clipped his weapon on his belt. He put on his hat and coat when he noticed Caleb frowning in his living room.

"What's wrong now?" Danny asked.

Caleb raised his brows. "If I didn't know better, I'd say you were the Grinch. Or Scrooge. Do you not like Christmas?"

"Not going to do this," Danny said as he grabbed his keys and stalked from the house.

Caleb was right on his heels. "I don't think I've ever been to your house during the holidays. Do you never put up decorations?"

"You're used to your sister. Not everyone likes to make their house look as if they've thrown up Christmas."

The laughter that fell from Caleb's lips grew louder and longer as the seconds ticked by. When he got into his truck and drove off, he was still laughing.

Danny shook his head and hurried into his vehicle to start the engine and turn on the heat. He really hoped he wasn't making a bad decision going to Skylar, but then again, he didn't care. He wanted to see her. Just one more time. There was nothing wrong with that.

He kept telling himself that, even when he pulled up to the entrance of the ranch and entered the code to open the gate. He had his own code. The gate shut behind him, but his attention was on the house—and Skylar.

His gaze skimmed the windows, pondering which room she had chosen. He wondered if her hair would be up or down, and if she was content at the ranch.

Danny parked and got out of the truck. His steps were slow on the way to the door. Then, through the many windows, he caught sight of Skylar walking from the living area to the kitchen with a mug in her hand.

She rinsed out the cup and set it aside when she glanced his way. She did a double-take, her body freezing when she spotted him. Then her face broke out into a wide smile, and Danny felt himself relax.

He hadn't realized that he was tense, waiting to see her reaction. Because no matter what Caleb said, he hadn't been certain that Skylar wanted to see him.

She opened the door and just stood there, waiting for him. "Hi."

His steps were long, quickly eating up the ground as he went to her. "Hi."

"Come inside," she said and grabbed his hand, pulling him through the doorway.

He immediately set his hat on the hook near the door and removed his coat, his gaze never leaving her. She looked so damn beautiful. Her blond hair was pulled over one shoulder in a loose braid. She had on a soft pink sweatshirt, white sweatpants, and fuzzy, pink socks.

"I'm making some tea. Would you like some?" she asked.

"I'm not much of a tea drinker." Then he found himself saying, "But I'll give it a try."

She beamed at him. "We can doctor it until you like it."

He'd try anything if she smiled at him like that. Danny had never thought himself the type to be smitten, but that's exactly what he was with Skylar. Perhaps he always had been.

"Did you have a good day?" she asked as if she weren't in the middle of a crisis.

He shrugged and settled on a stool at the island. He

knew he should go talk to Clayton and Abby, but he wanted a few more quiet moments with Skylar. "It was long. As most of my days are."

"You ate something, right?"

She was moving about the kitchen, getting teabags, spoons, and another cup. He liked watching her so at ease—it did something to him. Or rather *she* did something. She eased him. The tightness within him that had always been there receded.

"Danny?" she called. "You didn't eat dinner, did you?"

He shook his head. "I didn't get around to it."

"There's plenty of leftovers here if you'd like something."

Danny was about to refuse when he saw Clayton in the doorway. His friend smiled and grabbed Abby, who was about to walk into the kitchen. The two backed away, leaving Danny alone with Skylar.

"Sure," Danny answered as he looked back at Skylar.

He rose and went to the fridge to look through the containers until he found pork chops and mashed potatoes and gravy. He fixed a plate and heated it in the microwave then returned to his seat.

"You skip a lot of meals, don't you?" Skylar asked as she leaned over the island opposite him.

He stirred the potatoes and gravy to mix them. "More times than not. I don't like cooking, and cooking for one is difficult. I get tired of eating out, and while Abby and Clayton have opened their home to me, I don't want to be here more than once a week to eat. It just looks sad."

"I ate more cereal and avocado toast for dinners when I was single than I should probably admit. Lunch is different," she said. "You're at work, people are either ordering food or going somewhere together. But dinners, you're by yourself."

"Exactly," he said around a bite of food.

She lowered her gaze before looking at him, her blue eyes trapping his. "I'm so very glad you came by to-night."

Without thinking, he reached over and covered her hand with his as if it were something he'd always done.

Chapter 11

It didn't matter what Skylar tried to tell herself, her heart had actually leapt when she spotted Danny outside earlier. The happiness that swept through her had been strong, causing her knees to go weak.

Danny's hazel gaze lowered to his plate, but he didn't pull his hand away. Skylar had the feeling that while he wanted to be there, he also wasn't sure about it. And, sadly, she understood why.

Matt.

It all came back to Matt.

Why had she ever gotten involved with him? And how in the world had she missed the signs that would've told her who he really was? Had he been that good of a liar?

Obviously. She hadn't doubted for a moment that his parents were dead. Even his younger brother had gone along with it. Then there was his elder brother, Michael, who was in politics. Now that she knew that Matt was connected to him, she saw the resemblance, but it was something she should've realized from the beginning.

She was just too damn trusting.

And look where it had gotten her.

"I know it's tricky for you to be here," she told Danny.

He finished the last bite and pushed his plate to the side before looking into her eyes. "I'm here because I want to be."

"Do you really? Or do you feel as if you have to be because the others think I need you."

One side of Danny's wide lips tilted in a smile. "The one thing I noticed about you when we were in school was that you did things on your own. It didn't matter what it was. I remember you went to the Christmas dance by yourself."

She laughed, remembering. "That's right. I found out that my boyfriend cheated on me a week before the dance and I refused to go with him. Some friends said I could tag along with them, but it's never fun being a third wheel. I decided there was no reason I couldn't arrive by myself."

"That's not something people do, normally."

"I don't really follow the norm."

"That's my point," he said, his face sobering. "You've always blazed your own path. You left here after graduation without looking back. You made a life for yourself in Houston without letting anything stop you. You'll do the same with this fiasco, as well."

She cocked her head to the side, wishing she could see herself through Danny's eyes. "You have high expectations of me."

"Not expectations. A belief. Because you've proven it time and again."

She wanted to be as brave and courageous as Danny made her out to be, but she wasn't that woman anymore. "I lost some of that over the past few months."

"You didn't lose it. It's simply buried. You just need to find it again."

"I will, somehow." She glanced at their still-joined hands. "I'm really sorry that Matt and his attorney made this difficult for you."

Danny lifted a shoulder. "It was a tactic used to stall us a little. It didn't work."

"Perhaps not, but it's made you hesitant to spend any time with me."

"That's not entirely true."

She raised a brow, not believing him. "Yes, it is. And that's all right. I understand. You don't need to feel as if you have to check on me all the time."

Though she really liked it when he did.

"I do it because I want to," he said.

She smiled in response, deciding to let it go. She had said what she needed to say.

They sat in silence for a minute, and that's when she heard the TV and a Christmas song. The entire house was decorated for the season. Even her bedroom had a Christmas comforter and sheets. There was no doubt that it was the favorite time of year for Abby and her family.

"Walk with me," Danny urged.

She was surprised at the suggestion but agreed. They put on their coats, and once Danny had settled his hat atop his head, they walked from the house.

Skylar fell in step beside him, letting him lead the way. They made their way toward the nearest paddock where a mare and her two-month-old foal were kept. As soon as Danny came up to the fence, the sorrel foal trotted over, his little tail flapping excitedly.

She watched as Danny spoke softly to the animal while reaching his hand through the fence to pet the foal. The mother watched with a careful eye the entire time.

"Matt knows about the restraining order."

The smile on her face slipped. She tucked her hands

into her coat's pockets and looked off into the night sky where the stars twinkled above them. "How?"

"We don't know yet. His attorney was the one who discovered it. It could've come from someone in Houston or right here in town."

"It's Houston, I'm sure."

Danny dropped his arm and straightened to turn to her. "His knowledge of the proceedings won't stop it."

"It just goes to show that he'll know about everything we do. There's no getting a step ahead of him."

"Then we don't try."

She frowned and shook her head. "Why not? That's the only way to win."

"That's what he'll expect you to do. He has more money and people working with him. Let him think he's got you cornered. Let him believe you're scared."

Now, she understood. "Because then he won't try so hard to come after me."

"Precisely. I've seen it a hundred times with men like him. He likes to control things. Let him believe he is."

"It could all go wrong."

"That's true of any situation. The good thing is, you aren't alone. Leslie is a hell of a lawyer. Trust me, none of Matt's team will be prepared for her."

Skylar grinned and walked closer to him. "I like the thought of that."

"You won't be able to out-money him, and with his family connections, you won't be able to be heard by the press or anyone wanting your side to win. They're going to go to the family that will give them the fodder they want. What you can do is out-lawyer him as well as out-think and out-play him."

She drew in a deep breath. "It doesn't matter how I win, as long as I do."

"And I'll be beside you the entire time."

She bit her lip while scrunching her nose. "You have a great thing going here, Danny. I don't want to ruin that."

"You won't."

"You know that's not true. Matt and his lawyer have already put a spotlight on you. If you continue hanging around me and defending me, they'll come after you for sure."

Danny actually laughed and held out his hand. Once she took it, they walked toward the barn. "Let them."

"You could lose your job."

He shrugged. "There are others."

She couldn't believe he was so flippant about it. He opened the door to the stables, shutting it behind them once they were inside. "I don't want anything coming back on you, the Easts, or the Harpers."

Danny turned her to face him with a tug of his hand. "If you haven't noticed, my friends are a strong lot. They've been through a great many things together, and I was lucky enough to be there to help them out. If they didn't want any part of this, they wouldn't be helping."

"Okay," she whispered.

The lights were dimmed in the stables, creating a soft glow around them. She noticed that Danny's eyes were more gold than normal, the gilded flecks drawing her in like a beacon.

His hand was warm in hers, his hold steady, tender. She liked the dark stubble that shadowed his cheeks and jaw. It gave him a dangerous look. That was one adjective she never would've used to describe Danny before, but then she'd seen him come out of the shadows to stop Matt.

The man who had saved her had been one who was ready to do whatever he had to in order to stop Matt. The air around Danny had crackled with calmness while also showcasing the determined weapon he was in the face of such a menacing scene.

"I wanted to take you to that Christmas dance," he suddenly said.

She blinked, taken aback by his words until she remembered what they had talked about in the house. "Why didn't you?"

"I took a shift at work for a friend who wanted to bring his girlfriend to the dance. I hadn't intended to go. Besides, I wasn't brave enough to ask you."

"I would've said yes." She glanced at the floor and laughed softly. "I looked for you that night. I planned to ask you to dance."

His gaze darkened as his voice dipped into a husky whisper. "I missed out for sure."

Skylar lifted her free hand and tilted back his hat so she could better see his face. "There's still tonight."

There was a flash of hesitation, of doubt. Just when she thought he might step away, he wrapped his free arm around her and pulled her close. The moment their bodies touched, her blood ran hot.

She waited, her lips parted until he finally lowered his head. Just before their lips touched, he paused. She wound her arm around his neck, her fingers tangling in the dark hair at the nape.

Then—finally!—his mouth pressed against hers.

Skylar barely registered his soft, insistent lips before he brushed them over hers. She sighed, her body sinking against his. Both his arms came around her, allowing her to better wrap hers around his neck.

His tongue slid along her lips before slipping between them to tangle with her tongue. His kiss was . . . perfection.

They moved in unison, each taking and receiving until the kiss grew passionate, fiery. His hands were in her hair, gripping the strands firmly.

Then he spun her, pinning her against a stall with his

body. She felt his arousal. And her body burned for him. She hungered to feel his skin, his hard body—and most especially, his cock inside her.

Danny halted, his lips pressed against hers for a long moment. Then he lifted his head and looked at her. "You have no idea how long I've wanted to do that."

"Then don't stop."

"I'm not sure I can control myself."

She knew she couldn't control herself. "Maybe we don't need to."

He released her, taking a step back. "Having you back makes me crave you with a ferocity that should frighten you."

"You can't say things like that and not expect me to want to kiss you again."

"It's all I can think about."

Skylar didn't need to hear him say it again. She closed the distance between them and pressed her lips to his, reigniting the flame that he'd tried to stamp out.

His groan made her stomach flutter. His hands clutched her jacket as if he were trying to decide if he would push her away or pull her closer. Then they splayed on her back, pressing her tightly against him as he kissed her as if there were no tomorrow, as if the stars had finally aligned for them.

She surrendered to Danny, to the desire that blazed hot like an inferno between them. She'd never felt need so strong, a hunger so deep that it clawed up through her soul.

And she'd never tasted a kiss so absolute, so perfect. So . . . pure.

"I want you," he said between kisses.

Skylar couldn't form words to reply. Her body ached for his touch too much. She jerked off her coat and let it fall to the floor. When she shoved his jacket off his shoulders, he tore it away as if the thing offended him.

Then he lifted her until she wrapped her legs around him. With their lips still locked together, he walked them to a door and opened it.

Skylar briefly parted her lids to look inside and saw that it was the feed room. More importantly, it had bales and bales of hay.

Danny set her on her feet and pulled off his shirt before he spread it over the hay. "It itches like the dickens."

"I won't be feeling anything but you," she told him as she reached for him again.

Chapter 12

Skylar couldn't stop touching Danny. The moment his shirt came off, her hands needed to feel his body. And, oh, what a body it was. His shirts didn't hide his broad shoulders, but they did obscure his chiseled abs and rock-hard chest and arms. Her mouth watered at the sight before her.

She removed his hat and smiled up at him, slowly shaking her head. "Damn, sheriff. I wasn't expecting such a gorgeous body."

His cocky smile made her want to get him naked so she could get a look at the rest of him. But when she reached for his pants, he moved his hips away.

"Oh, no you don't," he said as he captured her hands and held them behind her back with one of his. "It's my turn to see you."

"Release me, and I'll be happy to take it all off."

The smile was gone, replaced by raw, unadulterated need. He let her go immediately.

Skylar grabbed her sweater by the hem and pulled it over her head. Her gaze was locked on his face when she reached behind her and unhooked her bra. A shiver went through her went she let it fall next to her sweater and saw the lust in Danny's eyes.

His gaze lifted to her face. "You're too far away."

She chuckled but didn't go to him. Instead, she took off her boots, jerking her chin to his so he'd do the same. He followed suit. Soon, they stood in nothing but their jeans.

"You first," she told him.

"I can barely keep my hands off you, so we'd better hurry."

Skylar smiled even as he took off his gun to set it on the floor, then unbuttoned his jeans and pushed them down his hips before stepping out of them to stand in a pair of orange boxer briefs.

She took note of the color but didn't say anything since it was her turn to remove her jeans. She didn't dally, and while she felt the cold, it didn't penetrate through the heat that each of them was giving off.

Then she stood in nothing but orange panties with white polka dots.

Danny's lips spread in a grin as he noticed. "Nice underwear. Looks like we both like orange. It's your turn to remove them first."

She was more than ready. She hooked her thumbs in the waist and pushed them down her legs before stepping out of them. Danny's gaze slowly looked her over from head to feet and back again. She didn't move, just let him look his fill since she intended to do the same with him.

"You're so beautiful," he said when he caught her gaze.

She looked down at his arousal, prominent through his briefs. "Your turn."

In seconds, the garment was gone. She walked to him and smoothed her hands over his chest, caressing his upper body from his shoulders to over his abs and down to his waist. After several passes, her hands went lower until they wrapped around his cock.

His breathing hitched, and his gaze burned into hers. "Skylar," he whispered.

She moved her hand up and down his length, but she didn't get the time she wanted. Before she knew it, he had her on her back and was leaning over her as he ran one hand from her breasts, down her stomach, over her hip, and then to her leg before moving back up.

She was so focused on the feeling of his hand on her skin that she jerked in surprise when his lips closed around her nipple, and his tongue began teasing the nub.

She was everything he'd dreamed of and more. Danny couldn't believe that he held Skylar Long in his arms. She was even more beautiful than he'd imagined.

Her breasts were large, filling his hands. And her nipples were sensitive, his every touch causing her to moan and arch her back.

He was pleased to find that she was devoid of any pubic hair. He spread her legs with his hand and lightly ran his fingers over her flesh while he tongued her nipple. And when he pushed a finger inside of her, he found her hot and wet. His cock jumped, eager to be where his finger was, filling her.

"Please," she begged. "I need you now."

Danny knew they wouldn't have long before someone came looking for them, and he didn't want to be interrupted. His entire high school career, he'd dreamed of all the ways he wanted to make love to Skylar. Now that she was naked in his arms, all he could think about was hearing her scream in pleasure.

He rolled on top of her, moving between her legs. She took his rod in hand and brought it to her entrance. Danny clenched his teeth when the head of his arousal breached her. He rocked his hips forward and filled her in one thrust.

Her nails dug into his sides as she moaned. He pulled out and thrust in again, going deeper this time. Her eyes opened as their gazes locked.

He began moving in and out of her, his hips pumping faster and harder. She wrapped her legs around him, locking her ankles as she met him thrust for thrust. Watching the pleasure cross her face was one of the most beautiful things Danny had ever witnessed.

She whispered his name as her breaths grew harsh. Then she stiffened, a cry falling from her lips. He covered her mouth so no one would hear as he ate up every sound that fell from her lips.

The sight of her in such a state of bliss broke the last vestiges of his control. His climax slammed into him with the force of a herd of horses. It took his breath away, locking it in his lungs.

The ecstasy was so intense that time stood still. All he felt, all that mattered was Skylar.

When he came to, she held him against her. He hadn't remembered falling forward, didn't recall her arms going around him. But he knew he was exactly where he wanted to be.

"That was amazing," she whispered in his ear.

He rose up on his elbows to look at her. "It certainly was."

"We're going to do that again, aren't we?" she asked pointedly, daring him to say otherwise.

Danny kissed the tip of her nose. It wouldn't matter what he wanted. Now that he'd had Skylar, there was no turning back. "Most definitely."

"Good, because that was something incredible. And I want more."

He pulled out of her, realizing when he saw his cock that they'd had unprotected sex.

"I have an IUD," she told him.

That was a relief, but he never had sex without a condom. It just went to show how Skylar made him forget himself.

Danny stood and gathered her clothes before handing them to her. They dressed in silence, but they couldn't stop smiling and looking at each other.

"I really wish we would've done that in school," she said.

He shook his head. "It wasn't our time then. We would've messed things up."

"You're saying that, despite our mutual attraction back then, it wouldn't have worked?"

He shrugged as he shook hay from his shirt and slid his arms into the sleeves before buttoning it. "I'm saying that everything happens for a reason. We weren't meant to be together then."

"But we are now? Yeah. I can see that."

Danny didn't tell her that anything could happen, that this could all be nothing more than a fling. He wanted more—so much more—from Skylar. But he knew better than to try and hold onto something that wasn't his. He'd tried to hold onto her in school, but she'd never been his.

She put his hat atop his head, and they left the feed room to retrieve their coats. They had just put them on when the door opened, and Clayton walked in.

He took one look at the two of them and backed out. "Sorry."

"Clayton, it's fine," Skylar called. "We just came out for a talk."

Danny didn't say anything because he knew Clayton had determined exactly what they had been doing.

Clayton returned to the stables and smiled at them, his gaze landing on Danny. "I'm glad you decided to come tonight."

"Me, too," Danny admitted.

Skylar put her hands into her pockets. "Matt knows I'm going for the restraining order in the morning."

Clayton nodded, his lips pressed together in irritation. "I heard. He can't do anything. It's up to you to submit the evidence."

"That, along with the arrest, will be enough to give you the order of protection," Danny said.

"Then why am I so scared?" she asked.

"Because it's a step in telling the world what a monster he is," Danny answered.

Skylar's blue eyes slid to him. "Will Matt be there?"

"I have no idea. If his lawyer is smart, he'll keep Matt far away. It won't be in his best interests to be there, fighting it."

Clayton nodded. "Danny's right. I don't think Matt will be at the courthouse, but you might want to prepare yourself just in case you see him nearby."

Danny wished he could give her an escort, but that would be like waving a red flag in front of a bull. He wanted Matt gone and out of Skylar's life, he didn't want to cause more trouble.

"You won't be alone," Clayton said to Skylar. "We're all going to be with you."

Danny nodded when she looked at him. "I'll be at the courthouse, as well. For you. The judge will have access to the arrest files, but she might want to ask me a question or two. She has in the past. Small towns and all that."

Skylar frowned then. "I'm from here, but I moved away. And Matt is from Houston. Will any of that make a difference in her decision?"

"Based on what Leslie told me, no," Clayton answered.

"That's a relief." Skylar shot Clayton a smile, but when her gaze moved to Danny, the smile widened.

He wanted to take her hand, to draw her against him. Hell, he wanted her in his arms again so they could fall asleep together.

"I'll leave you two to talk." Clayton's gaze lingered on Danny a beat before he turned on his heel and walked out.

Skylar shook her head and laughed when the door closed behind Clayton. "He knows."

"Yeah." No use sugarcoating anything.

She pulled her hand from her pocket and grabbed his. "I don't regret what we did, nor do I intend to stop seeing you. If you want to see me, that is," she said hesitantly.

He pulled her against him and held her with one arm. "I most definitely do."

"Just what I wanted to hear." She flashed a wide smile before clearing her throat and becoming serious. "But if Matt gets wind of this—"

"I know. It's why I tried to stay away from you. I thought it would be easier if I wasn't around, but I want to be with you during all of this."

Her gaze softened as she looked up at him. "I'd like that."

"But," he said, lingering on the word as he pulled away so she could look at him, "if at any time, it appears as if Matt might figure it out, I'll stop making an appearance with you. It'll only be for a short time. He needs to get out of your life."

"You're right," she said with a sigh. "I just hate giving in to anything regarding him."

"We may not have to. Just be prepared."

She rested her cheek on his chest. "We'll make sure

we only ever touch each other when we're here. No long looks, no obvious desire, no touching, and nothing but friendly smiles and courteous talk between friends. He'll never know."

"Sounds good."

But Danny knew they didn't have a chance in hell of Matt not noticing.

Chapter 13

December 5th

Waking up to the smell of gingerbread cookies was almost as good as kissing Danny. It was too bad he wasn't in bed with Skylar.

She couldn't stop smiling as she sat up and stretched. Not even knowing that today was the day she had to go in front of the judge and discuss the restraining order could diminish her happiness.

As she rose from the bed and got into the shower to ready herself for the day, she couldn't help but think about what Danny had said the night before and how it hadn't been their time for each other when they were in high school.

And she couldn't help hoping that now was their time. She couldn't explain her feelings for Danny. It was almost as if they'd always been there, but she hadn't noticed them. That wasn't entirely true. She had always felt . . . unsettled. Not in her everyday life, but in relationships.

Like a voice in her head had kept whispering words that the outside world had drowned out. Now, the world was quiet, and she could hear the voice—and it kept telling her that she was where she was supposed to be.

How ironic, since she hadn't been able to get out of this town fast enough. Yet it was her hometown—and Danny—that reminded her of who she'd once been. Both also helped her to find the strength that she'd thought she lost.

It saddened her to think that she had spent so many years not realizing how unhappy she was. She had a good job, but it didn't satisfy her as it once had. She had friends, but none she trusted enough to help her with the situation with Matt.

She'd thought the tightness she felt in her chest had been the knowledge that she'd chosen poorly by moving in with Matt. The real truth was that she had been unsure of them going forward.

Except when she tried to talk to him about it, he'd always had good arguments for them living together. It was only the second time in her life that she had moved in with a boyfriend. The first had lasted nearly two years before they decided to part ways.

That had been during college, and Skylar spent the rest of her time living alone. It's how she liked things. She'd had a few boyfriends through the years, and they would often stay a night or two with her, but each time they spoke about living together, she quickly shut them down.

She hadn't done that with Matt because he had treated her well, they had a lot in common, and they'd a great time together. She'd believed that none of her past relationships had worked because she hadn't put enough effort into them, and since she was getting older, it made her take a hard look at what she had with Matt.

What angered her the most was that she'd let age

factor into it. That was likely because she had listened to her friends talk about not wanting to be in their forties and single. One of the few times in her life that she'd let peer pressure help make a decision for her—and the outcome had been disastrous.

Though she couldn't blame her friends. None of them could've known what type of man Matt was. But Skylar had. At least, her intuition had warned her not to stay with him.

But she hadn't listened to her gut. In fact, she had flat-out ignored it, thinking it was just her indecision regarding what to do with her life.

By the time she'd finished with her shower and dressed, she knew for certain that no matter what happened with the restraining order and Matt, she wanted to see where things went with Danny. Skylar hoped that it wasn't just some fling.

For the first time in her life, she didn't have that gnawing uncertainty when she was with a guy. Because with Danny, everything felt . . . right. As if it were supposed to be.

As if it had always been meant to be.

On her way down the stairs, she thought back to the girl she'd been in high school. She'd been naïve and too cocky for her own good. Her first year of college had taught her a lot, and she'd continued to expand her mind and her thinking afterward. She'd known, even as a little girl, that it was her destiny to leave her hometown and experience the big city.

The past years had changed her, though, shaping her into a woman who was open to possibilities, one who accepted who she was and loved herself for it, someone who wasn't afraid to make changes.

She had been none of those things when she graduated high school and left home. Maybe Danny was right.

Perhaps they hadn't been ready for whatever was between them.

Because while she might not be sure of exactly what she and Danny were to each other, she knew for certain that he wasn't faking his passion or the desire. It had been clear in his kisses, in the way he held her. And most definitely in the way he looked at her.

"Good morning," Abby called when she spotted Skylar coming into the kitchen.

She glanced at Abby and returned the greeting but then headed to Hope, who was waving at her. "And how are you this morning?" she asked the toddler.

Hope just laughed and looked at her mother.

"I'm about to fix eggs. Would you like some?" Abby offered.

Skylar shook her head. "I don't think I could get food down this morning."

"I don't blame you. The water is hot if you want tea."

Skylar headed straight for the cabinet with the mugs and began steeping the teabag in the hot water. She then turned to watch Abby. "I really appreciate all you and your family have done."

"We're happy to do it," Abby said as she cooked her eggs. "Danny has done so much for all of us. He rarely asks for help with anything."

"He never did in school either." Skylar shrugged. "I just hope that nothing that happens with Matt puts your family in danger."

Abby snorted as she put the eggs on her plate. "This place is like Fort Knox, so I'm not worried about anyone coming here. We are aware that Matt could try something when we go out, which is why we've taken precautions."

"You shouldn't have to do that."

"And you shouldn't have to hide in fear for your life,"

Abby argued. "We wouldn't be doing any of this if we didn't want to. Danny is like family, and you obviously mean a lot to him."

Skylar looked away, unable to hold Abby's blue eyes. "He would've helped out anyone."

"That's true. But he wouldn't have brought just anyone to us."

That made Skylar's stomach quiver with excitement. "Have you ever been in a situation where everything suddenly makes sense? That you just *know* you're where you're supposed to be?"

"Actually, I have." Abby smiled, her expression becoming dreamy. "It was with Clayton. I wanted to hate him at first because I blamed him for Brice being arrested for cattle theft, but I soon realized that it wasn't Clayton's fault. It was mine."

"Yours?" Skylar asked in confusion.

Abby shrugged as she took a bite and chewed. Then she answered. "Our father died when we were young, and our mother skipped town the night I graduated. She left me to care for Brice and Caleb. I did the best I could, but we were barely making it. I was working all the time just to pay the bills and put food on the table, not to mention, keep my brothers in clothes. Brice had fallen in with a bad crowd, but he also knew how difficult things were. He thought if he could get some money, he could ease my burden."

"That didn't go as planned, I take it?"

Abby shook her head. "They got caught. The men scattered, leaving Brice to take the fall. Danny was the one who arrested him and called me. Thankfully, Clayton didn't press charges. He made a deal with Brice that my brother would work on the ranch to pay off the money owed for the stolen cattle and the prized bull. I knew Brice would be working for years to pay off such a debt, but that being at the ranch meant he wouldn't be hanging with that bad crowd he'd fallen in with either."

"I can't believe Clayton didn't press charges," Skylar said.

"He hoped to earn Brice's trust so my brother would give him the names of the thieves. It worked. With Brice being here, Caleb also wanted to work at the ranch. Clayton agreed, and soon, I was here all the time, picking them up and dropping them off. During all of that, things between Clayton and me fell into place somehow. But I know what you mean. Each time I was with him, I didn't want to be anywhere else. With him, the world made sense."

Skylar nodded, and her eyes widened. "Yes. Exactly that."

Abby grinned as she finished her eggs. "I take it you're talking about Danny?"

"Yes."

"Good," Abby said with a nod. "I figured there was something there by the way he looks at you."

Skylar wished she could see the look Abby was talking about.

Abby's face grew serious. "It complicates things, though."

"I know. Danny and I talked about that last night."

"Don't let that stop either of you," Abby stated firmly.

Skylar shrugged. "I wish I knew what to do and say to get Matt to leave me alone and go home."

"That's what Leslie is for. That woman is a shark, in the best possible way," Abby said with a chuckle. "Trust her like you trust Danny, and things will be all right."

Skylar sure hoped so. The closer it came to the time she needed to leave for the courthouse, the more nervous she became. She drank her tea while Abby wiped Hope's face after her breakfast and then cleaned up the kitchen.

Skylar found her gaze moving to the stables as she recalled the time she and Danny had stolen the previous night. It had been amazing, but she wished they could have had all night. Better yet, she wished they could be completely alone without anyone around.

Not that she wasn't thankful for having a place to hide from Matt, but she was ready for him to relinquish his hold on her and go back to Houston. Surely, once he realized that she didn't want anything to do with him, Matt would do just that.

Surely.

Because she wanted to put her past—especially the last few months—behind her for good. There was a future for her here, one she hadn't realized was there, and she planned to grab it with both hands and hold on for dear life. She was no longer afraid of Matt or what he might do to her. She had friends that she could count on. More importantly, she had found her inner strength again.

And she was going to fight with all she had.

The knock on the door startled her. She took a deep breath as Abby answered it, opening it wide to show Leslie. Skylar's attorney wore a black Armani sheath dress with white pinstripes and black heels. She'd draped a long, white coat over the dress to shield her from the cold.

"Perfect," Leslie said to Skylar when she walked in.

Skylar glanced down at her black turtleneck shirt, dress pants, and stilettos. She'd opted for gold studs to match her camel-colored coat that stopped at the top of her thighs. Her hair was gathered at the back of her head with a hairband.

She smiled at Leslie. "Is everything set?"

"Yes. All you need to do is stand with me before the judge. She'll ask a few questions and then make a decision on the order of protection. I don't see any reason she would refuse it, but be prepared either way."

"I always think of the worst, so I'll be prepared," Skylar said as she rinsed out her mug and set it in the sink.

Then she slipped on her coat and gathered the small black purse that held her cell phone, wallet, and nude lipstick. She faced the women. Hope smiled and waved, while Abby gave her a thumbs-up. Leslie lifted her chin and nodded her head once.

As Skylar walked from the house, she kept wishing Danny was there beside her. He said he'd be in the court-room, and she could hardly wait to see him. She would have to be sure not to let anything show if he did show up, no matter how excited she might be. Not that Matt would be there, but others would.

Skylar got into Leslie's silver BMW 8 Series and settled back in the heated seat as she pictured the future that she wanted.

Chapter 14

"You were right, Danny. Leslie and Skylar were followed."

Danny held his anger in check as he listened to Jace through the cell phone. He sat in his patrol SUV, staring at the courthouse. "How many?"

"Just one car with a single man inside."

Danny's gaze roamed over the vehicles in the parking lot before a figure walking toward the building caught his attention. "Matt's lawyer, Rodney, is here. I had a feeling he'd attend."

"At least Matt isn't there."

"Whatever is said in that courtroom will get back to Matt," Danny stated.

Jace blew out a breath. "Leslie and Skylar are less than five minutes away."

"Stay on the vehicle following them. Just don't let him see you."

"Oh, I'm better than that," Jace said before he disconnected.

Any other time, Danny would've grinned at the comment, but not this time. Danny had only gotten a few hours of sleep. He'd fallen asleep as soon as his head hit the pillow, but around five that morning, he'd had a dream about Matt attacking Skylar. Danny had woken up in a cold sweat and hadn't been able to go back to sleep.

He couldn't remember much of the dream except for Skylar's face, bloody from the beating. Danny rubbed his eyes with his thumb and forefinger. He never should have crossed the line by sleeping with Skylar. He'd known it was wrong before he ever kissed her, but he hadn't been able to stop himself.

His gaze dropped to his hand. He could still recall the feel of her velvety skin, the way her warm body felt against his. Even after satisfying himself, he'd been hard and needy that morning—for Skylar.

He sat up straighter the moment he spotted Leslie's car pull into the parking lot. Danny spotted a black Suburban drive past them, and he'd bet his pension that was who had been following them. Danny's gaze scanned the cars once more. The Suburban didn't pull in because someone else was here watching, someone besides Rodney. The question was: who?

Danny didn't see movement from anyone even after Leslie and Skylar had parked and exited the car. The women walked side by side to the courthouse, Leslie talking while Skylar nodded, listening.

He knew the moment Skylar spotted him. She didn't smile or show anything on her face, but her gaze lingered on him for two heartbeats before she looked away. He wanted to jump out and rush to her, but he stopped himself just as he was about to open his door. He had to remember that they were hiding this . . . well, whatever they had.

The goal was to get Matt to go away. He wouldn't do that if he believed Danny was interested in Skylar. Or worse, he thought that Skylar might want to be with Danny.

"Fuck me," Danny murmured. He'd really managed to put himself between a rock and a hard place.

All his training and instincts told him to keep watching for anyone who appeared to be following Skylar, or might harass her, Leslie, or anyone from the ranch. Not that Danny was worried about the men. Each of them had served in the military and were weapons unto themselves.

If someone was stupid enough to tangle with Clayton, Caleb, Brice, Jace, or Cooper, then that was their problem.

But Danny's heart told him to get inside the courtroom and be there for moral support for Skylar. He wanted to be there, and not just to hear what the judge might say. He also knew men like Matt. They were vindictive.

Danny's phone vibrated in the cupholder. He picked it up and recognized the sheriff's number. "Hello?"

"Sheriff, I wanted to let you know that you don't have to keep watch. I'm here."

"Where?" he asked Deputy Wilson.

"I'm in my fiancée's Wrangler. I'm also out of uniform."

Danny grinned when he spotted the navy Jeep situated in the back of the parking lot. "You have a good view?"

"Yes, sir."

"There is a black Suburban that followed Skylar and Leslie here."

There was a beat of silence. "I take that to mean you have others watching Miss Long?"

"Don't take it personally, Wilson. This is nothing against you."

"No, sir. I understand. The Gaudets' reach is long, and your job is to keep Miss Long safe."

Danny was glad the young deputy understood. "Matt Gaudet's lawyer is here."

"I saw him. You should probably get in there before it starts. I've got things covered out here."

Danny wished he had ten more deputies just like Wilson. "Let me know if anything comes up."

"Yes, sir."

Danny ended the call and adjusted his hat atop his head before he stepped out of his SUV. He shut and locked the door as he walked away without looking toward the Jeep. The moment Danny was inside the building, his gaze searched the faces for Matt's as he made his way to the courtroom.

The door didn't make a sound as it swung open. Danny took a seat, his eyes landing on Rodney first. The lawyer's gaze met his before he quickly looked away while typing furiously on his phone. Danny then swung his eyes toward Leslie and Skylar.

Both women looked confident as they sat with their heads leaning toward each other, talking in low tones. Danny wished Skylar would look his way, but he was glad she didn't. With Rodney watching her like a hawk, any little slip-up might send Matt into a rage.

Although, if Rodney were as good of an attorney as he was supposed to be, he would keep such things from his client in order to keep Matt under control.

Danny stretched out his legs and crossed his arms over his chest. If Matt did have another public display of anger, that could work in their favor. It could ensure that he never got near Skylar again.

Then Danny recalled how many times people disregarded orders of protection.

His stomach knotted at the thought. He didn't care if he had to watch over Skylar for the rest of her life, he'd do it. *If* she remained in town. If she returned to Houston . . .

He didn't even want to think about that.

"All rise," boomed a voice at the front of the court.

Danny and the others stood as Judge Harmon walked in and took a seat. She was a tiny thing, not even five feet tall. Her salt and pepper hair was slicked back in a bun, and she wore her customary pearl studs.

Dressed in black robes, she sank into the chair and looked out over the courtroom. "Ms. Ross, let's get started," she declared in a booming voice that seemed so at odds with the petite body it was housed in.

After everyone had been seated, Leslie rose again, and for the next twenty minutes, described, in detail, the timeline of Skylar and Matt's relationship. The pictures of Skylar bruised and battered were displayed on a large screen.

It didn't matter how many times Danny saw them, it turned his stomach. He never understood people's need to hurt others or animals. It was the aspect of his job that he hated the most. Although bringing an abuser to justice was very satisfying.

When Leslie got to the part of Matt's arrest, the judge flipped through the papers before her and nodded when she found the report from the sheriff's department. Both Danny and Wilson had filed reports. Danny because he was first on scene and had called it in, and Wilson because he was the one who'd cuffed and booked Matt.

"Ms. Long," the judge addressed Skylar. "Do you feel as if your life is in danger?"

Skylar got to her feet. "I do, Your Honor."

"Then I will grant an emergency protective order, effective immediately," she said.

Danny didn't smile, though inside, he cheered. He'd

had a feeling the judge would give Skylar the order of protection, but freakier things had happened, especially since the judge was friends with the Gaudet family.

Matt's attorney didn't seem at all shocked by the outcome. Rodney didn't look up from his phone even after the judge had left, and Skylar and Leslie quietly celebrated. Danny remained seated, even when the women walked past. He gave them a nod.

A few minutes later, when the room was setting up for another hearing, Rodney finally gathered his briefcase and put away his phone. Danny rose and stepped out into the aisle just as the lawyer approached.

"Morning," Danny said.

Rodney bowed his head. "Sheriff. What can I do for you?"

"I hope you'll tell your client that the sheriff's department will be enforcing the protective order to the fullest."

"My client isn't so foolish as to go against a court order like this," Rodney stated testily.

Danny heard the words and the firm voice, but he saw the uncertainty in the attorney's face. Not even Rodney was sure that Matt would adhere to the restraining order, and that meant more work for Danny and his deputies.

It was a good thing that Skylar was staying at the East Ranch. As long as she was there, Matt couldn't harm her. But that couldn't last forever.

"You remember that you can't arrest my client simply because you want to."

Danny smiled. "If I arrested everyone who irked me, you'd be in jail. Since that hasn't happened, I don't believe your client has anything to worry about. I follow the law. You should make sure he does, as well."

"He will."

"Do you have a sister? Daughter?" Danny asked when Rodney started to walk away.

The attorney halted and turned to face him. "Both. Why?"

"What would you do if a man hurt your sister or your daughter like what happened to Miss Long? What would you do?"

Rodney held Danny's gaze for a long minute. Then he took a deep breath and said, "Sheriff, I'm Texan, born and raised. I learned to shoot and ride when I was just a little thing. And I'm an excellent shot. I think that sums up exactly what I'd do."

"Yet you're representing a man who has hurt a woman. Isn't that a conflict of interest?"

Rodney took a step closer so their already whispered words went softer. "You have to do things in your job you don't like, I imagine."

"All the time."

"That's the same for anyone."

Danny looked into Rodney's dark eyes and nodded. He hadn't wanted to like the man, but it was turning out that he did. "It's too bad we're on opposite sides."

The lawyer flashed a small smile before he turned on his heel and left. Danny followed a few seconds later. When he got out to the parking lot, Leslie's car was gone, as were Rodney's and Wilson's vehicles.

Danny walked to his SUV. As he approached, he frowned when he saw something sticking out of his tire. He noticed that it was a knife as he got closer. Then he saw that his other tire was flat, as well. A quick look proved that all four tires had been slashed.

He pulled out his phone and called the station while looking around him. While he waited for someone to come and replace the tires, he walked back into the courtroom and the surveillance room so he could check the cameras. They were all over the place. One of them had to have caught the person responsible for such an act. And Danny really hoped it was Matt Gaudet.

Except when he found the footage, he was shocked to discover that it was a woman who had stabbed his tires.

Chapter 15

"It went just as I thought it would," Leslie said as she pulled out of the parking lot.

Skylar released a long breath. "This is one step in getting Matt to hopefully leave me alone, but we both know it won't stop him."

"You're right. It's a piece of paper, regardless that it's a legal document. Many stalkers and abusers completely disregard it. But it does help. Matt has been arrested, his abuse witnessed by the sheriff. Now you have the emergency protective order. If he comes within fifty feet of you, continues to threaten you, or does anything to make you feel as if your life is in danger, you can call the police."

Skylar didn't bother mentioning that it would take time for the police to arrive. It wasn't as if she had a security detail following her around all the time. If Matt came to her home, she might not even have time to call 911.

"Look, I'm not going to sugarcoat this," Leslie continued. "My cousin's friend got a restraining order, and unfortunately, it didn't help her. She died. But she also didn't take the advice given to her by the police or my cousin."

Skylar looked at her attorney. "And what advice was that?"

"Don't be alone."

"Alone?" Skylar asked with a frown.

Leslie nodded and turned on her blinker as she moved over into a turning lane on her way back to the East Ranch. "I know it's not optimal, but when your life is literally on the line, set aside comfort for a minute. There aren't many places in a two-hundred-mile radius as well-guarded and protected as the East Ranch. Stay there as long as you can. Because the minute you return to Houston, the very minute you're alone, Matt will come after you."

"Maybe."

Leslie snorted loudly as she turned the car. "There's no maybe about it. He will. I saw the look in his eyes."

"When did you see him?"

"It's not hard to find a new arrival in this town. Especially one that's being talked about like Matt Gaudet."

Skylar shrugged, knowing Leslie was right. "What did you think of him?"

"I think he's handsome, and he knows it. It's obvious by the way he dresses and acts that he's used to wealth."

That made Skylar frown. "What do you mean? I didn't notice anything like that with him."

"Because he was hiding it from you. He didn't want you to know who he really was."

Skylar shook her head. "It's exhausting to keep up such lies. Why would anyone do that?"

"Because they can. He manipulates. Not to mention, he's a narcissist."

Just great. Boy, she really knew how to pick them. "So, what did you see in his eyes?"

"He feels wronged that you left him. Add in his arrest and this protective order, and he'll want revenge. I, personally, think he'll have a hard time deciding if he just wants payback or if he wants you back."

Now that shocked Skylar. She gave Leslie a look of doubt. "He doesn't want me anymore."

"Contrary to what you may think, he wants you more than ever. I'm not a psychiatrist or anything, but I've seen enough cases like this. He likely feels offended that you chose to end things. In his mind, he believes he's the one in control, and you took that away from him. He could very well want you back long enough to end things himself."

"That's ridiculous."

Leslie chuckled. "You aren't wrong."

She pulled up to the ranch gates and punched a button to wait for Abby or someone to let them in. Skylar looked across the huge expanse of pasture to the house and thought about Danny.

The moment she'd seen him enter the courtroom out of the corner of her eye, she'd been elated. It had taken great willpower not to turn and look at him. Even walking out, she had only given him a brief glance.

But the moment his hazel eyes met hers, it felt as if the sun were bathing her in light.

"I normally take my clients to lunch after a win," Leslie said as the gate opened and they drove forward. "But I don't think it'd be wise to test things out so quickly."

"Actually, it probably would have been the best time. Matt is likely with his attorney."

Leslie braked, halting the car as she looked at Skylar. "You're right. Want to go back out?"

"Thanks, but we're already here. And, really, it should be me taking you out after jumping into this so quickly and getting to work."

Leslie rolled her brown eyes and continued driving. "This was nothing. A few forms entered in and showing up in front of the judge. I'd like to think this is over, but that's far from the case. The Gaudets will consider this a loss, and families like theirs don't take defeat sitting down."

Skylar waited until the car had stopped once more in front of the house before she eyed Leslie. "You aren't coming in?"

"I'm going to stay one step ahead of things for you."

"What do you think the Gaudets will do?"

Leslie shrugged and shook her head. "I don't know exactly. I'd stay away from any sort of social media and news for the next week. The family could come after you."

"For what? I'm not the one who did anything."

"The thing you need to remember is that nothing about this is fair. You aren't on equal footing with them, and even though you're the one who was abused, they could make you out to be the bad guy. All I'm saying is prepare yourself."

"I guess I'd better call my parents, then."

Leslie's lips twisted as she wrinkled her nose. "That might be wise. Do they know what's going on?"

"I wanted to keep them out of it so they wouldn't worry. I'm really glad they no longer live here."

"You still better warn them."

Skylar grabbed her purse and smiled. "Thank you. I'm glad I have you on my side."

"Everything is going to be all right. You not only have me, you have Danny, and I can't remember this county ever having such a great sheriff. Then there are the Easts and Harpers and their friends. Honey, you have a strong ring of allies around you that Matt will never get through."

By the time Skylar made her way to the door of the house, she felt really good. She turned and waved to

Leslie. The woman honked while driving away. When Skylar turned back around, Abby stood with the door open, a bright smile on her face.

"Congratulations," she said.

Skylar laughed. "You already heard the news, then?"

"Danny texted us as soon as he left the courthouse, but I'm not surprised by the outcome. With the evidence, Matt's arrest, and the details of the night in question, the restraining order was a pretty sure deal."

Skylar followed Abby into the kitchen and set her purse down as she took off her coat. "I wasn't sure about any of it. Matt's family has connections everywhere, even with the judge."

"That may be true, but she ruled in your favor."

Everyone was so excited, and Skylar felt she needed to be, as well. After all, the restraining order was a big deal. Why then didn't she feel protected?

Because she knew if Matt really wanted to get to her, he wouldn't let a piece of paper stop him.

"I know you're still worried," Abby said. "I would be, as well. Anyone would."

Skylar hopped onto a barstool and propped her elbows on the island counter. "Leslie said the key is for me to stay away from Matt for a little while."

"It's good advice. Matter of fact, Danny said the same thing over text. And I don't need to tell you that you're welcome to stay here as long as you like."

"I don't want to wear out my welcome."

Abby gave her a flat look. "That's not going to happen. Like I told you the first night, this house is big enough that you don't even have to see us if you don't want to."

Skylar chuckled because the house really was that huge. "The point is that I shouldn't have to hide."

"When you come up against men like Matt, you do what you have to in order to stay safe."

That was true. Besides, Skylar wanted a future. She wasn't ready to die or live her life in a constant state of fear. "I took a week of vacation, but I can't take more than that."

"You might get paid more in Houston, but I bet you could find something here. If you want to stay, that is."

Skylar knew Abby was not so subtly reminding her of their talk about Danny earlier. Not that she needed that prod. She couldn't stop thinking about him.

"I thought I'd feel different if I ever came back here," Skylar said. "But when I'm riding around, it all looks the same. There are changes, of course. New buildings, renovations, and city improvements, but it still *feels* the same. Like I never left."

"You haven't come back at all since graduation?"

Skylar shrugged one shoulder. "A few times for holidays, but I didn't go see anyone. Just my parents, and then I headed back to Houston. The last time I was here was about ten years ago when I helped my parents move."

"Wow," Abby said, her eyes wide and her brows raised. "Do you still feel the need to get out?"

She shook her head. "Not at all. It could be because of Matt."

"True. You might be connecting him to Houston, so now the city is tainted in your mind. Or," Abby said, drawing out the word, "you might have discovered that you belong here."

"I asked Danny last night why we didn't date in school. He said it hadn't been our time."

Abby nodded and crossed her arms over her chest as she leaned back against the counter. "You each had living to do."

"Growing up, you mean," Skylar said with a chuckle.

Abby grinned. "Well, that too, but I'm talking about dating other people, discovering who you are, what you like, and all of that. It's not something you can do when you're tied to someone else because you inadvertently take on their traits. Are you considering moving here?"

"I don't know." And that was the truth. Skylar didn't want to make a rash decision out of fear.

Abby gave her a comforting smile. "I think you need to do what makes sense for you. It might be returning to Houston. It might be going to another city. Or . . . you could remain here, but nothing has to be decided now."

"Good point." Skylar got to her feet. "I think I'm going to go change out of these clothes and into something more comfortable. Thank you again, Abby. For the friendship and hospitality."

"Any time."

Skylar made her way up the stairs, her mind considering the option of remaining in her hometown. At one time in her life, that'd seemed like a death sentence, and yet, it no longer felt that way.

There were stores and workers in Houston who recognized her face from frequent visits, but it wasn't the same as living in a small town. People looked out for others. The drawback was how nosey everyone was, but that went hand-in-hand with the rest.

After she'd changed into jeans and an oversized maroon sweatshirt that hung off one shoulder, she found herself searching real estate listings in the area. The first house she pulled up was one that she had loved when she was growing up. It had a lot of charm. It was on the small side, but it was one of those houses that you wanted to go in and explore.

Skylar clicked on the photos and was amazed at the updates that had been done in the home. She loved everything about it—aside from the yellow paint in the bedroom. That would have to go, but everything else was good enough for her to move in right away.

She stopped, shocked that she was actually considering purchasing the house. Her gaze dropped to the price, and she smiled. Yet her finger hesitated over the button to contact the realtor.

Was it because she wasn't sure about moving? Or was it because she didn't want Matt getting wind of her decision?

Or was it both?

Skylar put away her phone and went downstairs to find Abby.

Chapter 16

December 9th

Shit, he was tired. Bone-weary and just exhausted. Danny rubbed his eyes with his thumb and forefinger before he reached for the cup of coffee. He'd stopped keeping track after his sixth cup.

He flipped through the reports on his desk, trying to get through all the paperwork. He had a meeting with the mayor that he had to attend in about an hour, so he was trying to get as much of his desk cleared as he could in the meantime.

There was a knock on his door that drew his attention. Danny waved in Wilson, who slipped inside the office and shut the door before taking a seat.

"I take it you have news," Danny said.

Deputy Glen Wilson licked his lips. "Mr. Gaudet is still in town."

Danny ran a hand down his face and sighed loudly, leaning back in his chair. It had been four days since the restraining order had been issued. Danny had thought that Matt would get the hint and go back to Houston but, apparently, they hadn't been so lucky.

Or should he say that Skylar hadn't been that fortunate?

"And his lawyer?"

Wilson crossed his ankle over his knee. "He hasn't been back since Miss Long was in court."

"Well, Matt stayed for some reason."

"I think I know what that is," Wilson hedged.

It was obvious that the deputy didn't want to say whatever it was. "Spit it out, Wilson, before it sours your mouth more."

"Two hours ago, Mr. Gaudet's youngest brother arrived."

That news wasn't great, but it wasn't horrible either. "Okay. We'll just have two of them to watch now."

Wilson's lips compressed as his face puckered in unease. "Actually, there's more. Just a few minutes ago, Matt's parents were seen getting food. I checked the hotels in town, but they aren't staying here. They're staying about thirty minutes away."

Of course, they were. Because their little town didn't have a five-star hotel. But Danny kept that part to himself. He had no use for people with egos, and that's exactly what the Gaudets had. "Thanks for the update."

"It's bad news for Miss Long, isn't it?"

Danny shrugged, but he had a bad feeling in his gut. "It might be nothing. Perhaps they're here to get their son back to Houston."

"Let's hope that's the case, sheriff, because the only other reason they're here would be because of Miss Long."

Danny forced a smile to his lips. "Miss Long is in a safe place. We don't need to worry about her."

Though Danny had been doing just that. Hell, he'd even stayed away from the ranch for the past five days, waiting for Matt to leave town. He'd asked that Clayton try and explain that to Skylar.

Clayton's texted response was simple—DUMBASS.

Danny had to agree with his friend. He should've gone to see Skylar, but he'd played it safe. Now, more Gaudets were in town, and that could only spell trouble for everyone. As much as Danny wanted to spend all his time protecting Skylar, he had an entire county to look after, not just one woman.

He was so engrossed in his thoughts that it took Danny a moment to realize that Wilson was still in his office. He focused on the deputy and noticed that Wilson was looking more uneasy than before.

Danny raised a brow in question while waiting for the deputy to get on with whatever he had to say.

"I'm guessing you haven't seen the latest."

With his stomach growing more queasy by the second and tightening with apprehension and worry, Danny shook his head.

Wilson cleared his throat and drew his cell phone from his uniform pocket. After a few seconds, he handed the device over. Danny didn't want to take it, but curiosity got the better of him. Besides, knowledge was power, right? At least, that's what he told himself.

At the top of the screen in bold letters was the headline: *Scorned woman lashes out at prominent Houston family.*

Danny didn't want to read the rest. He knew it was all lies, but he scrolled down. A picture of Skylar leaving the courthouse with Leslie was next, and right below that was a picture of Skylar smiling up at Matt with his arm wrapped around her.

The article went on to paint Skylar as nothing more than a gold-digger who'd trumped up lies when things didn't go her way. Danny had to admit, the writer did a good job of pointing out everything that would make others believe that Skylar was lying about the abuse since she hadn't gone to the police. No one had ever seen any marks on her, and she had moved in with Matt.

As a policeman, Danny knew that none of that mattered when it came to evidence. But most people reading the article didn't know the ins and outs of such a situation, which was exactly what the Gaudet family wanted. The simple fact was that social media and any news articles could swing the tide of the public's opinion. It happened more times than not.

And the Gaudets were proving what a well-known, wealthy family could do.

"When did this come out?" Danny asked Wilson.

The deputy scratched his jaw. "About ten this morning."

Which meant there was no doubt that Skylar knew about it. And Danny wasn't there to comfort her. That would change, though. He planned to go see her later tonight.

"Two days ago, our own newspaper came out with an article."

Danny noted Wilson's wide smile. Obviously, he needed to stay more up to date on the goings-on with the local paper. "And?"

The deputy pulled a folded-up paper from his back pocket and handed it to Danny. "That's not just circulating here. Someone—I'm guessing our very own Beverly Barnes—sent it to a Houston news station. It was on the six o'clock news tonight."

Danny opened the paper to find the front page showing a picture of Matt Gaudet in handcuffs being led into the courthouse. Not far below it, though much, much smaller, was a picture of Skylar's smashed driver's-side window where Matt had broken it to get to her.

The article detailed the facts, though Beverly leaned heavily on Matt as an abuser. And while Beverly didn't print the pictures showcasing Skylar's injuries, it was mentioned about them being used in the court case requesting the restraining order.

"I might like this article, but I think it'll do more harm than good. For Skylar." Danny folded it back up and set it aside to read a second time later.

Wilson folded his hands together. "Someone needs to stand up for Miss Long."

"I don't disagree, deputy, but the Gaudets' reach is very long. And their money is endless. Skylar can't fight them head-on like that."

"Then maybe she doesn't."

Danny frowned. "Meaning?"

"Miss Long doesn't do anything. She lets justice do its job."

"As a sheriff and cop for nearly two decades, I'd like to agree with you, but the simple truth is that doesn't work. Do you know what happens to people who don't stand up and have their voices heard?"

Wilson paused for a moment, his lips flattening. "They get run over."

"Exactly. In Skylar's case, Matt will continue doing what he's been doing."

"Is there no way to stop him?"

There was one way. Danny had been hoping he'd hear from Cooper about his PI friend, Cash. So far, there had been nothing.

Danny gave a nod. "There's a chance. It's being looked into."

"By us?"

"No."

Wilson's brows snapped together. "I don't understand."

"Our laws are there for a reason, but sometimes, they prevent us from doing what should be done. There are other means by which a citizen can seek aid."

It took half a minute or so, but Wilson's eyes suddenly widened in understanding. "A private investigator."

Danny didn't confirm or deny anything. He merely stared at Wilson.

The deputy smiled as he got to his feet. "I got into this job because I wanted to help people and put the bad guys away. Matt Gaudet is one of those guys."

"Yes, he is. And if everything works out, he will get the justice he deserves."

Wilson bowed his head before walking out. Danny glanced at the clock and folded the file he'd been reading to set it aside for later. He then picked up the paper and gathered it along with his keys and cell phone as he headed out for the meeting with the mayor.

Unfortunately, the meeting went far longer than Danny wanted. He was in his truck on the way to see Skylar when dispatch hailed him over the radio. He immediately answered.

"Sheriff, we found who she is."

He frowned as he recognized Jeanie's voice over the radio. She had been a dispatcher since he was a teenager. "Found who?"

"The woman who slashed your tires," she said irritably.

Danny bit back a grin. Jeanie was a bit cantankerous. "It's taken long enough. Who is she?"

"Madeline Gross from Katy, Texas."

Katy was a suburb of Houston, and Danny had a feeling that Matt and Madeline knew each other well. "Is there a connection between Ms. Gross and Matt Gaudet?"

"I was hoping you'd ask that."

When Jeanie didn't elaborate, Danny rolled his eyes and said in his most sarcastic tone, "And?"

She laughed, the sound accenting the fact that she'd spent most of her life smoking. "It's good to show some emotion every once in a while, sheriff."

"I show emotion," he stated defensively.

"If you say so," came the stern response. Before he could say anything else, Jeanie said, "From what Deputy Wilson found on social media, it seems like Matt Gaudet and Madeline Gross have been seeing each other off and on for years. There are pictures of them together as recently as last week."

Danny blew out a breath. "And she came to his defense."

"It appears that way."

Danny really didn't want to share this with Skylar. It was bad enough that Matt had lied to her about his family and abused her, but now they could add cheating to the list, as well.

"What do you want us to do?" Jeanie asked.

Danny gripped the steering wheel. "Have Wilson contact the sheriff's department over there and get them to issue a warrant for Madeline Gross."

"Glen heard you, and he's headed to his desk to do just that," Jeanie told him.

"Thanks."

"Sheriff?" Jeanie said.

"Yeah?"

"We're going to have the entire state of Texas looking at us."

He knew that. It had weighed heavily on his mind for the past few days, but he'd held out hope that Matt and his family would leave well enough alone and let all of this die down.

Danny and his deputies would be under a microscope. Everything they did had to be completely by the book. Everything.

He pulled off the road and came to a stop. Which meant that if reporters weren't already following him, they would be soon. He didn't want anyone to see him going out to the ranch and creating more issues—regardless if they were true—when this was about something else altogether.

"I just want you to know that we have complete faith in you," Jeanie said. "We all have your back."

He closed his eyes for a heartbeat. "Thanks. I appreciate that. If anyone needs me, I'm headed home."

"Sure thing, sheriff. See you in the morning."

Chapter 17

"This is risky, Matt."

He ignored his younger brother as he stared at the sheriff's SUV that was pulled off to the side of the road. Matt knew without a shadow of a doubt that Danny was going to see Skylar. Just as he knew that Skylar and Danny had been seeing each other behind his back.

And he'd prove it.

"Matt," Spencer said, his voice pitched louder. "Mom and Dad are here, and they're pissed."

"I don't give a shit." He hadn't for a long time. It was time his family found that out.

Spencer blew out a loud breath. "Look, I know it's not always easy living in both Dad's and Michael's shadows, but you've got to make peace with it."

Matt slid his gaze to Spencer. "Make peace with it? Is that what you've done?"

"Yeah," Spencer said with a shrug of his shoulders. "What else can we do? Dad is good at business. Did he get lucky in falling into the job he did? Sure."

"He also had family money," Matt pointed out.

Spencer's lips twisted. "We all have."

Matt snorted, not bothering to answer.

But Spencer wasn't finished. "Michael fell into politics. He's just like Dad with his golden tongue. I don't have that gift, but I'm okay with that."

"That's because you have your sculpting."

It seemed everyone in the Gaudet family had something they were good at. Everyone, except for Matt. For as long as he could remember, Michael and his parents had said they were always cleaning up his messes.

Because the Gaudets had to be absolutely perfect. There could be no mistakes, no messes—and definitely no skeletons in anyone's closet.

"You have . . ." Spencer began but trailed off.

Matt barked with laughter. "Exactly, little brother. I have nothing but the family money."

Spencer ran a hand down his face. "Matt, you can't keep following the sheriff around. It's already been proven that he and Skylar didn't collude against you. You've got to let it go. But most especially, you need to let Skylar go."

"Why?" Matt asked as he looked back at the sheriff's vehicle that was pulling back onto the road. "She's mine."

"Skylar left. That pretty much says it all. This time, you were arrested. It's not like the other times where the family could make it all right again."

Matt ignored him and pulled behind the sheriff, following at a safe distance. Matt had learned all about how to tail a person without being seen, and it had certainly come in handy many, many times before now.

"You aren't even listening, are you?" Spencer asked with a shake of his head. He looked out the passenger window. "Why did you want me to come with you, then?"

Matt grinned without looking at Spencer. "So I

wouldn't be alone when the lecture was delivered. For the first time, you'd get it as well as the disappointed looks from Mom, Dad, and Michael."

"Do you hate our family so much?"

Instead of replying, Matt kept his focus on Danny. Except when the sheriff should've moved over to make the turn to the East Ranch, he kept going. Matt thought he might be going another route, but ten minutes later, Danny turned into a driveway and parked before a dark house.

Matt pulled off and watched as Danny exited his SUV and made his way to the front door that he opened with a set of keys. A light flicked on in the kitchen, but there was no other movement that Matt could detect.

"You brought us to the sheriff's house? You really have lost it," Spencer stated indignantly.

"You can tell Mom and Dad all about it when they show up," Matt said.

Spencer shifted in his seat. "Look, he's not seeing Skylar. Let's just go get some food. Mom and Dad are in town and looking for us."

"I'm not finished here."

"Matt, please. You're not making any of this easier. You were arrested, the assault on Skylar witnessed by the sheriff, no less. Not to mention the restraining order she took out on you. The best thing for the family is for all of us to get back to Houston and work on things as we always do."

Matt shook his head. "I'm not going anywhere."

"What do you think to accomplish? You can't get to Skylar while she's at the ranch with the Easts."

"She won't be there forever."

Spencer's eyes widened. "Why are you so besotted with her? Or is it that she left you?"

The truth was, Matt never liked anyone leaving him. If anyone were going to end things, it would be him. That's just how things were.

But Skylar was different. He didn't intend to give up on her. He would win her back. He would prove that they were good together, remind her of the year that had bonded them. No one, and certainly not some piece of legal paper, was going to stand in the way of that.

"It's the same with every girl you date," Spencer said and propped his elbow on the car door. "Look, we all get dumped. Some relationships end badly, some end quietly, but most all of them end. Why can't you let the women go? You hold on to them too tightly. It's like you suffocate them."

It was sheer reaction. Matt reached over and punched his brother. Blood poured from Spencer's nose, getting on his clothes and the seat of Spencer's Porsche Boxster.

"What the fuck?" his brother bellowed as he covered his nose with his hands and leaned his head back.

"Watch your fucking mouth. I might take shit from Michael, but I'll be damned if I take it from you."

Spencer's blue eyes cut to him. "Because the truth sucks that bad, huh? You're a fucking asshole, Matt. I'm not helping you anymore. Get out of my car."

Matt laughed. "Make me."

"My God. We're kids again."

There was a tap on Matt's window. He looked over to see Danny standing outside the vehicle with his pistol in hand. Matt debated whether to throw open the door and slam it into the sheriff to catch him off guard so Matt could tackle him. The only thing that held him back was knowing that Spencer wouldn't have his back.

If Matt had been alone, he would've done it. But, like usual, there was always a member of his family near, preventing him from doing what he really wanted.

The sheriff motioned for Matt to roll down the window.

Matt lowered it a few inches, taking a jab anywhere he could. "Is there something I can do for you, sheriff?"

Danny Oldman stared at him for a long moment before he leaned down and looked into the passenger seat at Spencer. "Stop following me before I have you arrested for harassment, Mr. Gaudet."

"You couldn't do that."

"Actually," Spencer said, "he could."

Danny peered closer at Spencer. "Do you need some help?"

Spencer glanced at Matt before he shook his head. "I get nosebleeds all the time."

Matt could tell by the look of doubt on Danny's face that he didn't believe a word of it. Not that it mattered. The sheriff had no reason to arrest either of them.

"Go home, Mr. Gaudet," Danny ordered him.

"It's a free country, sheriff. I can go wherever I want."

Despite the shadows, Matt could see the hard edge that filled Danny's face. "This is my county, and I don't care who your family is or what connections they have, I will enforce the law."

"For what exactly?" Matt smiled, knowing he had the sheriff. "I've not done anything. So what if I followed you? There's no law against that."

"I was the officer who facilitated your arrest."

Matt narrowed his eyes. "Meaning?"

"Meaning," Spencer piped up, "that the sheriff could take you into custody to make sure you don't cause any more harm."

Matt snorted, though he wasn't quite sure if his brother and the sheriff were making it all up or not. He opted to play on the side of caution because if he were in jail, he couldn't get what he wanted—Skylar.

Not that he'd stay in jail long. He'd bail himself out quickly enough, but that was beside the point.

Matt started the car and shot the sheriff a wide smile. "I'll be seeing you around, Danny."

"You better hope not," the sheriff replied.

Matt rolled up his window and drove away. He glanced in the rearview mirror to see Danny standing there, watching them leave. The sheriff had yet to holster his gun.

"That was stupid," Spencer mumbled.

Matt glanced at him. "You had the chance to get me arrested, but instead, you chose to say you have nosebleeds."

"The sheriff knew I was lying."

"So?" Matt said and shrugged. "You still lied. If you really didn't want to help me, you would've done something about it then."

Spencer sniffed loudly and reached into his glove compartment where there were tissues. He pulled out several and wiped at his nose, face, and hands. "Whatever. Let's go meet Mom and Dad."

"No."

His brother's head snapped to him. "What?"

Matt couldn't hold back the grin at the high-pitched, shocked sound of his brother's voice. "You heard me."

"They're waiting for us."

"I don't care."

Spencer sat up straighter, worry settling over him like a cloud. "We don't keep them waiting. Ever. They tell us to do something, and we do it. You know that, Matt."

"I'm a fucking adult, Spence. I don't have to jump every time they tell me to."

"You do if you want them to keep helping you."

Matt threw back his head and laughed. "God, you're such an idiot. As long as Michael is in politics, and they worry about the precious Gaudet name, they'll do whatever they have to in order to keep anything bad from leaking to the press."

"You really know how to alienate people."

"Maybe, but you know I'm right."

Spencer shook his head. "That's not the point. We're a family. We stick by each other."

"Really?" he demanded as he pressed the accclerator, propelling them faster down the road. "When has anyone ever stood by me?"

"Every fucking time!" Spencer yelled. "Now slow the fucking car, you maniac."

Matt grinned and looked at his brother. "About time you let the cap off your anger."

"I hate you," Spencer said and looked out the side window.

"Feeling is completely mutual."

Matt drove toward the East Ranch. He'd hired a couple of world-class hackers to break the security system so he could get to the house. He had enough money to throw out that someone would get him what he wanted. He just had to be patient.

In the meantime, he planned to remind Skylar, Danny, and anyone else who thought they could get in his way that he wouldn't be sidelined.

Restraining order or not, nothing would keep him away from Skylar. Especially not some family who thought they had money. No one had money like the Gaudets. The Easts were a poor replica of what it really meant to be wealthy.

And Matt was going to show them exactly that.

As for the sheriff and his deputies, he would take care of them in time. Same with the judge. That bitch was supposed to have refused the restraining order. Instead, she'd almost gleefully signed off on it.

But with enough money, anything could get done.

Chapter 18

December 10th

She'd been warned, but Skylar still wasn't prepared to read the article about her. It was just so . . . wrong. She felt dirty afterward, as if she had done something terrible by standing up for herself and wanting to be safe.

"I'm sorry," Leslie said.

Skylar looked up at her attorney with Abby and Clayton sitting on the other side of Leslie. Skylar forced a smile as she looked at the trio. "I'm fine."

"No, you aren't, and it's okay not to be," Clayton said.

Abby nodded. "He's right. What was said is just . . ." She paused, searching for the right word.

"Shit," Leslie offered.

"Yes. It's shit," Abby stated firmly.

This time, Skylar's smile was easy. "Thank you. All of you. I'm glad I have y'all, because the thought of doing this alone is frightening."

"It isn't easy to call someone out like you have Matt," Leslie said. "But I'm glad you did it. More women need to do it. But sometimes, it's easier just to go about their lives."

Movement out of the corner of Skylar's eyes caught

her attention. She spotted Hope outside with the ranch manager, Shane, and his partner, Beverly Barnes. Hope was running and laughing as Shane chased after her, and Beverly snapped photos of them.

"It is easier," Skylar admitted while continuing to watch Hope. "It shouldn't be, though. I didn't want anyone to consider me a victim or look at me with pity. But if I have to endure that in order for others to stand up for themselves, then I'll gladly do it. The abuse has to stop. The abusers have to realize that they can't get away with it. And those who've endured the abuse need to feel that when they do take a stand, they'll be heard and can gain back their lives."

Leslie beamed at her. "Damn, girl. If you batted for our team, I think I'd make you mine."

They all laughed, but it brought to mind that Danny hadn't been by in days. Skylar tried not to let it affect her, but she couldn't help that any more than she could stop reading the things being written about her.

She went to bed each night thinking of him. And he was the first thing on her mind each morning. It didn't seem fair to have finally found someone she wanted to be with only to realize that it was most likely nothing more than a fling.

No matter how many times she told herself that Danny was staying away to protect her, she couldn't help thinking the worst. It was something she always did, but this time, she truly believed the worst would happen.

"Not all the articles are putting you in a bad light," Clayton pointed out as he jerked his chin to Beverly. "You have someone on your side."

"That's true." Skylar was aware that it had more to do with the fact that Beverly didn't like Matt than anything having to do with Skylar herself, but she was fine with that.

Leslie checked her phone when it vibrated. Her face fell into a deep frown. "I hate to be the downer, but it looks as if the Gaudets are suing you for slander."

For a moment, Skylar couldn't move. Then it felt as if the world had tilted on its axis and she was desperately trying to hang on.

"You can't be serious," Clayton said angrily.

Leslie handed him the phone while her gaze slid to Skylar. Skylar couldn't speak, because her brain had yet to process the information. It was all just so surreal. She was the one who had been abused, and they wanted to sue her?

"I have no words for how utterly ridiculous this is," Clayton stated as he got to his feet and walked a few paces away.

Abby took the phone from him and read it before she slowly handed it back to Leslie. Then she asked the attorney, "Can they really do this?"

"Absolutely."

"But Skylar didn't make a false statement," Abby pointed out. "As a matter of fact, Skylar hasn't said anything."

Skylar cleared her throat. "That's not entirely true. I spoke to the judge."

"That's not the same thing," Abby argued.

Leslie's mouth twisted ruefully. "Actually, it is."

"What does Skylar do now?" Clayton asked while pacing.

Skylar's gaze was locked on Leslie while her lawyer considered her next move. The seconds that ticked by felt like eons, and the longer the silence filled the room, the more Skylar was tempted to pick up and disappear somewhere with a new life and a new name. Maybe the Caribbean. Perhaps Europe.

Surely, if she put enough distance between Matt and her, he would eventually give up.

"In order to throw out the lawsuit, we have to prove what Matt has done," Leslie said.

Clayton halted and looked her way. "Cooper has already brought in an old buddy of his who now works as a private investigator. Cash is looking into Matt's past."

The hope that sprang through Skylar was so intense that she got dizzy. She realized how tenuous and perilous it was for her to pin everything on one PI and what he *might* find.

"While I like the initiative, I can't wait for the PI to find something," Leslie said.

Abby's brows furrowed. "But what if Cash finds something that could help?"

"Then we'll use it," Leslie stated.

Clayton crossed his arms over his chest. "We're hoping to dig up an old girlfriend or two. Matt abused Skylar. Chances are, he's done it to others."

Leslie nodded. "I agree completely. However, we've got to get ahead of this thing."

"How do you get ahead of such a lawsuit?" Abby asked.

Skylar stopped listening to them. She was on a roller coaster of emotions. Not to leave Matt, then to leave Matt. Knowing her freedom was within reach, then having it snatched away briefly, only to get it back again.

Finding Danny and the passion between them, only to fear that it was now over before it'd even begun. Obtaining the restraining order, which was a win in her book, but also knowing that it wouldn't stop Matt. Reading horrible lies about herself, only to accept it all in exchange for standing up to being abused. Then to learn that she was being sued by Matt's family for slander.

Skylar wasn't sure how much more she could take.

It was all so much more than she'd ever expected. Then again, she hadn't known what to imagine.

It all came back to one simple question: why should she give up her life because she wanted out of an abusive relationship?

She shouldn't have to. Matt was the one who should be worried about his future. Instead, she was holed up, afraid to go out by herself, simply because he was still in town.

Skylar looked at Leslie, Clayton, and Abby as they sat together in the office, trying to come up with a solution for her. She suddenly needed some air. It felt as if the walls were closing in on her.

None of them noticed when she got to her feet and quietly slipped out of the room. She left the house and grabbed her coat, putting it on as she walked outside. Skylar walked in the opposite direction of Hope, Shane, and Beverly. She wanted to be alone, didn't want to answer more questions or be asked how she was doing.

She wasn't a victim!

And yet, that's exactly what she was.

Skylar stuffed her hands into her pockets and lengthened her stride. She had no idea where she was going, but there was plenty of land in front of her that she could walk. And since Matt couldn't get onto the ranch, she didn't have to worry about being alone.

Her mind wandered as she walked. She didn't pay attention to where she was or how long she had been gone. Skylar followed the fence, knowing it would take her back to the house when she decided it was time to return. Right now, she just wanted to be on her own.

She'd always been independent. It'd never bothered her to be alone. In fact, there were times she preferred it. It allowed her time by herself with her thoughts to figure things out. Now, more than ever, she needed to get her head on straight.

Because while she had expected the write-ups about her, she hadn't anticipated being sued. She was just so flabbergasted by the move that she didn't know what to think. Though with Leslie and her new friends by her side, Skylar wasn't worried. It would work itself out somehow.

She thought of the private investigator. It would be nice if he dug up one of Matt's old girlfriends who might have dealt with something similar to what Skylar had, but she knew the odds of that happening were slim.

If the Gaudets were suing her for simply getting a re-straining order and telling the truth, even if there were others abused by Matt out there, they likely wouldn't be able to come forward. No doubt non-disclosure agree-ments had been signed, and who knew what else. Fami-lies like the Gaudets took care to protect themselves and their family name. Add in the fact that their eldest was in politics, and things became even more complicated.

They shouldn't. In fact, it should be extremely easy. But that's not how their society operated.

Skylar stopped and looked around. She saw the big live oak to her right and walked to it. The sky was bright blue without a cloud marring it, and while the tempera-tures were a bit nippy, it wasn't too cold that she couldn't remain outside a little longer.

She sat down with her back against the tree and simply looked out over the pasture with the cattle grazing in the distance. There was something incredibly peaceful about the scene. Even surrounded by rodeos and cattle ranches, she'd never felt the desire to know anything about it while growing up.

Looking over the land now, she realized everything

she'd missed out on. She let go of the anxiety and dread that had overtaken her in the office. Skylar drew in a deep breath and slowly released it. She had once meditated daily. Perhaps she should do that again to help center herself, especially with everything that was going on.

But that was for later. Right now, she wanted to continue enjoying the beauty. The quiet was only broken by the occasional moo from a cow and the sounds of birds, and it eased her little by little. She was able to relax and put everything into perspective.

When she felt she was ready to return, she got to her feet and dusted herself off, then headed back in the direction of the house. Except after fifteen minutes when she came to a junction in the fence, she didn't know which direction she'd come from.

She'd been so wrapped up in her thoughts that she hadn't paid proper attention. And no one knew that she was gone.

Skylar turned in a slow circle, trying to orient herself and pick out something—anything—that looked familiar. But there was nothing. She had to make a decision. She had a one in three chance of getting it right. After a few seconds of internal debate, she went to the left.

She had only walked another five minutes when she saw something or someone coming toward her. It wasn't long until she made out that it was a horse and rider.

Her heart leapt when she recognized Danny. He nudged the horse into a gallop to reach her quickly. Skylar wore a smile when he pulled the horse to a stop and dismounted.

"You scared the hell out of me," he stated angrily.

She blinked, taken aback. Before she could respond, he enveloped her in his arms. She held him, her eyes closing as his warmth surrounded her.

"Don't walk off like that again," he said.

She nodded. "I just needed some time alone. I didn't mean to worry anyone."

He pulled back to look at her. In the next instant, their lips were pressed together as they kissed. And everything else faded to nothing for Skylar.

Chapter 19

Danny had never been as scared as he was when he got
the call from Clayton that they couldn't find Skylar.
Everyone on the ranch was looking for her, but that
wasn't enough for Danny. He'd driven as fast as he could to
the Easts' and then immediately got on a horse and rode,
praying that someone found her.

He couldn't believe he'd been the one to stumble
across her, though. He hadn't meant to kiss her, but one
look into her blue eyes, and he hadn't been able to help
himself.

Somehow, he was able to rein in his desire and end the
kiss. Then he pulled out his phone and sent Clayton and
the others a text to let them know that he'd found her.

"I'm sorry," Skylar said again.

He shook his head as he pocketed his phone. "I understand why you needed to get out."

"I should've told someone. It was careless. I just didn't
want to talk to anyone."

Danny pulled her against him and simply held her. He
rested his chin atop her head. "You don't need to justify
anything to me."

"Actually, I do. I just assumed I'd be safe out here."

"You are." The simple fact was that everyone overreacted.

She held him tighter. "Am I? I can't help feeling that I'm not safe anywhere."

Danny didn't intend to tell her about discovering Matt and his brother following him. Skylar had enough to worry about without adding that to the mix. Besides, Danny had taken care of it.

It also helped that Jace and Cooper were still following Matt and his family. Though there was just Jace and Cooper, compared to five members of the Gaudet family, and their attorneys. That's why no one realized that Matt had been following Danny until he spotted them.

"They're suing me," Skylar told him as she pulled back.

Danny nodded. "I heard. It'll be thrown out."

"Will it? I'm not so sure."

"You think their money wins every time? There are good people in the justice system. People who don't care about anything but doing their jobs like they're supposed to. Judge Harmon is one of those."

Skylar nodded slowly as she glanced away. "It's just that every time I feel as if I've found my footing, they knock me down again."

"Keep getting back up. They don't expect that."

That made her smile. "I hope I can."

"You can. You've got friends who will help you. And that's not even including your shark of a lawyer." He smiled when she laughed at his comment.

Now that was the Skylar he wanted to see. Not the fearful and apprehensive one that he'd come upon.

"I'm thankful that I came this direction while driving from Houston," she told him. "I still don't know why I did it."

"It doesn't matter why. You were meant to be here, and you're surrounded by people who want to help you and keep Matt from getting to you."

Her blue eyes softened. "I was worried I wouldn't see you again."

"I didn't stay away because I didn't want to see you. I didn't come because of Matt."

She nodded slowly, a frown on her lips. "I thought it might be something like that."

"But you weren't sure, and you couldn't ask me," he finished. What a fool he'd been to keep her in such turmoil. "I'm sorry, Skylar."

She put a finger on his lips. "Don't. You have nothing to apologize for. You're the sheriff. Your duties require you to look after an entire county, not just me."

"I should've contacted you."

"You're here now."

He smiled and took her hand. "I am. Let's take advantage of it since I won't be coming by as often as I'd like."

"Because of Matt?"

"Because of Matt," he admitted.

She made a face. "Is there some law you can enact to kick him out of the county?"

"I wish," he said with a laugh. "I wouldn't hesitate to do it."

"Danny, I want to ask you something."

He grew serious to match her expression. "Ask me anything."

"Do you want me because you feel sorry for me?"

"No," he answered immediately. "I want you because I've always wanted you. I thought you were just a high school crush, the one that got away."

"The kind that lingers because you didn't get to find out if things could work out?"

He nodded. "Exactly. When I saw you—" He paused,

unable to find the right words. "I thought you were a dream. When I realized you were real, I couldn't believe my luck."

"I've spent my life in a constant state of flux, at least when it comes to relationships. I wasn't happy when I was alone, and I wasn't happy when I was dating someone. Nothing fit properly. I was always looking ahead, thinking of what was down the road waiting for me." She shrugged and swallowed. "I don't feel any of that when I'm with you. It all feels . . . right."

Her words made his heart soar. "Skylar, you know I've always had a thing for you. I just want you to be sure it's me you really want."

She blinked, her brows drawing together. "You think I want you because you came to my rescue with Matt?"

"That's not what I'm saying. Just as you wanted to be sure I didn't want you for any other reason than wanting you, I need to know the same."

The anger that had been growing faded. "You're right. You should ask that. And, no, I don't want to be with you simply because you stopped a bad situation that night. I want to be with you because of the man you are and the way you make me feel when I'm with you."

"You should know that I've not dated anyone in a few years."

She lifted one shoulder. "Then you should know that I've got a crazy ex-boyfriend who used to beat me. His family is suing me for slander now."

"Hmm," Danny said as he shook his head. "That sounds like a lot to deal with."

She playfully punched him in the arm. "Hey!"

They both laughed as he pulled her into his arms. He wasn't sure how this was going to work, but he knew he wanted to try.

"You're right," he admitted. "This does feel right."

"Yes, it does."

He closed his eyes and breathed easily for the first time in days. Having Skylar close somehow calmed the turbulent sea within him. There were risks involved because of Matt, but Danny didn't care any longer.

"I'm going to move here," Skylar suddenly said.

Danny looked down at her. "When did you decide that?"

"Just now." She laughed and took a step back. "I've been contemplating it for a day or two. I even looked at real estate and found a house."

"Oh? Which one?"

"The Taylor house out on Greenbriar Lane."

He nodded. "I know that house. It's always been a nice one. I didn't realize it was for sale."

"The parents died, and the brother and sister decided to gut it and redo everything in order to get more money out of it, but they kept the charm of the outside. I used to drive by that place every day on the way to school and think about how pretty it was."

"You really going to buy it?"

She shrugged. "Maybe. I don't know."

He was about to offer for her to move in with him to save her some money, but he realized that their relationship was probably too new to talk about things like that. As odd as it sounded, he could see them together far into the future.

"Will you come look at it with me?" she asked.

"I'd love to."

She beamed. "Good."

"We should probably get back."

"And you have work."

He hated to admit it, but he did need to get back to the office. "Yeah. I'll be back tonight, though."

"Are you sure? What about Matt?"

"What about him?"

She hesitated, then smiled. "I need to stop thinking about him, don't I?"

"Not until he's out of your life, but you are safe here. You won't be staying here forever," he said when he saw her argument forming. "Just a little longer."

He reached for her hand, and their fingers twined as they walked to the horse he'd ridden over, which was now grazing nearby. Danny gathered the reins and tugged the equine after them as they started toward the house.

"I suppose you saw the article," he asked.

She glanced at him. "About me? Yeah, it was hard to miss. I also saw the one from Beverly. Smart woman to send that to a Houston news station."

"Beverly is tenacious like that. Matt and his family think they'll be treated the same here as they are in the city. It doesn't work like that."

"I'm glad of that."

Danny squeezed her hand. "Maybe you subconsciously knew that, and that's why you came back home."

She smiled as she looked at him. "You may be right."

"Don't worry about the lawsuit. The Gaudets are doing it to make themselves look good."

"That may be, but it puts me in a poor light."

"Not if we can prove the abuse."

Skylar chuckled. "I wish it were that easy."

"Well, it may be. As I was out looking for you this afternoon, I was thinking about the lawsuit and proving things. I think everyone forgot that the rest stops have cameras set up by the state. Leslie needs to petition the state for the footage of the night that Matt was arrested. It'll show his attack."

Her eyes widened. "That would be great, but is it

enough? I mean, couldn't his lawyers say that I provoked him or something?"

"That video, along with my testimony of what I heard and witnessed, as well as the photos of what he did to you in the past should be all the proof you need."

Skylar stopped walking and turned to face him before she wrapped her arms around him. "Thank you for being so amazing."

"Just doing my job," he said, though he was pleased by her words.

They took their time returning to the house. By the time they got there, both were smiling easily, their hands still joined.

Skylar remained with him when he unsaddled and brushed the horse he'd ridden. She fed the animal a carrot as a treat, and then they walked into the house.

The only ones missing were Jace, Cooper, and Brice. Caleb and his brother were taking turns helping their friends trail the Gaudets, and right now, it was Brice's turn.

"I'm so sorry," Skylar told everyone.

Naomi shook her head. "No one blames you for needing to get away."

"I wouldn't have survived as long as you have," Audrey admitted.

Abby walked to her and took her hand. "We were so involved with everything, we didn't even pay attention to how it was affecting you."

"That was our bad," Leslie said with an apologetic smile. "We won't do it again."

Clayton smiled at her. "Are you better?"

Danny felt Skylar's gaze on him and looked her way. They shared a smile before she said, "Much. I can face anything now."

Chapter 20

Chapter 20

Skylar really hated seeing Danny drive away, but knowing he'd be back made it easier. She hadn't realized just how much she'd missed him until he was with her again.

The talk they'd shared had also done wonders. Not knowing where she stood with him had also played havoc with her head. Now that she had some answers, she could concentrate on putting all her energy into Matt and his family. Because she wasn't going to take any of it lying down.

She checked her phone and found several missed calls and texts from her parents. Skylar had spoken to them the night before to prepare them, but obviously, she needed to talk to them more.

"Hey, Mom," she said when the phone connected.

"Skylar, I think we should come and get you."

She frowned at the thread of fear and worry she heard in her mother's voice. "I'm fine. Really, Mom. This place is like a fortress."

"You're not hearing your mother," her dad's deep voice said, joining the conversation. "We think you should be with us."

Now this was too weird. Her parents had always been big proponents of independence. Not that they hadn't been there for her as parents, but they thought it was good that she stood on her own.

"What's going on?" Skylar demanded. The beat of silence only made her anxiety deepen. "Mom? Dad? Tell me."

Her father released a long breath. "Some attorneys visited us an hour ago."

"What? Why?"

"They were from the Gaudets," her mother explained.

Skylar gripped the phone tightly. "What did they say?"

"They offered us two million dollars, and you eight million, if you disappear and drop everything having to do with Matt and the restraining order," her father answered.

It took her a minute to get her anger in check, but even after, she couldn't hold it in. "You've got to be kidding me."

"I wish I was, pumpkin," her mother said.

Skylar wasn't sure if she was more appalled, shocked, or outraged at the entire scenario. "Do they really think I can be bought?"

When neither of her parents replied, she frowned, wondering why they hadn't voiced their agreement.

"Honey, you need to understand that while we saved, we didn't save enough for retirement," her father said.

Skylar slowly sank into the nearest chair. Skylar didn't need to ask if her parents had accepted the deal. Her father's words told her that they had. "You're calling to convince me to agree to the money."

Her mother then said, "Think what you could do with it. You'd never have to work again if you invested it right."

"What if I like working?"

Her father guffawed. "No one likes working. You're just being obtuse."

"I make good money, Dad. I've saved and invested really well. I'm not in need of anything."

"Everyone always needs money," came her mother's reply.

Skylar shook her head. "Not me. I live simply."

Her mother barked in laughter. "Right. And that car you drive says you live simply."

"That car is paid off," she retorted. "Three years early, I might add. I doubled up on the payments and got an incredible interest rate. I have no debt either. Like I said, I live simply. I don't need millions."

"What of your children?" her father asked.

Skylar had had enough. "And what of your daughter? Matt beat me. Do you understand that? Do you comprehend what he did to me? Not once. Not twice. And it wasn't just physical abuse. It was mental, emotional, and verbal."

"The Gaudets aren't saying it didn't happen," her mother said, using the soft voice she used to use in order to get Skylar to do something. "They know what he's done, and they want to make up for it with money."

Her father added, "You were strong enough to get away and stand up for yourself. You're free of him. Take advantage of what they're offering you."

Skylar closed her eyes and shook her head. "What they're offering you, you mean."

"Well, that as well," her father mumbled.

Skylar opened her eyes and took a deep breath. "Take the money if you want, but I don't want anything from the Gaudets."

Her mother made a sound in the back of her throat. "We don't get a penny if you don't agree."

"Do you know they're suing me for slander?" she asked her parents. "Did the lawyers happen to mention that part?"

"Um," her father said. "Actually, they did. They said it would go away as soon as you sign the papers."

"Papers?" she asked.

"An NDA," her mother answered.

Of course, the Gaudets would want a non-disclosure agreement from her. What good would it do now that her statement had already been filed with the courts? Skylar was so fed up with the entire situation that she wanted to scream. And her parents? She didn't even know what to think about them.

"Skylar?" her father called out. "Why don't you think about this? No need to make a hasty decision."

There was something in his voice that set off warning bells in her head. "Dad, what else did the lawyers say?"

"They weren't here long," her mother responded.

"Dad?" Skylar pressed.

Her father cleared his throat. "It's a one-time offer that expires in twenty-four hours. They said if you reject it, they'll come after you with everything they have."

"And you. They'll come after both of you, won't they?" Skylar asked.

Her mother sniffed, unable to hide her tears anymore. "Yes. They'll come after us, as well."

Skylar wrapped her free arm around her middle and bent forward. She was sick to her stomach, knowing that the Gaudets had gone after her parents. They hadn't been a part of this at all.

"Listen," she told them, "don't answer anyone's calls other than mine. Don't answer the door, and don't go anywhere until you hear from me. Do you understand?"

"Yes," her dad replied.

Her mother was crying loudly now. "Skylar, we're appalled by the fact that you were abused. We raised you to stand up for yourself."

"I know, Mom." And she did understand now. Her parents had been trying to convince her to take the money without telling her the rest of it so she wouldn't get upset. Now that she knew the full truth, it only angered her more.

"Honey," her dad said, "if you want to take the money, we'll support you. We're not worried about ourselves. We've lived a long, good life. We're more concerned about you and what that family can do to you."

Skylar wiped at a tear that leaked from the corner of her eye. "I need a little time. I'm going to think some things over and get back with you. Just remember what I said. Stay in the house, don't let anyone in, and don't talk to anyone but me."

They ended the call. Skylar remained seated for a little longer to settle her stomach that roiled with rage. Then she got to her feet and walked down the stairs to the kitchen, where Leslie was saying her goodbyes.

"Do you have a little longer?" Skylar asked.

Leslie took one look at her face and frowned. "Something's happened."

"Yeah, it has," Abby said. "Do I need to get the others?"

Skylar hesitated before nodding. She glanced down at her phone and contemplated calling Danny, but she decided against it. She could tell him later that night. Besides, he needed to work.

Once Clayton, Brice, Naomi, and Audrey were seated in the living area with Skylar, Abby, and Leslie, Skylar took a deep breath and opened her mouth to begin. About that time, Hope woke up from her nap.

"Go ahead," Abby said as she jumped up and jogged to the stairs. "I'll be back as soon as I can."

Skylar licked her lips and folded her hands in her lap. Then she proceeded to tell the group what had transpired with her parents.

"I'm really not liking these Gaudets," Naomi stated.

Clayton didn't seem at all fazed by the story. "I figured they would offer some money as an incentive, but I didn't expect the rest. Leslie, can you use this against them?"

The attorney shook her head. "Since the Longs didn't get anything on tape or video to prove it happened, it would be their word against the Gaudets'."

"Damn," Audrey said.

Brice leaned forward and braced his forearms on his legs. "The Gaudets were quick to make an offer, and a sizable one at that."

"You think they've done this before," Leslie said.

Brice nodded, his brows raised. "I do. I think we need to get this information to Cash to see if it'll help."

For a minute, Skylar forgot who Cash was, but then she recalled that he was the private investigator the Harpers knew. "You think he can discover if Matt's family has paid off others?"

"Absolutely," Leslie said.

Audrey raised a brow, uncertainty on her face. "Um . . . don't you need a court order to look into someone's financials?"

"Not when there's that kind of money involved," Leslie explained. "If we have an idea which individual may have received a payoff and was connected to Matt, all we need to do is look at their lifestyle to see if anything changed drastically."

Skylar rubbed her hands together. "I just want my parents safe."

"We should bring them here," Clayton replied.

"You can't keep opening your house to others," Skylar told him.

Brice laughed and shook his head as he smiled at his brother-in-law. "Obviously, you don't know Clayton and Abby well enough to know that they'll do just that."

Clayton shrugged. "The fact is that your parents have been threatened. They need somewhere safe to go, and we have room."

"I'm not sure we should move them," Leslie said before Skylar could respond.

Skylar slid her gaze to her attorney. "Why do you say that?"

"Because the Gaudets already know you're here."

Brice's face scrunched up in confusion. "Why does that matter?"

Leslie gave a little shake of her head. "It doesn't. We all knew they would figure it out, but they expect you to bring Skylar's parents here."

"Again," Brice said, "so?"

Clayton's lips turned up at the corners. "I see where you're going with this, Leslie."

Brice threw up his hands. "I don't."

Leslie turned her brown eyes to Skylar. "With your and your parents' permission, I'd like to set up their home to record conversations."

"You think the lawyers will go back to them?" Skylar asked.

Leslie flashed a quick grin. "I do. When your parents don't leave, and you don't arrive to bring them here, the Gaudets will think that either your parents didn't tell you of the offer, or that you're planning something else."

"Could it also look like Skylar and her parents don't get along?" Naomi interjected.

Leslie lifted one shoulder in a shrug. "I'm betting that Matt knows how close Skylar and her parents are."

Skylar nodded. "He does. And, yes, Leslie, do whatever you need to. My parents will agree, as well. I told them not to leave the house or let anyone in until they heard from me."

"Good," the attorney said as she tucked a strand of dark hair behind her ear. "I can get this taken care of quickly."

"Thank you," Skylar told the room. She was saying that a lot, but without the friends she had around her, she wouldn't know which direction to turn.

Clayton gave her a nod. "Talk to your parents. We'll do the rest."

Chapter 21

How in the hell was he supposed to concentrate on work after learning what the Gaudets were doing to Skylar? Danny squeezed the bridge of his nose with his thumb and forefinger.

"Your silence tells its own story," Clayton said through the phone.

Danny lowered his hand and sighed. "It's either that or I let the cuss words fly."

"You get pretty creative with those. I say spew."

Danny grinned as he was sure Clayton intended, but it was fleeting. "How is Skylar?"

"She's holding up well, but I can't help but wonder how much more she can take."

"A lot. She's strong."

"Everyone has a breaking point, Danny."

He was well aware of that. "Have you heard from Jace, Cooper, or Caleb?"

There was a beat of silence. "No. Have you?"

"Not in the past few hours. They usually check in regularly."

"For all three to be radio-silent isn't good. I'll contact Caleb."

"And I'll try to get in touch with Jace or Cooper," Danny said. "Please keep me posted on Skylar."

Clayton made a sound through the phone. "Of course. It's none of my business, but it looks like something is developing there between you."

"It is," Danny said, smiling. It was the first time he'd admitted it to anyone else, and he liked how he felt when he said it aloud.

"Good. I like her. She'd be good for you."

"Because you're worried about me being alone?" Danny asked.

Clayton grunted. "Because I know you're lonely. It's the first time I've seen you really take an interest in anyone in years."

"There's always been something about Skylar that drew me."

"Then I'm glad she's in town. And, Danny, I'll tell you what I told her, as bad as this business is with Matt and his family, it'll go away eventually."

Danny drew in a deep breath. "You aren't wrong, Clayton, but I've seen the other side of these things. They can go really, really bad."

"But we aren't going to let that happen."

Danny briefly closed his eyes. "Thanks for everything. I know it's not great that I brought this to your door."

"I'm glad you did. It means you trust me enough to keep someone you care about safe."

"Yeah, but it also puts your family in a spotlight that might take a bad turn like it has with Skylar's parents."

There was a hard edge to Clayton's voice when he said, "I dare the Gaudets to come after me."

A few seconds later, the call ended. Danny immediately dialed Cooper's number, but it went to voicemail. He tried Jace next, but it also went to voicemail.

Danny was about to go looking for them when his phone buzzed. He looked down to see a text from Cooper.

BUSY. CALL BACK IN A BIT.

That made Danny feel a little better, but he still didn't like that they hadn't checked in. It also worried him that he hadn't heard their voices. Anyone could send a text.

He drummed his fingers on the desk before he dialed Jace's number again. This time, he answered on the second ring.

"Hey," he said in a whisper.

Danny winced. "A bad time?"

"Just don't want to be heard."

"You still following Matt?"

"They're all together."

Danny sat back in the chair. "The parents, Matt, and his brother?"

"And the lawyer."

The fact that Jace kept everything at a whisper told Danny that the group was nearby. "Where are you?"

"Farmer's market."

Danny nodded, mentally placing them in a map off Old Sawmill Road in his head. "Public place."

"Yep."

"Anything good happening?"

"We have to get pretty close to hear anything. I fell back while C-squared moved in."

Danny knew Jace was referring to Caleb and Cooper. "They haven't recognized any of you, have they?"

"If they have, they haven't said anything. And before you ask, no one is following us."

For just a second, Danny thought about asking if Jace was sure about that, then he remembered the military training the three of them had. "Y'all should know that they sent some lawyers to Skylar's family and offered them several million between them and Skylar if she'd disappear and forget about Matt. Skylar has twenty-four hours to make a decision, and if she refuses, they're going after her parents and doubling down on her."

"The hell they are," Jace said in an even tone, but Danny wasn't fooled. He, like the Harpers and Easts, knew that Jace wasn't someone you wanted to get riled.

Danny drew in a deep breath. "Y'all have been trailing them for a few days now, and nothing has happened."

"Not since Matt trailed you."

There was that. "None of them are stupid enough to try to get onto the ranch. As long as Skylar stays there, she's safe."

"She's a prisoner, Danny, and you know it. No matter how nice the surroundings, she can't live her life."

Danny fisted his hands, hating that he'd forgotten about Jace's past. "You're right. It is a prison. The quicker Matt and his family leave, the sooner she can have her freedom."

"Cooper tried to get ahold of Cash earlier. I'll nudge him to call again. We'll be in touch soon."

"Thanks."

Just as he was about to hang up, Jace whispered, "Wait."

Danny concentrated on listening through the phone as voices got louder. He picked up Matt's easily enough.

"I'm not a fucking child anymore," Matt said.

A man replied with, "No, but you are my son. If you want to continue pulling from your trust fund, then you'll listen."

Danny put the voice to memory and labeled it with: *Sean Gaudet, patriarch.*

Right on the heels of Sean's voice was a woman's. It was refined and dripped with annoyance. Michelle

Gaudet told her son, "We've bent over backward for you. Perhaps we should stop and let you take care of things yourself. Without the family money."

"Right," Matt replied with a laugh. "We both know that won't happen. Michael is gearing up his campaign for governor, and the family has to be perfect."

"Every family has a black sheep," replied another male voice.

Danny recognized that as Spencer, the youngest Gaudet brother. This conversation was enlightening to be sure, but it also told him the lengths the Gaudets had gone to for Matt before. Now, if Cash could only find a bread trail to Matt's past, that would be great.

"This isn't a conversation for public," Rodney stated, reminding the family where they were.

Matt issued a loud bark of laughter. "You're the one who wanted to walk around among the regular folk. Mom in her pearls and diamonds, and Dad in his thousand-dollar shoes. Yeah, we fit in real good here, Rodney."

The crack of a palm on skin could be heard even through the phone. Then Michelle said, "I've had enough. I'm going back to the hotel."

"Me, too," Spencer said.

Unfortunately, nothing else was said. Danny pressed his lips together and went over the conversation as Jace ended the call after a whispered goodbye.

Danny turned to his computer and pulled up the file on Matthew Gaudet. He looked for any previous arrests, but there was none. In fact, Matt's arrest with Danny's department was the first time a Gaudet had been in the system since the sixties. The family was squeaky clean.

Or they just knew all the right people.

Matt hadn't been wrong when he said that the family stood out in their community. Houston was only a few hours from them, but city life was vastly different than country life, and it was never more obvious than with the Gaudets' arrival.

Danny devoted another hour to looking into the Gaudet family but came up with very little. He searched the national database, looking for anyone who might have made a complaint against them.

There had been a housekeeper who had gone to the police in Houston, but if there was any paperwork filled out, it hadn't been entered into the system. Either that or the housekeeper had changed her mind.

With how easily the Gaudets threw money around, Danny wouldn't be surprised if the housekeeper had been paid off. It seemed to be how the Gaudets did business. And it was certainly one way to keep the family name out of the papers and in a good light.

If no one was around to make waves, then the family could remain looking impeccable to most. With their wealth and picture-perfect looks, it was no wonder the family was one of the most photographed in Houston.

Danny rubbed his tired eyes. He reached for his cup of coffee, only to find it empty. He rose to go get more when there was a knock on his door. It opened far enough for Jace to poke in his head.

"I didn't expect a visit," Danny said.

Jace pushed the door open wider to walk in. "I was headed to get something to eat. Brice took over, so I'm done for the night."

"What did you learn?"

"That the Gaudet family is fucked-up," Jace said as he sank into one of the chairs before the desk. "And that they don't hesitate to do whatever they need to for their family."

Danny lowered himself back into his chair. "Yeah, I figured that."

"You didn't see the mother slap Matt, though. I don't think it's something she does often, but she was furious. Not sure if it was at Matt or the fact that he made her lose her temper in public."

"Probably a bit of both."

"For a moment, I actually thought Matt might hit her back, he was so irate. The others walked away, and Spencer went with Michelle. I followed them back to their hotel, where Brice met me."

Danny nodded as he listened. "Dissension in the family. If only that meant they would stop helping Matt."

"Yeah, that's not going to happen."

"I know. Wishful thinking."

Jace yawned and scrubbed at the shadow of a beard on his jaw. "This thing could go one of two ways. Either they'll stick it out and continue fighting, or they'll leave."

"From what I've seen, the Gaudets don't run from anything."

Jace blew out a long breath. "I have to agree with that assessment. Skylar needs to be prepared for anything."

Matt stared at his red cheek in the public restroom. Everything in him had wanted to lash out at his mother for daring to slap him. And in full view of everyone, no less.

His parents had drilled into him and his brothers that nothing untoward could happen in public. That anything, even the slightest of disagreements, should be kept to the house where no one could see or hear.

And yet his mother had hit him.

That was the last straw. He'd been under his family's thumb for too long. It was time he showed them just what he could do on his own. He didn't need them. Not before, and certainly not now.

In his mind, their actions against Skylar were putting

more of a spotlight on him, and that's the last thing Matt wanted. He'd handled things before without his parents' knowledge. He would again.

His phone buzzed. He looked down to see a number he didn't recognize. Usually, he ignored those calls, but he took a chance and answered.

"Matt?"

He perked up at the feminine voice, but he didn't recognize it. "Yeah?"

"It's Crypto. I'm still working on hacking into the East Ranch. Whoever set up the security system is a genius. It's set up on several different servers. I've only been able to get into one. It's the video feed. Thought you might be interested in what I've seen over the last six hours."

He frowned, remembering that she spelled her name CRYP70. Hackers were weird. The woman talked fast and didn't seem to give a rat's ass who he was. Then again, he'd paid her handsomely, and that was just the first half. If she succeeded, she'd get the other half of the money and a big bonus. "Video? What good does that do me?"

"I don't know, nor do I care. You wanted to see if I could hack in. This is how far I've gotten. I just sent you the link. The copy I made is on my server."

There was a threat in her tone that he didn't like. "Why is that important?"

"I want to make sure that you pay me what you've promised."

"When you deliver, sweetheart."

"Oh, I'll deliver," she promised and disconnected.

Matt pulled his phone away from his ear as a text came through from Crypto. There was a link that he clicked. It took him to a video feed.

He smiled when he saw the various camera views situated around the ranch. He focused on the ones nearest the house. It would take hours for him to search through it all, and that was better done on his laptop back at the hotel.

Just as he was about to lower his phone, a flash of blond hair caught his attention. He chose one of the video feeds and enlarged it so it filled his screen. And there, before his eyes was Skylar, holding hands with none other than Danny Oldman.

"I knew it," Matt murmured angrily.

Chapter 22

Everything was set up with her parents. Skylar hated that they had been brought into the middle of things, but once she explained what Leslie wanted to do, her parents had quickly agreed.

Skylar wasn't in a good mood that morning. Danny had been called out to a bad wreck and hadn't made it back to the ranch the night before. Skylar knew it was just part of his job, but she couldn't help wondering if Matt and his family had had something to do with it.

Then she realized how silly that thought was. Matt had no idea about her and Danny, and it was going to stay that way. Mainly because she had no idea how Matt would react. And the last thing she wanted was for Matt to turn his anger on Danny.

All of this was turning into such a fiasco. It was one thing when it was just her that Matt was bothering, but his family had joined in and had turned their wrath on her parents. All she could hope for was that the Easts and Harpers—as well as Danny—escaped the Gaudets' viciousness.

Skylar rubbed her temples. She had a pounding headache

from the constant worry. No matter what she did, she couldn't seem to stop her mind from going from one bad scenario to the next, each worse than the last.

Which was silly because Matt hadn't killed anyone. It didn't matter how much money his family had, they couldn't cover that up.

Skylar frowned as she realized that no one in the Gaudet family—especially Matt—would get his hands dirty with such business. They'd hire it out.

"Oh, shit," she murmured.

Skylar went downstairs. On her way down, she heard voices from the kitchen. As she approached, she caught her name.

"Speaking of," Abby said and plastered a smile on her face when she spotted Skylar.

But Skylar wasn't fooled. Her gaze moved from Abby to Clayton to Leslie. "What is it?"

Clayton asked, "Do you know anyone by the name of Madeline Gross?"

"No," Skylar said with a small shake of her head, her gaze moving between the three of them. Then something clicked in her head. "Wait. Matt has an old girlfriend named Madeline. I don't know her last name."

Leslie took a deep breath and released it as she said, "It's safe to say that the Madeline you heard Matt speak of is the same Madeline Gross."

"Okay," Skylar said, trying not to get too worked up. "What about her?"

Abby put her hands on the island. "It seems that Madeline and Matt have had an on-again/off-again relationship for some years."

"Meaning that he cheated on me," Skylar guessed.

Clayton nodded once. "Yes."

Somehow that didn't surprise Skylar, but oddly enough,

she wasn't that upset about it. "What does Madeline have to do with me?"

"She was here," Abby replied.

Now that got Skylar's attention. "For Matt?"

"That's our guess," Clayton said. "However, she stabbed Danny's tires at the courthouse."

Skylar wished Danny had told her about it, but he did have his hands full, so she wasn't going to hold it against him. "Have they caught her?"

"She's been arrested in Houston," Leslie said.

Skylar thought about that a moment. "That's a good thing, right?"

Clayton grabbed a slice of bacon and took a bite. "It is. And it isn't. You see, she's claiming that Matt had nothing to do with her coming here and slashing Danny's tires."

"Which means we can't connect Matt to the crime," Leslie explained.

Skylar took one of the seats at the island. "I don't suppose Madeline is lying?"

"Houston PD checked everything, and then Danny and his deputies double-checked," Clayton said. "There's no connection."

"That we can prove," Abby added.

Skylar shoved away a lock of hair that had fallen into her face. "Well, we'll get them on something else."

"That's what I dropped by to tell you," Leslie said. "Your parents' house is all set up and ready. We're recording both video and audio."

"That's great." Skylar didn't point out that there was a chance that the lawyers wouldn't return to talk to her parents. It was another long shot, but right now, it was all they had.

"This won't last forever, you know?" Leslie rubbed her hand up and down Skylar's arm.

Skylar looked around at all the Christmas decorations. "I'm supposed to be buying gifts and going to parties to celebrate the season. I'm supposed to be planning Christmas dinner with my mom and thinking about what I'll do for New Year's Eve this year. I'm surrounded by Christmas everywhere, and it's the first year that it doesn't even feel like the holidays."

Abby's brows puckered. "I'm sorry. I can take it down."

"Don't you dare," Skylar quickly said. "I love it. I'm just feeling sorry for myself this morning. I'm sorry."

Clayton shook his head as he finished the last of the bacon. "Don't apologize. You're holding up remarkably well considering the events. Maybe you need to get out of the house."

"No," Abby and Leslie said in unison.

But Skylar was staring at Clayton. "Do you think that would be possible? There's a place I'd like to go."

"Absolutely." His pale green gaze swung to Abby. "It'll be fine, darlin'."

Leslie's lips were pursed. "I don't like it, but I also know that you need to get out."

"While I'd like nothing more than to go alone, I'm not stupid." Skylar looked at Clayton. "Would you or someone else accompany me?"

Clayton smiled. "I'd be happy to. And I have a feeling Abby will be coming, as well."

"You bet I will," Abby stated, then smiled at Skylar.

Matt stared coldly at the monitor, watching Skylar and Danny over and over again. It had taken him all night, but he'd seen every second of footage from every camera angle on the East Ranch—and there was a lot of it.

Seeing Skylar and Danny holding hands had made

him angry, but when a camera had caught them kissing, Matt had lost his temper and destroyed the hotel room.

Spencer had knocked on the door, but Matt hadn't let him in. He'd even ignored the calls from his parents because his mind had been crafting a plan. It was going to take a lot of moving parts, but it was perfect in its elegance.

He dialed Crypto's untraceable number. She answered on the third ring with a bored, "What?"

"Have you gotten into the entire system yet?"

There was a loud sigh. "If I haven't contacted you, then nothing has changed. It's a tough system. One of the toughest I've seen in a while. It's going to take me a few days."

"How easily can you get into someone's phone?" he asked.

"In seconds."

"What about making a recording from someone's voice from other voicemails? Could you do it if I needed it?"

There was a bored sigh. "Of course. That's child's play."

"Just what I wanted to hear. I need you to get into two phones," he told her.

Crypto chuckled softly. "Is that right? Why would I do that?"

"Because there's another two hundred and fifty grand in it for you."

"What do you need?"

Matt gave her the details of what he wanted. When he finished, there was a smile on his face.

"Just one problem," the hacker said. "I need phone numbers."

"You're a hacker. Can't you figure that out on your own?"

There was a beat of silence. "You're a dick, you know that?"

"A rich dick who is going to give you a lot of fucking money. Can you do it or not?"

"Yeah. What are the names of the people?"

"Skylar Long and Danny Oldman. How soon can you set it up?"

Crypto made an almost inaudible sound. "Give me four hours."

"You've got two, and I'll double the money."

"Then I better get to it."

The line went dead. Matt pocketed his cell phone and packed up his few belongings. Then he walked out of the hotel room and to his truck. As he got in and started the engine, he looked up to find his parents and Spencer looking out their hotel window at him.

He didn't bother to even wave at them as he backed out of his parking space and drove away, headed toward Houston.

Now that she was in a much better frame of mind, Skylar used the morning to set up a time to view the Taylor house with the Realtor. She was going to send Danny a text, but she thought better of it once she realized that he might be either sleeping or working.

As if her thoughts had summoned him, a text came through from Danny. The smile on her face dimmed as she read it.

BUSY. NOT SURE WHEN I'LL GET TO COME BY.

She tried not to let the disappointment consume her, but it was a losing battle. It was stupid, too. Danny had an important position, an elected one. He had duties that took precedence over everything and everyone. If she was going to be a part of his life, she needed to understand that.

Danny wasn't like other men, and that's why she was attracted to him. He'd always put others before himself. It was just something she would have to get used to. And that was definitely something she could do because she wanted to be with Danny.

Skylar sent off a quick reply.

I UNDERSTAND. COME BY WHEN YOU CAN.

She added a smiley face emoji.

After she'd let Clayton and Abby know what time they were going to the house, she started looking at her finances. She was going to have to do something about her job, and while she wanted to give a two-week notice, it just wasn't possible in this situation.

Skylar bit her lip and then dialed her boss. She wasn't looking forward to the conversation, but she wasn't going to leave him hanging either. The sooner he knew about her plans, the quicker he could begin looking for someone to replace her.

The discussion went as she'd expected it to. He was upset that she was leaving, but he understood the reason and supported her in it. When she hung up, she knew that her life in Houston was well and truly over. And she felt good about it.

Really good.

She checked her image in the mirror before she headed downstairs, where Abby and Clayton were waiting. Skylar grabbed her coat before they walked out to Clayton's truck. The tinted windows would make it difficult for anyone to see who was in the back seat, which gave her some anonymity.

Her excitement climbed as they drove toward the house. There was a reason the Taylor house had always caught her attention. Maybe she'd known all along, somewhere in her subconscious, that she was going to buy it.

Now, all she could hope for was that the house looked as good in person as it did in the pictures online because she had her heart set on buying it.

It seemed to take forever to get to the Taylor place, and then the Realtor wanted to chat before opening the door. Finally, it was Clayton who politely asked if they could get inside.

As soon as Skylar walked through the front door, she knew this was where she would start her new life.

Chapter 23

Every time Danny tried to leave the office to take his lunch and see Skylar, something came up. If he didn't know better, he'd think someone was intentionally doing it to him.

He was still upset that he hadn't gotten to see her the night before, even after promising that he would, but he couldn't control what happened with his job. When he was needed, he had to go, and the previous night had been no exception.

Danny hadn't gotten home until after three in the morning. He'd been so dog-tired that he hadn't even taken off his clothes before crawling into bed. When his alarm went off at six, he'd stumbled into the shower with his eyes closed, barely remembering to remove his clothes before stepping beneath the spray.

Not all days were as bad as the previous, but when they did come, they were doozies for sure. The day hadn't gotten any better when he arrived at the station.

"It's a full moon, sheriff," the deputy at the front counter told him when she handed over a stack of files.

He grunted because there was something about a full

moon that brought out the crazy in humans and animals alike. Danny went straight to his office, returned some phone calls, looked through files, and signed off on paperwork. He couldn't believe everything he'd accomplished before lunch.

Then he called in a special order at the steakhouse that he planned to pick up and drive out to Skylar to surprise her. Only something else came up that required him to stay at the station, so he hadn't been able to make it. Instead, he'd had Wilson pick up the food and take it to have a nice lunch with his fiancée.

Danny was in the process of calling Skylar when the mayor arrived. He hung up and set his phone aside while talking to the mayor about the dangerous curve on one of the main roads that had caused the accident the night before. It was the fourth one that year, and there had been three the year before. It was time to do something about that stretch of highway.

It was two hours later before the mayor left, and Danny was free. He rose from his chair and headed out of his office. He was halfway to the door leading to his SUV when someone called his name.

He turned to find Wilson. The deputy wore a grin as he strode up. "Good news, sheriff. Madeline Gross will arrive here within the next forty minutes."

That was good news. It wasn't normal for a misdemeanor offense to be extradited from another county, but the sheriff in Harris County owned Danny a favor, and Danny had called it in. "Great news."

"Did you want to talk to her?"

"You should handle it. I want to watch the interrogation, though."

Wilson's lips twisted. "You really think she'll tell us anything different than what she told HCSD?"

"I'm sure she'll stick to her story," Danny told him.

"The fact that she's here and being charged should be of interest to Matt Gaudet. We can prove the two were having an affair, but while we can't prove Matt had her do anything, the fact they were a couple doesn't make him look innocent."

Wilson shifted his feet as he rested one hand on the butt of his weapon. "What are you charging her with?"

"Criminal mischief, which will be a Class-A misdemeanor."

"I'll be sure to let her know. By the way, this isn't her first run-in with the law. She was arrested for disorderly conduct about four years ago and has a criminal mischief charge from seven years ago."

"Do you know what the CM was?"

Wilson grinned. "She keyed Matt Gaudet's car after they had an argument at a bar. There were over a dozen witnesses, and someone called it in, which is why the police were there."

"No doubt the family would've preferred that not have been witnessed or involve the police. Good work, Wilson."

"Thanks, sheriff," the deputy replied.

Danny turned his head when he saw someone enter the station. The moment he spotted Caleb, he excused himself from Wilson.

"What is it?" Danny asked Caleb when he made his way over.

Caleb pulled a face. "Matt left town. I followed him all the way to Houston last night. He drove out first thing this morning and went straight to work. I think he may be done here."

Could it really be that easy? Danny sure hoped so. "He seems to have given up quickly. I'm still going to keep an eye out for his Audi."

"Maybe he realized he couldn't get Skylar back. Or

maybe his family finally talked some sense into him," Caleb said.

Danny shrugged. He should feel better about Matt leaving, but for some reason, he didn't. In fact, he was even more worried now.

"You aren't happy about this turn of events," Caleb guessed.

"No. Not after everything Matt and his family have done. What of his parents and his younger brother?"

Caleb smothered a yawn. "According to Brice and Cooper, they've not left yet."

"Why would they stay behind?" That didn't make any sense to Danny at all. If Matt left, they should have all returned to Houston. Then it hit him. "Shit. Matt didn't tell them he was leaving."

Caleb made a sound in the back of his throat. "That's a possibility, especially after the altercation between Matt and his mother yesterday. With Matt gone, there's no reason for them to stay."

"Then let's hope they leave soon."

"Agreed. I'm headed home for some rest. Cooper is already gone, and Jace is stepping in to help Brice for the next shift."

"I can't thank y'all enough for this."

"I'm offended you feel the need to say that at all," Caleb told him. "We're family, Danny. You know that. Now, go do your sheriff thing. We've got this covered."

Danny watched Caleb leave the station. There wasn't enough time for him to run out to the ranch and see Skylar before Madeline Gross showed up, which meant that it was going to be much later before he was finally free to see her.

He managed to get more office work done before Madeline arrived. Then he stood behind the glass, watching as Wilson interrogated the woman. Cross-examinations were usually something Danny enjoyed, but all he could think about was that it took him away from Skylar.

And Madeline Gross was taking all the blame for the vandalism of Danny's SUV, without putting any on Matt Gaudet.

When it appeared that Wilson wasn't getting anywhere with her, Danny called the deputy outside of the room. "Lead her to believe that Matt and Skylar were thinking of getting married. I want to see if we can push her into admitting something besides the same lines she keeps repeating."

The deputy returned to the room and did just as Danny suggested. There was a tightening in Madeline's face, giving away her surprise and anger. Wilson saw it as well and kept mentioning how Matt loved Skylar so much that he'd followed her all the way out here just to win her back.

Every time Wilson said it, Madeline grew angrier, but she still didn't break. Not until Wilson shared that it was Matt who'd told the sheriff's office where to find her to serve the warrant. It was a lie, but Madeline didn't know that.

She believed every word, and by her expletive-filled tirade about how Matt had promised her they would be married, and that Skylar meant nothing to him, Danny knew they could get whatever they needed from Madeline now.

It took nearly fifteen minutes and four deputies before Madeline calmed down. Danny watched it all behind the glass, monitoring the suspect as well as his staff. He took note of the deputies who were involved and intended to praise them for their quick thinking and calm demeanor during all of it—even when Madeline called them names.

But when Madeline was once again seated and quiet,

Wilson asked her, "Do you have anything new you'd like to tell us about Matt Gaudet?"

"As a matter of fact, I do. I've been in a relationship with Matt for eight years. He's always had an eye for the ladies," Madeline said, venom in her words. "But he always came back to me. Skylar is no different than the others."

"Did he live with any of the other women?"

Madeline took offense to the question, but she still answered. "Our relationship was on and off again. I was the only one who ever lived with him until Skylar."

Wilson nodded as he sat back in his chair. "So, it was serious between them?"

"He was still sleeping with me the entire time," Madeline stated. "I don't call that serious."

"Has he hit you?"

Danny held his breath, waiting for the reply.

Madeline lifted her chin. "I like things rough during sex, so yes, he's hit me."

"What about when you weren't engaged in intercourse?" Wilson asked.

Danny nodded because it was the same question he would've asked.

Madeline shrugged. "Like I said, we've been together for a long time. I can't remember every moment."

Danny ran a hand down his face. To get so close but still not get the information they needed was frustrating. Damn. It just wasn't a good day.

Unable to wait another minute, Danny called Skylar. To his disappointment, she didn't pick up. Instead, it went to voicemail. "It's me. Another long day, but I'm hoping I'll get to stop by tonight. Really want to see you."

He returned his phone to his pocket and his attention to Wilson and Madeline. For the next hour, Wilson kept asking her the same question in different ways, and there were several times that she came close to admitting that Matt had hit her outside of sex, but it was never enough to get them what they needed.

Danny was about to go into the room to join Wilson when a deputy came to get him because Danny had a visitor in his office. He hurried there and smiled when he saw Clayton.

"I didn't expect you to come by," he said.

Clayton held up his mug. "I was on my way into town to get some things and thought I'd stop in for some coffee."

It was a running joke that the sheriff's department had the best brew in town, but the simple fact was that it was true. And with as much of it as Danny drank, he was grateful.

"How is Skylar?" Danny asked.

Clayton nodded and set the cup of coffee down on Danny's desk. "Good. She's going a bit stir-crazy, but you can't blame her. Everything is set up at her parents' if anyone returns to threaten or bribe them. Not sure that's going to happen with Matt going back to Houston."

Danny shrugged as he sank into his chair. "The family seems intent on keeping their name spotless. I think they'll keep on the path regardless if Matt is on board or not."

"You're probably right. Just wishful thinking on my part."

"Does Skylar know Matt is gone?"

Clayton took another drink of coffee. "I've not told her yet."

"Why not?"

"Thought you might want to be the one to share the good news. Besides, she has news for you, as well."

Danny perked up. "Oh? What is that?"

"I don't want to spoil anything. You think you'll get by tonight?"

Danny pressed his lips together as he looked around him. "I'd like to say I will, but I can't promise anything."

"I understand. You might want to call her, though."

"I tried. Just left a message."

Clayton scratched his cheek. "I'll be sure to let Skylar know."

"Was she upset about last night?"

"I think disappointed is a better word, but I also believe she understands about your job."

Danny really hoped so.

Clayton scooted to the edge of the chair. "Look, why not just come by no matter what time it is? You know how to get in the gate. Plan on staying the night. I'm sure Skylar would love that."

That was definitely something Danny could get on board with.

"Oh, and now that Matt is gone, Skylar will want to know if she has to remain at the ranch. She knows she's welcome to stay as long as she wants."

"But she's eager to get on with her life," Danny finished. "I'd like to give it another few days just to be cautious, but I don't think we'll be able to keep Skylar there."

Clayton laughed. "She is rather headstrong. I like her, and I think you make a great couple. Don't let her get away, my friend."

"I don't intend to."

Chapter 24

She bought a house. Skylar still couldn't believe she'd made the offer, or that it had been accepted. Since she was putting such a large cash payment toward the price, the closing would go through relatively quickly. On top of that, she and the sellers had drawn up a rental agreement for the couple of weeks in the interim of the closing. Which meant that she had a place to live.

Not that she would be stupid about it. She was well aware that Matt was still out there.

To say she was giddy was putting it mildly. Already, she was thinking of the things she needed to purchase to furnish the house, especially since she'd gotten rid of everything when she moved in with Matt.

Her new place was on the small side—cozy, she liked to call it—but she loved everything about it, down to the backyard that was ripe for flowerbeds and even a deck. And she couldn't wait to tell everyone. Especially Danny. It would prove to him that she planned to start her new life here.

Skylar checked her phone, but the last text she'd gotten from him was the one that'd said he was busy earlier that morning. She tried not to focus on that as she made her way to the kitchen to help Abby prepare dinner.

No sooner had they begun than Clayton arrived home. He'd barely gotten to hang up his hat before Hope launched herself at him. He scooped her up easily and gave her a big kiss before setting her down to remove his coat.

"Hey, honey," Abby called.

Clayton walked into the kitchen and kissed her before he turned his attention on Skylar. "Just got back from a visit with Danny. He plans on dropping by tonight."

Skylar brightened. "Did he say when?"

"He's got a lot going on, but he knows the code to get into the gate. No matter the time, he's coming."

Abby grinned at Skylar. "About damn time."

Skylar had to agree, but she kept that to herself. Instead, she asked, "Did you tell him about the house?"

"Nope. I'm leaving that to you," Clayton told her. "Please don't rush off. You're welcome to stay as long as you want."

Skylar had already thought about this. "You two know my thoughts on being a burden, but I have no desire to become a casualty either. As soon as I've got everything in place to be safe, I'll move to my new place."

"Smart," Abby said as she quickly moved about the kitchen, managing to miss Hope as the child played near her feet.

Clayton kissed Hope on the cheek. "I'm going to take this little bug and go find her siblings. I'll spend some time with them before dinner unless you need me for something."

Abby shook her head. "Go, have fun. I'll call you when it's ready."

Clayton took a few steps, then stopped beside Skylar. "Danny is one of the smartest men I know. He's dependable and honest, but sometimes, he gets wrapped up in his work too much. He needs someone to remind him that he has a life."

"I can do that," Skylar assured Clayton. "And I understand how much his work needs him."

After Clayton had walked away, Abby asked Skylar, "Are you really okay with his job?"

"It's an important position," Skylar said. "I've never had someone in my life with such a job before, and it'll take some time getting used to him working such hours, but it's not something that's a deal-breaker for me."

"The two of you haven't gotten to spend a lot of time together."

"Not as much as I'd like," Skylar said as she thought about taking him to her house. "But that will change soon enough."

Abby stirred the pot and glanced her way. "I hope you're right."

"Matt has always made snap decisions about everything, but he'll grow weary of all of this and move on. At least, that's what I keep telling myself."

"What about his parents and younger brother being here?"

Skylar shrugged nonchalantly. "I'm not too worried about them. They've already done so much. How much more can they do?"

"Don't ever ask that," Abby cautioned. "Anytime you say something like that, then things go south and quickly."

"Good point."

Abby put on some Christmas music as the talk turned to the gifts she still needed to buy while they finished cooking.

Dinner itself was a loud affair with three kids, but Skylar enjoyed it. She kept looking toward the back door in the hopes that Danny would arrive, but he never did. Skylar tried not to let her disappointment show, but she wasn't sure she succeeded.

She insisted on cleaning the kitchen herself, though Abby put up a fuss. That is, right up until Clayton told her he'd run a bath for her. Alone, Skylar didn't have to put on a smile, not that she felt she had to be someone she wasn't in front of Clayton and Abby. But they knew how badly she wanted Danny there, and she felt their eyes on her all through dinner.

With everything going on with the Matt fiasco, she didn't want to be the person others thought couldn't handle disappointment.

She rinsed off the last plate and was drying it when there was a knock on the back door. Her head snapped to the side, excitement rising at the thought of it being Danny. When her eyes collided with hazel ones, she set down the plate and hurried to him.

"Hi," she said when she opened the door.

He smiled and pulled her against him with one arm. "Hi," he murmured before he kissed her.

Skylar melted against him as their kiss deepened. The sound of the kids approaching drew them apart.

"You made it," Clayton said as he followed his kids into the kitchen.

Danny didn't get a chance to answer as the children swarmed him. Skylar stood back and watched as he interacted with each of them, making sure not to give one more attention than the others.

"Hungry?" Skylar asked when there was a break in the talk.

Danny shook his head. "I grabbed something earlier."

Clayton jerked his head toward the stairs. "Y'all go and spend some time alone."

Danny took her hand and pulled her after him. Skylar

smiled at Clayton as she followed Danny up the stairs. When he reached the top landing, he stopped.

"Which one is your room?" he asked.

This time, she was the one to lead him. "This way."

When they got to the room and stepped inside, they found a bottle of champagne on ice with two glasses, along with some strawberries and some cheese and crackers.

"This was Abby," Danny said.

Skylar shook her head. "I think it might have been Clayton."

"Hmm. You might be right, but in truth, I don't care. Food isn't what I'm hungry for."

She eyed him. "Is that right? And just what is it you want, sheriff?"

"You," he replied huskily.

She ran her hands up his chest and then over his shoulders. "It feels like years since I last saw you."

"I know what you mean. You're all I can think about."

That made her giddy. "You're all I can think about, as well."

He gave her a soft kiss before pulling back and looking down at her. "I'm sorry about last night."

"Don't apologize. Just kiss me some more."

"I can do that."

Her eyes slid closed as his mouth pressed against hers. She sighed as his arms came around her and held tight. She was the one who began unbuttoning his shirt before yanking it out of his pants. They stopped kissing long enough for him to pull her sweater over her head, and then they were kissing again.

He maneuvered her to the bed. Once there, he managed to get out of his boots and unbutton her jeans. She had to unzip her boots, and every second she wasn't touching Danny, she felt lost. She tossed her boots aside and got out of her jeans in record time. Then she removed her bra and panties.

"Damn, woman. You are beautiful," he said and kissed her.

She had only gotten a brief glimpse of his body after he'd shed his clothes, but she wasn't worried. They had all night. No one was going to interrupt them this time.

Skylar reached between them to his arousal and wrapped her fingers around it. He groaned into her mouth. She pulled back and began kissing down his chest before kneeling in front of him and taking his hard cock into her mouth.

"God, baby, that feels so good," he murmured as he grabbed a fistful of her hair.

She liked the noises he made, but more than anything, she liked that she made him feel good. Yet she didn't get to remain there for long. Danny quickly had her on her back on the bed as he kneeled between her legs.

The moment his mouth touched her, she arched her back. His tongue licked and laved, urging the fire inside her higher and higher as she came ever closer to orgasm.

His finger pushed inside her while his tongue swirled around her clit. The pleasure surrounded her like a thick cloud. She didn't think it could get any better. Then his free hand found her breast and thumbed her nipple.

She fisted the comforter as he brought her to the brink of climax, but he didn't take her over. Instead, he flipped her onto her stomach and entered her.

The feel of him filling her was exquisite. He buried himself deep, then grabbed her hips and began slowly moving. His thrusts grew deeper, harder as his tempo gradually increased.

Already on the cusp of an orgasm, he kept her there for several minutes until he reached around and moved a finger over her clit.

Skylar bit back a scream as the climax swept through her with the force of a hurricane. She could do nothing but experience it as Danny controlled everything, and as someone who was always in control, she liked how he took over when they had sex.

Just as she was coming back to reality, his hand left and grabbed a fistful of hair. There was something about him holding onto her in such a way that brought on another climax.

"I can feel you around me," he said.

His hands tightened on her hip and hair, and then his body jerked as he pulled out of her and spilled his seed on her back.

Skylar pressed her cheek against the comforter, her body sated and her heart full. She stayed there while Danny cleaned them off, then he took her in his arms as he lay beside her, their legs intertwined.

"I've missed you," he said and kissed the top of her head.

She smiled and hugged him tightly. "I've missed you, as well."

"Clayton said you had news?"

"I do." She tilted her head to look at him. "I bought the Taylor house today."

His eyes widened. "Congratulations."

"Don't worry," she told him before he could say anything. "I'm not moving in just yet. I'd like your and Clayton's help picking out the perfect security for the house. I'm going to make sure I'm safe."

"Good. I just found you, Skylar Long. I don't want to lose you."

"You won't lose me, Danny Oldman. I'm yours forever."

"I like the sound of that."

She did, too. A lot.

Chapter 25

December 12th

Danny woke to the sound of an alarm. It took him a moment to realize that it was his. Normally, he was awake before the alarm even went off.

Careful not to disturb Skylar, who was still lying on his chest, he reached over the side of the bed and found his jeans then pulled out his phone. He shut off the alarm and checked his texts. Several had come through during the night, but nothing had been pressing enough for the station to call him.

He set the phone on the bedside table and closed his eyes. Skylar sighed against him, snuggling deeper. He smiled. He felt rested for the first time in . . . hell, he couldn't remember. The fact that he'd actually slept the entire night was a feat in itself.

And he knew it was all because of Skylar.

He tightened his arm around her, rubbing his palm along her bare back. He could wake up to this every morning and be perfectly content.

Danny was in the process of rolling her over and waking Skylar by making love to her when his phone buzzed. With a sigh, he grabbed the cell and looked at the screen to see it was a call coming in from the office. He answered in a whisper, hoping not to wake Skylar.

"Sheriff, you might want to get down here quick," came the voice of one of his deputies. "Someone vandalized Sean Gaudet's Cadillac Escalade, and he's fit to be tied."

Danny sighed. Knowing the Gaudets, they would likely hold a press conference about the matter. "I'll be right there," he whispered.

After he'd hung up, Danny managed to gently roll Skylar onto her side so he could get out of bed. As he dressed, he looked at her, wishing with everything he had that he was still in bed with her. But they would have other mornings. In fact, he was due some vacation time. Perhaps he'd take it, and they could spend the entire week together.

He pocketed his phone, strapped his gun to his belt, and ran his hand through his hair before he walked to Skylar's side of the bed and kissed her forehead. Then he got his boots and quietly exited the room. Once in the hall, he put on his boots and made his way downstairs.

"I've not seen that look in a long time," Clayton said when Danny walked into the kitchen.

Danny couldn't stop smiling. "It sure does feel good."

"So, this thing between y'all, is it a fling?"

"Not on my part."

"Well, I can honestly say I don't think it is on hers either. That makes me happy for you, my friend."

Danny put on his coat and hat. "I'm pretty damn happy, as well."

Clayton frowned. "You leaving already?"

"Got called in. The Gaudets' vehicle was vandalized."

"Yeah, you better get down there."

Danny set his hat on his head. "See you later."

Clayton held up his mug of coffee and smiled in response.

The sunrise was striking, and Danny wished he was showing it to Skylar. He chuckled as he got into his SUV. Every time he thought of anything, Skylar was in his thoughts. And it felt damn good.

He was still smiling when he arrived at the station. Not even the sight of the Gaudets could dim that. The moment they spotted him, they turned to him, talking over each other.

Danny slid his gaze to the side to find Spencer sitting in one of the chairs on his phone, seemingly unperturbed about it all. Odd that there hadn't been any sign of the eldest son, Michael, during all of this. Then again, he wouldn't be caught anywhere there was a scandal involving his family.

"What are you going to do, sheriff?" Sean Gaudet demanded.

Danny tipped back his hat and glanced at the counter where three deputies watched, relief to have someone other than them taking the brunt of the Gaudets' obvious disdain clear on their faces. "I'm going to do what I do with every person who comes in to file a report. I'm going to give it to a deputy to handle."

Michelle's eyes narrowed. "We deserve better than to be handed off."

Danny took a deep breath to stay calm. "Mrs. Gaudet, you're a visitor in this county, and that gives you the same rights as everyone else. Unless you saw who did it, we will write up the report for you so you can give it to your insurance to handle."

"Have you even seen the vehicle?" Sean demanded.

"I haven't."

"Perhaps you should."

Danny glanced again at the deputies, but none of

them would meet his gaze. With no other choice, he said, "Let's go have a look."

Michelle crossed her arms over her chest and turned away, leaving Sean to take Danny outside. The two of them exited the building and turned to the right. Since Danny had parked at the back of the building, he hadn't seen anything upon his arrival. But now that he was outside, there was no missing the tow truck that had the Escalade hooked up.

The black vehicle had *SCUM* spray-painted in red on both sides. A metal pole had been pushed through the windshield and was embedded in the driver's seat. All four tires were slashed, and the other windows were also broken.

Whoever had done this had been in a rage. If Matt were still in town, Danny would've hedged his bets on him.

"Is this what your visitors can expect here?" Sean asked.

Danny shook his head. "I've never seen anything like this done in my county, Mr. Gaudet. It could be in retaliation for what you and your family have been doing to Miss Long."

"I knew you were going to bring that up." Sean glared at him as if he were the Devil himself. "You're supposed to be impartial, sheriff, but I see where your loyalties lie."

"My job is to protect the citizens of this county, and that's exactly what I'm doing. That means even you, despite the harm you've caused."

"I've caused harm?" Sean said, taken aback. "You can't be serious. This was done to *my* family!"

Danny wasn't going to get drawn into a debate about it. "Your son was arrested for physically assaulting an individual. And I witnessed the entire thing. It's even on video if you'd like to see it. You can lay the blame on others if you want, but you can't get away from the truth."

A muscle worked in Sean's jaw. "What are you going to do about my vehicle?"

"Exactly what I said I'd do. Until the culprit can be identified and located, you should get a rental car." Danny turned to walk away, then hesitated. "And you might want to be nicer to folks. No one around here gives a shit how much money you have or what your family name is. Respect around here is earned."

Danny strode back into the station. Spencer was still playing on his phone, and Michelle glanced at Danny as she talked to someone on hers. He ignored both as he made his way to the front desk.

"Someone go take some pictures of the Gaudet SUV immediately. Detailed pictures, both in and outside the vehicle. Get the report done ASAP so they can get on with things."

"Yes, sheriff," the three deputies replied in unison.

Thanks to the Gaudets, Danny's mood wasn't as sunny as before. He walked through the door to the back of the station and his office.

He sank into his chair and closed his eyes as he thought of Skylar. It didn't take much to bring the smile back to his face. When he opened his eyes, he decided to get as much done as he could so he could get out of there early and take Skylar to dinner.

With Matt gone—and hopefully his family soon, as well—there was no reason they had to hide their relationship. Danny's stomach quivered at the word.

Relationship.

He couldn't believe he was thinking it, especially when he'd resigned himself to a life alone. Then, out of the blue, Skylar had shown up and changed everything—for the better.

Danny called Jace to see if he had seen anyone damaging the Gaudets' vehicle, but they had been watching the hotel, not the SUV.

Danny then went through some case files from other deputies, all the while fully expecting the Gaudets to demand to see him again. Thankfully, that didn't happen.

A few hours later, he was on his way to get some coffee when Deputy Carlos Pena called him into an office. The deputy had been working a case that had stalled out. Danny went over the evidence and read the statements by the witnesses, as well as the recorded video of the two suspects that had been brought in for questioning. While he did this, Pena went out and got them lunch.

Danny and Carlos brainstormed ideas regarding who Carlos should focus on next as a suspect as they ate. Pena even asked Danny if he wanted to ride along to find their suspect.

It wasn't something Danny was going to pass up. He glanced at his watch and gave a nod before they headed out together. In three hours, they had found the suspect and spent an hour questioning him and gaining new information.

"Thanks, sheriff," Carlos said after they'd let the suspect go.

"Anytime."

Danny checked his watch, happy that it hadn't taken all afternoon. He sent Skylar a text asking if she wanted to go to dinner, and she replied with an immediate YES.

He texted her a time he'd be by to pick her up, and then Danny went back to his office. He checked his emails and phone messages to make sure there was nothing pressing. On his way out, he spotted Wilson.

"How's it going?"

The deputy shrugged, his lips twisting ruefully. "Ms.

Gross is set to go before the judge in the morning. She still hasn't admitted to Matt abusing her."

"She probably won't. Well, we can't say we didn't try."

"I'm not done trying to get it out of her," Wilson said. "I think she's afraid of the family."

Danny grunted. "No doubt that's true. Maybe use that next time. If she believes the family won't harm her, she might give us what we need."

"Will do, sheriff. You outta here for the day?"

"I sure am."

Wilson smiled. "You deserve it. Go have some fun."

"I think I will."

Danny's steps were light as he walked to his truck and drove home. He took a long shower, then took his time shaving. He actually used the aftershave he usually ignored. Then he stood in his closet, looking at the two clean—and nice—shirts he had. It had been a while since he'd replaced any of his clothes. Maybe it was time to do some shopping.

But that would have to wait for another time. He had other plans for tonight.

Danny chose the olive green button-down and tore it out of the dry-cleaning package. Then he dressed, even going for his nice boots instead of the everyday ones he wore for work.

With one last look at himself in the mirror, Danny put his weapon on his belt and settled his hat atop his head. Then he slipped into his coat and climbed inside his vehicle. He started the engine and backed out of his drive.

He had gone a few miles when he looked in his rearview mirror and spotted a truck behind him, which didn't mean anything. But Matt had followed him recently, so Danny decided to take the long way around the town to see if he was being paranoid or not.

Turned out he was. The truck turned off after a few miles. Danny then did a U-turn and headed back toward the ranch. He could barely contain his excitement. He was going on a date, and that hadn't happened in a couple of years. But more than that, he was taking out the woman he'd been in love with for years.

He grinned. Yep, he was in love. He could hardly believe it, but there was no denying it. In fact, he'd been in love with Skylar Long since high school, though he hadn't realized that's what the emotion was at the time. He'd thought it was just lust or infatuation.

When he thought of all the years they could've spent together, it made him sad. But he also truly believed that this was their time. Had they tried it at any other time, it likely wouldn't have worked.

But it would this time.

Danny pulled up at the ranch and turned off his engine. He got out and went to the door, but he didn't get a chance to knock. Clayton and Abby's eldest, Wynter, held it open for him.

"Hey, Uncle Danny. You look nice. And you smell nice, too."

He gave her a wink as she stared up at him with her big eyes. "Thank you."

"You should see Miss Skylar. She looks beautiful."

Something out of the corner of his eye caught Danny's attention. He lifted his head and saw Skylar. Her blond hair fell free about her shoulders. She wore a thin cream sweater and cream pants, along with matching heels. Around her shoulders was a cream, taupe, and black plaid wool shawl.

"I told you," Wynter said before walking off.

Danny only had eyes for Skylar. He walked to her as her smile grew. He stared into her blue eyes. "You look amazing."

"You look pretty hot yourself," she replied. Then she frowned. "Are you sure we should be doing this?"

"Definitely."

She then flashed him a bright smile. "Then I'm game."

"You two kids don't do anything I wouldn't do," Clayton said.

Danny looked over to find Clayton and Abby and their three kids all watching. Danny laughed and held out his hand for Skylar. She took it, and with one last wave to his friends, they walked from the house.

Chapter 26

To go from such a low period to *this*! Skylar couldn't remember being so happy or content. Through one of the roughest, darkest months of her life, she had come through the other side to find where she truly belonged.

She wasn't naïve enough to think that things with Matt and his family were over yet, but she believed they were on the downhill side of things. And that was just fine by her. Skylar wanted that part of her life to be well and truly behind her while Danny and their future together were before her.

Tonight was a turning point for them. Their relationship had been unconventional to say the least, but she wouldn't change a thing. It didn't matter that they'd had to hide things for a little while. Now, they were going to show the world.

"Are you sure you're okay with this?" Danny asked, glancing her way as he drove.

She smiled and nodded. "I am."

"Good, because I am, too."

"You surprised me, though."

Danny laughed, his eyes crinkling at the corners. "I like being able to do that. Does steak sound good?"

"Sounds perfect. Did you have a good day?"

"It started off amazing because I was in bed with you."

Skylar grinned at him. "You weren't there when I woke up."

"I'm sorry about that. I got called in."

"I hope it wasn't serious."

He grunted and shrugged one shoulder. "Someone vandalized the Gaudets' SUV. The rage was apparent in how they destroyed the vehicle. Even going so far as to put an iron rod through the windshield and into the driver's seat."

"Damn," Skylar murmured. "Could it have been Madeline Gross?"

"I thought of her, but she's still being held in the jail. I also thought of Matt."

"It could be him."

"I never got a chance to tell you last night. He left town."

Her eyes widened as she grinned. "Really?"

"Yesterday, he went back to Houston and straight to work, but I still think the security system on the house is a must."

"I agree." Skylar frowned as she thought about the case. "I'm glad he's gone. That makes things easier for us, and for me. However, that doesn't leave you with a lot of suspects for the vandalism, does it?"

"It has to be someone from my county. I know the community doesn't particularly care for the Gaudets or their treatment of you, thanks to the articles in the paper and the pieces on the local news, but I never would have thought anyone would do such a thing."

"People react different ways to different things.

Maybe the Gaudets did something to someone that you don't know about."

"Maybe." He shrugged again and pulled into the parking lot of the restaurant. "We might be far from city life, but we still have crime here. I shouldn't be bothered by such an offense, but I am."

She waited until he turned off the ignition before she said, "You'll find out who did it."

"I hope so. The Gaudets sure are hell-bent to find out who wronged them. They're used to people in Houston deferring to them, and that doesn't happen here."

"No, thank goodness."

They shared a laugh and exited the vehicle. They then walked hand-in-hand into the restaurant, where they were led to a table. Skylar wouldn't have cared if they went to a sandwich shop, she was just glad to be out with Danny.

"If we're going public, does that mean that you don't fear Matt returning?"

Danny raised a brow. "I didn't say that."

Skylar shook her head. "We're holding hands and eating dinner together. If you thought Matt was coming back, we wouldn't be here. Not to mention, you don't seem too worried about his family seeing us."

"There are a lot of restaurants in the area," Danny responded. "What are the odds of the Gaudets eating here? Besides, they're in the next town."

Skylar was disappointed in his words. "So, you're still concerned?"

Danny leaned forward, his arms on the table. "Honey, let me put it to you this way. Ten, twenty years from now, I'm still going to be looking for Matt to come back into your life."

"He won't bother us anymore. He's gone. Otherwise, he wouldn't have left."

"I wish I had your confidence. I've seen too many crime scenes."

She took a deep breath and opened the menu. "I've found that to make something real, you have to believe it's going to happen."

"Well, I imagined you as mine for long enough," he replied with a smile.

Their talk paused as they ordered. Once they were alone again, Skylar said, "Now I know why Abby and Clayton kept asking me to stay longer. I'll stay at the ranch for a couple of days, but I can't stay there forever, especially now that I bought the house."

"I still can't believe you bought it."

"As soon as I walked in, I knew it was meant to be mine. It's perfect," she said, hearing the dreamy tone in her words.

Danny gave her a lopsided grin. "I'm glad."

"I wanted you to see it with me, but I couldn't wait. The offer was past my lips before I even realized it."

"And the sellers agreed that quickly?"

Skylar scrunched up her face. "Well, I made it worth their while. We also agreed to a short-term lease so I could begin moving in before the papers are signed."

Danny nodded, concern on his face.

"I learned a lot about real estate from my boss. Well, old boss now," she said with a laugh. "He's brilliant at it, and when I asked him to teach me, he agreed. And before you ask, Clayton showed me a couple of security systems today. He also called his people to go take a look at the house to give their recommendation. They'll give it to us tomorrow."

Danny glanced down at his mug of beer. "That doesn't surprise me at all. I'm really glad you're taking your safety seriously."

"I don't want to be scared again. I don't care how

much the system costs, I'm going to get the best one there is."

"It would be just like Clayton to pay for it, you know."

"I don't need him to do that," she said.

Danny chuckled. "Get used to it, honey. Clayton, Abby, and that whole gang are some of the most giving people I know."

"You've surrounded yourself with great people."

He thought about that a moment before nodding. "Yes, I have."

"I didn't do the same," she lamented.

"You are now."

She smiled then because it was the truth. "I'm going to run to the ladies' room."

Danny winked at her as she rose and walked away. On the way to the toilet, all she could think about was how happy she was. It didn't matter what she had suffered at Matt's hands. Not anymore, at least. Not when she had someone like Danny.

Skylar finished and walked from the restroom, only to have a man step in her way. "Excuse me," she said and tried to walk around him, but he prevented her from going.

She looked into his dark eyes and angry face, and without having to be told, she knew this man was somehow affiliated with Matt. The happiness she'd felt was gone in the blink of an eye.

"If you're going to say something, then speak. Otherwise, get the hell out of my way," she told him, trying not to let him see that her hands were shaking from anger and more than a little fear.

Danny was out of sight, but she knew all she had to do was scream his name, and he would come running. But that wasn't the point. She had foolishly believed that Matt's departure meant that he was done with her.

The man glared at her, then with a sinister smile, he

stepped around her. Skylar turned to watch him as he walked from the restaurant. Then she hastily looked around to see if anyone had witnessed it, but no one had their gazes turned to her.

She took a deep breath and returned to the table to see that the waiter had delivered their food. It gave her another moment to compose herself, but it didn't matter. Danny noticed. His smile was replaced by a frown.

The moment they were alone, he asked, "What happened?"

Skylar didn't want to tell him and ruin their night, but she knew that was stupid. Matt was still a problem for her, and Danny needed to know.

"Skylar, you're scaring me."

She took a drink of her wine to fortify her, then she recounted the quick encounter for him, detailing as much of the man's face, attire, and actions as she could.

"Stay here," Danny ordered her as he rose and hurried out of the restaurant.

Skylar looked at the delicious steak, but her appetite was gone. Matt had ruined something again—and he wasn't even near. Was this how it would always be?

No. She wouldn't let it. She wouldn't shut herself off from everything and everyone because she was afraid. That's what Matt wanted. She'd lived in fear for months, worrying about every word that came out of her mouth, or that he might not like some outfit she wore.

Enough was enough. She'd made a stand when she came here. She wouldn't falter now.

But the false hope she'd when he left was like a rug being yanked from beneath her. She didn't like the feeling at all.

"He's gone," Danny said as he resumed his seat. "You're sure it was someone involved with Matt?"

Skylar took another drink of wine. "Who else would

give me such a look? He was menacing and threatening. There was no doubt in my mind that he wanted to hurt me."

"I'm not saying you didn't experience any of that. I'm just making sure. Do you want to leave?"

She did, but she wasn't going to. "Our dinner is here, and we're out for our first official date. I don't want to go anywhere until I've finished my steak."

"That's my girl."

He was cutting into his steak when she said, "You called deputies here, didn't you?"

"Damn straight, I did," he said before putting a bite into his mouth and smiling.

Skylar laughed. "Life with you will always be entertaining."

"I hope you don't mind."

"Mind? I love it."

Danny swallowed the bite and set down his utensils. "Are you sure about us? Is it too soon? Do you need time? I should've asked all of that before, but I was thinking how much I wanted to be with you."

She also set aside her fork and knife. "No, it isn't too soon. If I believed that, I never would have gotten involved with you. I meant what I said the other day. As soon as I saw you, it was like everything fell into place. For the first time in my life, I knew where I belonged, and it's right here. Do I like that I had to go through abuse to find my way here? Not at all. But it was part of my path, and I'll accept that."

Danny blew out a breath. "Thank God, because I wasn't sure I'd be able to keep my hands off you."

"You better not. And just so you know, I like a lot of affection," she said with a wink.

His smile was slow and sexy. "Then we're going to get along really well."

They laughed and went back to their meal. Between

bites, Danny asked about her plans for the house. Skylar loved decorating, so she pulled out her phone and showed him some of the furniture she was thinking of purchasing.

"I like the leather couch. I wouldn't have thought of black, though," he said. "But with the colors you've picked out, it'll look good."

She shrugged. "I've never been into florals or pink. You know, the typical feminine look. I've always been partial to richer, darker colors."

"I like them. Quite a lot, actually."

"What does your house look like?"

He winced. "Um . . . it's . . . plain."

She laughed. "There's nothing wrong with that."

"When I bought it, it had been freshly painted. I didn't particularly care for the colors used, but I didn't have the time to paint it again, and I didn't want anyone in my house, so I decided to wait."

"How long ago was that?" Skylar asked.

He shrugged as he looked into her eyes. "Twelve years."

"No way," she said with a laugh.

He nodded, joining in her laughter. "I'm not joking. It needs help, but I'm only there to sleep, so I've not really paid much attention to it. I do the minimum amount of maintenance, which is sad, really. I think I just needed someone to come home to in order to change that."

She put her arm on the table and opened her hand, waiting for him to take it. "Then come home to me."

"I plan on it."

Chapter 27

December 14th

Danny never imagined that his life could be turned around on a dime, but that's exactly what had happened. He'd wanted to spend another night with Skylar, but as he was headed back to the ranch, Ryan Wells, the police chief, notified him of a big narcotics bust that the local PD was about to undertake. Danny and some of his deputies were asked to participate, especially since Danny had given the police the tip several months ago.

He dropped Skylar off with a lingering kiss, then headed straight to meet Ryan and get geared up. The bust went flawlessly with more than ten people arrested and multiple drugs confiscated. It was one of the biggest busts in the area in three years.

The fact that it had fallen under the police's jurisdiction didn't bother Danny at all. What he cared about was getting the streets clean.

He slept well that night, despite not having Skylar in his arms, and woke refreshed once more. By the time he entered his office, he was already planning the next two days off with Skylar. He didn't particularly like shopping, but if she needed to buy furniture for her new house, he'd gladly walk the stores with her. Because it was about being with her.

Plus, it would give him time to look over the security systems she was looking at, as well as put in a way for her to contact him immediately should she find herself in danger.

He sighed as he thought about Matt Gaudet. It was good that the bastard had left town, but Danny knew Matt wasn't finished with Skylar yet. That meant Danny—and Skylar—needed to stay alert and not let their guards down.

After meetings with his detectives, Danny spent the morning writing his report on his involvement with the drug bust the night before. He was about to send a text to Skylar to see if she wanted to meet for lunch when he recalled the man in the restaurant.

No matter how hard his deputies had searched, they hadn't found anything. Not that he expected they would. He had no idea what the make or model was of the vehicle that the man had left in—if he had left at all.

But it made him wary about Skylar getting on the road by herself. Danny didn't want to ask Abby or Clayton to drive her. His friends were already doing so much. Brice, Caleb, Jace, and Cooper had taken days off from their jobs to help him, so he wasn't going to turn to them either.

Which meant that he would need to get Skylar himself. The only problem was that it wouldn't leave any time to come back into town to eat.

Danny wanted to spend every minute he had with her, but he realized that wasn't going to be possible quite yet. They didn't have to steal moments anymore, but those moments weren't going to be as often as he liked either. At least, for now.

He ended up going to lunch with Ryan Wells. They

worked well together, and that hadn't always been the case between the previous chiefs and sheriffs. Danny knew how essential it was for everyone to get along and work cohesively. During his first year in office, he'd gone out of his way to mend the fences his predecessor had destroyed with Chief Wells.

It wasn't until his second year that the chief had actually been receptive to him. From then on, the two met at least once a week over lunch to keep their working relationship going. Danny went so far as to call Ryan a friend.

Both were young for their offices, but Ryan was one of the best cops Danny knew. If Ryan hadn't already been snapped up by the police department, Danny would've recruited him. The fact that Ryan had risen through the ranks so quickly was a testament to his skill. And his men were as loyal to him as they came.

"I heard you've had your eye on a certain family that's come into the area recently," Ryan said as he began eating his grilled fish and veggies.

Ryan was a health nut. Their long hours, little sleep, and vast amounts of coffee weren't exactly good for the body. With Ryan's prodding, Danny had actually started eating healthier four years ago. It was now a habit, though every now and again, he'd get his favorites—a hamburger with bacon, cheese, and jalapeños along with a mound of curly fries.

Danny shrugged as he finished chewing. "I knew you were focused on the drug bust. I didn't want to take any men off that."

"You should've called."

Danny looked into Ryan's green eyes and nodded. "I should have. I would've expected you to."

"Exactly. So, want to fill me in? I heard you were part of Matt Gaudet's arrest."

For the next fifteen minutes, Danny told Ryan everything—even about him and Skylar seeing each other.

Ryan finished his last bite and pushed the plate away as he crossed his arms on the table. "Damn."

"That's one way of putting it."

"And you say a man approached Skylar last night while the two of you were out?"

Danny nodded. "I never saw him. I couldn't see the bathroom area from our table. I thought all of that was done."

"I would've believed the same. You took precautions, Danny. It's not on you."

"It is if she gets hurt."

"That's not going to happen. I'd feel the same myself. I've already told my men to keep a lookout for anyone fitting Matt's description. If he shows back up, we'll know. He won't get within a mile of Skylar."

Danny grinned, once more thankful for the friends he had in his life. "I figured out of the two of us, you'd find someone first."

Ryan snorted loudly before sitting back in his chair. "I always knew it'd be you."

"Actually, I thought we'd be single forever," Danny confessed.

Ryan threw back his head and laughed loudly. "Me, too."

Danny noticed the many women in the restaurant looking at Ryan with interest. He was a prime catch, but he'd gone through a nasty divorce seven years earlier and had buried himself in his work. He hadn't looked up since, but Danny knew all it would take was the right woman.

He should know. It had just happened to him.

The smile was gone from Ryan's face. "What about the rest of the Gaudet family? Do you think they pose a threat to Skylar? And what about Clayton and his family?"

"You've not been able to spend too much time with Clayton, or you'd know he's the last one I'm concerned about. Anyone stupid enough to break onto that ranch gets whatever Clayton and his men dole out."

Ryan smiled, nodding. "My cousin was a SEAL and had a chance to work with Clayton once. He said Clayton is one of the most badass people he's ever met."

"It's true. And Clayton passed that onto his brothers-in-law, Caleb and Brice."

"Don't leave out Cooper and Jace."

Danny chuckled. The seven of them would have a poker night every few months, though it had been a while.

"But I don't think the Gaudet family will physically harm Skylar," Danny said, getting back to Ryan's question. "They went the direction of a smear campaign to call her word into question."

"People like that will resort to anything. Their main focus is their eldest son, you can't forget that."

Danny would never forget such a thing. "Skylar just bought a house."

"I heard. The old Taylor home."

"She wants to move in soon. I've convinced her to stay a couple more days with Clayton and Abby, but I don't know how much longer she'll do that."

Ryan rubbed a hand over his jaw. "You can't watch her every second of every day. Can she defend herself?"

"She carries a handgun and has her concealed carry permit, but I don't know about defending herself without the weapon."

"You should talk to her. Hell, even Clayton could show her a few things."

"I will. I know Clayton is helping her out with a security system, and she doesn't intend to move in until that's installed, which alleviates some of my worry. I'm going to make sure there's a way for her to get ahold of me at any time if she feels threatened by anything."

"Your concern is valid, Danny. Don't think it isn't."

He nodded, swallowing. "I could go on all day about this. So we better change the subject. How are things in your department?"

"Pretty good. The new recruit that came up from Beaumont is working well, but the one from Waco isn't meshing with the rest. I'm going to have to do something about that soon."

"Unfortunately, you will. You've got a great group over there, but one officer can disrupt everything."

"As I'm learning." Ryan sighed loudly. "Sometimes, I envy the fact that your position is elected. You can't get fired."

"Oh, I certainly can."

Ryan twisted his lips and grunted. "Not as easily as I can. The mayor sure is eyeing everything I do, and election year is coming up. I'm not looking forward to that."

"Just keep doing what you're doing. You're an amazing chief."

Ryan looked around and leaned closer. "I had a visit from a Texas Ranger last week."

Danny's brows shot up. "No kidding? That's great. You interested in joining them?"

"I've always wanted to be a Ranger. Always. But . . . I don't know. I'm happy where I am."

"But you can't go any further."

Ryan shrugged. "True. I have another meeting with them in a couple of weeks. We'll see how it goes."

With their lunch winding down, they paid and made

their way outside to their vehicles. After another few minutes of small talk, they parted ways.

Before Danny drove off, he checked his phone for texts. He was a little disappointed that he hadn't heard from Skylar, so he sent her a text to let her know that he was thinking about her.

He waited a few minutes to see if she'd respond, but she didn't. Thinking she was busy, Danny started the SUV and drove back to the office. His mind went over what Ryan had said about the Gaudet family. He turned his vehicle around and drove to the next town over where the Gaudets were staying.

A brand new white Cadillac Escalade was in the parking lot, and Michelle Gaudet was putting her luggage in. No rental car for this family. They'd just gone out and bought a new one. He shook his head as he pulled into the parking lot and drove up to the Escalade.

"Ma'am," he said when she looked at him.

Michelle's eyes narrowed on him. "Come to gloat?"

"I came to see how you were faring."

"That's a lie. You wanted to see if we had left."

He shrugged. "That, too." No use lying.

She rolled her eyes. "We might be going home, but we're not done with Skylar Long."

"As I told your husband, ma'am, I'll be happy to show you the video footage of Matt assaulting Skylar. Maybe then you'll stop thinking of your son as the victim."

She folded her arms over her chest as she faced him. "People who don't have money don't realize the cockroaches that come out of the woodwork to get their grubby little hands on anything they can. Matt told us what happened. When he told Skylar they wouldn't be marrying and she wouldn't get any money, she got angry and retaliated. He followed her here, hoping to win her back."

"I really think you should see the footage, Mrs. Gaudet. You can see for yourself who is doing the lying here, and it isn't Miss Long."

She smiled, a cat-who-got-in-the-cream type of grin. "Oh, sheriff, I know exactly whose side you're on. I heard about you and Skylar at dinner last night. You can have her. I say, good riddance."

"Mrs. Gaudet, don't you think it strange that your son dated a woman for a year and had her move in with him, but you didn't know about her?"

"My family is none of your concern," she replied.

But Danny could tell that he'd hit a nerve. He bowed his head. "Have a safe trip home, Mrs. Gaudet."

He drove off, rolling up his window as he did. Things would get much better once the family was gone, but he knew their attacks on Skylar weren't nearly over. He'd be with her through it all, no matter how tough it got.

His phone dinged, alerting him to a text. He pulled over to read it, hoping it was from Skylar. He smiled when he saw her name, but it melted away as he read her text, his stomach knotting in apprehension.

DANNY, I HAD A GOOD TIME LAST NIGHT, AND I REALLY WANTED THIS TO WORK. BUT I NEED MORE TIME. SO MUCH IS UP IN THE AIR, AND I NEED TO MAKE SURE MY FEET ARE SQUARELY ON THE GROUND BEFORE I CAN COMMIT TO ANYTHING. I HOPE YOU UNDERSTAND.

He blinked, hoping he was dreaming. But Danny knew it was all too real. Things had developed quickly between him and Skylar. Really quickly. But when he knew, he *knew*. Why take things slow if she agreed?

But, obviously, she didn't agree now. What did the text mean, though? Was it over between them before it had even gotten started? Or was this just the pressing of a pause button?

Chapter 28

"Everything okay?"

Skylar looked up at Abby as she put away her phone that she'd looked at constantly, waiting for Danny to reply to her text. "Yeah."

Abby quirked a brow. "I don't quite believe you, but I know it's also none of my business. Just want to make sure you don't need to talk."

Skylar folded the last towel and gathered the bundle in her hands as she followed Abby to one of the bathrooms to put them away. "I just need to chill out. Danny's working. He can't reply the instant I send a text."

"Unless he's in the middle of something, he's normally pretty quick to respond to Clayton."

That didn't make Skylar feel any better.

Abby stepped back from putting away her towels and winced. "I didn't make things better, did I?"

"Not really," Skylar admitted.

They returned to the spare room where they'd set up to fold laundry so they didn't have to go up and down the stairs.

"I know Danny really likes you. In all the years Clayton

and I have been together, Danny's never stayed the night here before. But he did for you."

Skylar returned Abby's smile. "I know he cares. And it's silly, really, but I have this feeling that something more is going on."

"Danny is an upfront guy. If there's an issue, he'll talk to you about it."

"I'm just being paranoid." That had to be it. Skylar began folding little Hope's pajamas. "I'm not usually like this, by the way."

Abby made an indistinct sound. "You don't need to explain yourself to me. I've been here through a lot of it. I know just how chaotic and trying the last week has been. It would make anyone a wreck, but you've done great."

"Have I?" Skylar wasn't so sure.

She didn't normally get so worried about a guy not returning a text right away. Then again, she'd never been so head-over-heels in love with one either. Skylar stopped folding and just smiled as she stared into the distance.

"Skylar?"

She looked at Abby and said, "I love him."

"Oh, girl, we've known that from the first moment he brought you to the house."

"Really?" she asked with a laugh.

Abby nodded her head. "It's clear in the way the two of you look at each other."

Skylar sank onto the bed and sighed. "Things should be easy, then."

"Nothing worthwhile is ever easy all the time. There will be times when things seem to fall together nicely. And other times when you have to work for it."

"I want to work for it," Skylar said. "In all my life, I've never wanted anything more than I want Danny. I just can't help but feel there's a cloud above us that has to do with Matt."

Abby rolled her eyes and sat beside her. "I've never been in your situation, so I can't really give you an opinion. What I can tell you with certainty is that Danny won't let anything happen to you. He'll have every deputy who works for him on the lookout for Matt. Also, in case you didn't know, Danny is very good friends with the chief of police here, and I've no doubt Danny will talk to him about Matt, as well."

"It doesn't seem fair that I get such treatment."

"The hell it doesn't," Abby admonished her. "If you have that kind of connection, then you'd be a fool not to use it. Though it isn't like Danny wouldn't help you, no matter what you said."

Skylar grimaced. "That is a good point. I can't help thinking of all the other women out there going through something similar. I've been very fortunate, I know this. Not only was Danny there that night, but I've also had somewhere to stay that kept Matt away."

"This is definitely something that has become a problem, but so many people don't talk about it. I wish there was some way I could help."

Skylar suddenly had a thought. "I've done well in my life. My boss paid me well, and he taught me about investing in real estate to more than triple my money in the first two years. I've kept at it all this time. While I've enjoyed my job, I think I've found something else I can do."

"Helping others get out of abusive relationships," Abby said with a knowing smile.

"Is it too much?" Skylar asked hesitantly. "I want to do something, and now that I've been in the middle of it, I know what's worked for me. It won't work for everyone, but everyone has to start somewhere, right?"

"You're absolutely right. And I don't think it's too much at all. Anyone who wants to help in that kind of scenario is always great, in my opinion. And I plan on helping out, as well."

Skylar smiled, joy rippling through her. Not only had she found the love of her life, she'd also found the place she was supposed to be, and now, she'd found her calling. "That would be great."

"You've got great resources around you. Make use of them. And there are others who can introduce you to those you don't know. Personally, I think it's a great idea," Abby said.

Skylar got to her feet to continue the laundry, her mind racing with possibilities. As they finished folding, she and Abby talked about the locations she could set up as safe houses where women and their children could go.

She got another ten minutes out of it before she looked at her phone again to see if Danny had replied. Still nothing. Skylar really tried not to take it to heart, but she couldn't shake the feeling that something was going on.

That afternoon, they set up in the office, where they looked at everything she needed to do to be able to become someone who could help abused women. There was a plethora of information out there, and it wasn't long before she had been pulled down the rabbit hole of one article after another.

She had a notepad with her, jotting down ideas and notes as she read them. Abby was in and out of the office, tending to the children, and answering calls.

The sound of her name being called pulled Skylar from her reading on the laptop. She looked up to find Leslie in the doorway.

"Hey," Skylar said as she set aside the computer. "I didn't know you were coming by."

Leslie blew out a breath and walked to sit on the sofa next to her. "I had some news that I thought would be better delivered in person rather than over the phone."

"That sounds ominous."

Leslie turned sideways and set her hands in her lap as she looked at Skylar. "You remember Cooper calling his friend Cash, who is a PI?"

"Yeah."

"Well, about two hours ago, Cash walked into my office."

Skylar sat up straighter. "Did he find something?"

"Did he ever." Leslie looked away for a moment. "We were all right. This isn't the first time Matt has abused a woman. There are more."

"How many more?"

"Cash is still digging into that. It took him forever to locate the first woman, and she refused to talk to him at first. It wasn't until he told her about you and showed her what the Gaudets were doing to you in the papers that she finally relented and admitted that she and Matt had dated."

Skylar swallowed hard. "And?"

"He broke her collarbone and dislocated her shoulder, and that was just the first time he hit her. The next time, he went after her with a baseball bat. She was pregnant at the time, just a few weeks, but she ended up losing the baby."

"Oh, God." Skylar wrapped her arms around her stomach. "How did she get away?"

Leslie pressed her lips together. "Like you, she tried several times to leave. Matt had convinced her to quit work and said that he'd support her."

"That way, he would know where she was at all times."

"That's my guess. After trying four different times and having Matt drag her back, beating her each time, she knew she only had one choice. She got him drunk and waited until he passed out. Then she went to the police."

Skylar shook her head. "Did they not do anything?"

"The officer who took the statement happened to be one of Matt's friends. He called the Gaudets and let them know what was going on. The parents arrived and took the woman away, where they bullied and threatened her to take the millions they offered and to change her name and leave the area. She had family there, so she refused to leave, but she did change her name."

"Did Matt not look for her?"

"Oh, he did, but his family, with the help of others, made sure he never found her. Also, the Gaudets made her sign an NDA. If she says anything, she has to give back the money."

Skylar was sickened by all of it. "Please tell me the non-disclosure agreement won't hold up in court."

"You're damn straight it won't," Leslie stated. "I'm going to make sure of it."

"With you on her side, the Gaudets don't stand a chance."

Leslie didn't smile in response. "There's more. Once Cash got her talking, she gave him another name. It was a woman Matt dated before her."

"That's good, right?"

"Yes. Cash got more information on Matt and how quickly his family covered things up. Along with the pictures from the first woman, he got more proof of abuse from the second. And he got another name from the second woman. This went on for five more until he looked into the last one."

When Leslie paused, Skylar frowned. Her heart was racing. She didn't want to know the rest, but at the same time, she had to know it all. "Tell me."

"The timeline of this goes all the way back to his sophomore year in college. Cash went looking for the woman and discovered that she was dead. Killed, actually."

"By Matt?" Skylar asked in a whisper.

Leslie lifted one shoulder. "He was the prime suspect, but he had a rock-solid alibi where over thirty people saw him while the murder was taking place."

"He had her killed."

"That's what we all think. Even the police believed that, but they had no proof."

Skylar released a deep breath. "He started the beating in college then?"

"Actually, it began in high school with his first steady girlfriend. No one did anything about it, and they went to separate colleges, so she got away."

Skylar looked into Leslie's brown eyes. "You think he would have me killed?"

"I think it's something that isn't just in the past, and that you should take the threat seriously. You've done what none of the others have. You not only got away, but he was also arrested. I don't think Matt is the type of man to take that in stride."

"There was a man last night at the restaurant," Skylar said. She went on to describe the incident.

Leslie tucked her chin-length dark lock behind her ear. "We all hoped that with Matt leaving that he was giving up. I don't think that's the case now at all."

"Then that means he knows about me and Danny. If that man last night works for Matt, then he reported back about who I was with."

"Cash is filling Clayton and the others in on all of this as we speak. You're safe here."

Skylar leaned back and looked at the ceiling. "I hate Matt for taking away my freedom. What right does he have to try and control me like this? Can't he just get on with his life like other couples do when they break up?"

"Matt's brain isn't right. You can try to tell him that a million times, and it'll never sink in."

"Is anyone telling Danny?"

Leslie nodded. "Cash said he would have Cooper bring him over to fill Danny in."

"Just when I thought I could get on with my life, Matt rears up again."

Leslie reached over and covered Skylar's hand with hers. "Don't crumble. Now is when you need to be the strongest."

Skylar thought about all the other women out there scared out of their minds about their abusive partners. Many got free. So many others didn't. For whatever reason, she wasn't done walking this path. But everything she learned would be used to help other women—because she was going to survive it.

Chapter 29

No matter how hard Danny tried, he couldn't stop thinking about the text that Skylar had sent. It went against everything they'd spoken about, but he had asked her the night before if she was ready to date. Maybe she hadn't really thought about it until he brought it up.

"Way to go, Oldman," he chastised himself.

If only he'd kept his mouth shut.

But he'd known that she would eventually realize that she needed more time. It was better that it happened now rather than months later when they were more serious. Still, it stung.

Badly.

Danny needed to remember that this wasn't about him. It was about Skylar and everything she'd endured for three months, as well as what she was going through now with Matt and the Gaudets coming after her. He shouldn't be upset that she was putting their relationship on hold, but he couldn't help it. He'd fallen hard for her years ago and had tried to forget her for many more years after.

Then she'd walked back into his life. As soon as he'd

seen her, he'd known what had been missing from his world—her. She was perfect for him in so many ways. He was glad she had come back to town, but he hated that it had been under such circumstances.

He was so wrapped up in his thoughts that it was impossible for him to get any work done. He did all he could, then he called it a day early. With all the extra hours he'd put in over the last month, he could afford to leave two hours early.

Danny let the front desk know that he was leaving and made his way to his vehicle. He got behind the wheel and sighed. He didn't want to be at work, but he didn't want to go home, either. And he couldn't go see Skylar. So, where did that leave him?

Needing something to do, Danny drove out to the horse rescue he'd gotten involved in after meeting Audrey months earlier. Everyone who volunteered came whenever they could and worked for free. Danny often bought feed or had hay brought in to help offset some of the costs.

He was glad that he didn't see Audrey. He wasn't in the mood to talk. Instead, he grabbed a brush and went to the stables to find the dapple-gray gelding that had caught his eye from the first visit.

The horse had been abused and neglected in a dried-up field, left to starve to death, but Danny had been working with him to gain his trust. Thankfully, the horse had taken to Danny almost instantly. In fact, Danny was one of the few people the gelding would allow near him.

"Hey, boy," Danny said as he walked into the stall and held out his hand.

The gelding turned back his ears and lifted his head in agitation.

"I know. I'm sorry. I've not been around as much as usual. It's been a busy week. And, if I'm honest, I met someone. Actually, I've known her for years, but she recently returned to town. Can you believe that she actually wanted to be with me?"

As he talked, the horse perked his ears forward. Then he moved to Danny, giving Danny permission to pet him. For the next thirty minutes, Danny brushed the horse and continued to speak softly, all about Skylar.

Oddly enough, it helped. The horse might not understand the words or be able to issue advice, but sometimes, the simple act of talking about what was bothering him helped Danny. And today was no different.

He scratched the gray's ears. "I can't wait until the day I get to ride you."

It had taken a great amount of patience just to get the gelding used to having a saddle where he could see it. The last time Danny had brought it out, he'd set it on the stall door, and the horse hadn't batted an eye. That had been a couple of weeks ago, though, and Danny didn't want to test it this time.

"You forgive me for being away?" he asked the gelding.

The horse turned his large head to Danny and looked at him with soulful eyes.

"I've missed you. I won't stay away this long again."

Feeling better, Danny decided to head home. Maybe he'd stop off at the grocery store and buy a few things and then do some laundry. He might even watch a movie.

He was on the way to his SUV when he saw the rescue office. Before he knew it, he was standing inside and offering to buy the gelding.

The woman behind the desk didn't seem surprised at all. She smiled and gave a price. Danny didn't even try to negotiate. Few of the horses were ever bought and given another home. Once at the rescue, most remained until their deaths because no matter how much rehabilitation they got, they would never be ridable again.

Few people wanted such an expensive pet just to have them put out to pasture. But Danny and the gelding had a bond. It was time he did something about it instead of just coming by to see him.

"I'm happy you decided to take Gray," the woman said.

Danny blinked. He'd been unaware that the horse had a name. Or maybe he did know and hadn't paid attention to it. Not something a cop usually did.

"I'll be by tomorrow to pick him up," Danny told her.

He walked out into the sunshine and looked up at the cloudy sky. He had no place for a horse. Nor did he have a horse trailer. While he hated to ask it, he would need to use either Brice and Caleb's place or Clayton's. Since Caleb was such an expert at training horses, that would be the best place for Gray until Danny found a proper home for him.

His decision made, Danny got into his patrol vehicle and started the engine. He'd wait to get home before he called Caleb because he still wasn't in the mood to talk to anyone. No doubt Caleb would ask about Skylar, and Danny didn't want to answer any inquiries that might make anyone curious and ask more questions.

Danny headed back to town to get groceries to stock his refrigerator and pantry. Every station had Christmas music playing, and it reminded him of Skylar and all the things she wanted to do to her new place for the season. He'd thought to be a part of that, but that wasn't going to happen now.

As he passed the wooded drive to the house Skylar had bought, he saw a suspicious-looking black SUV stopped a little ways off the driveway. After the altercation Skylar had had with the man at the restaurant, Danny wasn't about to let anything out of the ordinary go without investigation. Danny turned his vehicle around and parked behind the SUV. He went to call in the stop to alert the station. It was protocol in case something went wrong for the police.

He was reaching for the radio when the passenger window suddenly shattered. Danny turned his head away so glass didn't get in his eyes. When he looked back, a semi-automatic rifle was pointed at his face.

"Put the radio down, sheriff," the man said.

The attacker was muscular with beady gray eyes and virtually no lips. His hair was shaved on the sides with only a little sticking up on top—a typical military haircut.

Danny knew then that whoever this man was, he'd been sent by Matt. And no doubt there were others like him. Danny slowly lowered the radio and lifted his hands.

"Good. Now, turn off the engine and unlock the doors. *Slowly*," the man stated in a threatening tone.

Out of the corner of his eye, Danny saw another man approaching his side of the vehicle. The moment the doors were unlocked, the newcomer opened the door and held a pistol in Danny's face.

"Unbuckle your seatbelt," the first man said.

Danny looked into the man's cold eyes and knew he was a killer. They both were. And they were here to kill him. With two guns trained on him, there was no time to reach for his own weapon and try to get the drop on them.

"Get out," the second man ordered in a deep, raspy voice.

Danny swung his gaze to him. He was a big brute of a man, several inches taller than Danny. The brute's blond hair was so closely cropped that it made him look bald.

Danny had spent enough time with Clayton, Brice, Caleb, Jace, Cooper, and even Ryan to know the look of someone just out of the military. And both of these men fit the description.

Keeping his hands up, Danny exited the SUV while his gaze stayed locked on the man closest to him. The brute waved the gun, indicating that Danny should move away from the vehicle. The beady-eyed one came around the SUV and climbed into the driver's seat. The two men exchanged a silent look before the first started the engine and drove the patrol SUV into a thicket of woods so it couldn't be seen from the road.

Danny kept hoping a car would pass and see them. To his delight, one did, but it was an older woman with her gaze locked on the road as she gripped the steering wheel tightly. She didn't even look his way.

So much for anyone helping him.

Then he had a gun barrel in his back as the brute barked, "Move!"

Danny was put into a black SUV with his hands bound with a zip tie, and a hood pulled over his face. Then they drove away. He knew the county like the back of his hand, so he had no problem knowing where they were headed. Right up until they drove around in circles to disorient him.

Unfortunately, it worked. Danny lost track of which direction they were headed, and consequently had no idea where he was being taken.

They drove for an extended period of time, but he wasn't sure if it was distance they covered, or if they just drove around aimlessly to fool him. Regardless, Danny knew he was going to his death. There was no way to get out of this. None of his training as a cop ever put him in such a scenario. And no one knew where he was because he hadn't wanted to talk to anyone.

Finally, the SUV slowed and then stopped. Danny's heart thumped in his chest. The two men got out of the vehicle, slamming the doors behind them. Suddenly, his door was opened, and someone grabbed his arm, yanking him out.

He lost his balance and fell hard to his knees. Danny bit back a cry of pain as one knee landed on a rock. He clenched his jaw as he was roughly pulled to his feet. No matter how he tried, he couldn't walk without a limp. But he ignored the pain shooting up his leg as he listened to every little sound.

They weren't near a main road because he didn't hear any cars. The bright light around him dimmed as if he were being led into a building. He tried to discern his location from sounds, but got very little that way.

The air was stale and filled with the scents of old wood and rotting hay. If Danny had to guess, they were in one of the ramshackle stables from the abandoned ranch in the next county over. He knew about the property because it was one that Brice had looked at before buying his.

Unfortunately, no one would ever look for Danny out here.

The bag covering his head was unceremoniously yanked away. He blinked, letting his eyes adjust to the dimness of the interior. He glanced around, confirming that he was in a stable. Then his gaze landed on the man who walked from the shadows.

Matt Gaudet's smile was that of someone who had gotten exactly what they wanted. "Hello, sheriff."

Danny didn't bother to reply.

Matt laughed and put one hand in the pocket of his trousers. "I'm surprised at how easy it was to take you. But then again, when you hire people who have been trained by our government and do this exact thing all over the world, you expect it to go off without a hitch."

Danny's hands were still bound, and he had the two

men standing near him. They might not have their weapons trained on him at the moment, but it wasn't as if he could do any damage in his current position.

"You should've left well enough alone," Matt continued. "You just had to interfere with me and Skylar. We were doing great, by the way. Until you poked your nose in."

"You think hitting her and tracking her every move means you were doing *good*?" Danny snorted at the idea. "You're fucking delusional, Gaudet."

Matt just smiled. "Skylar is mine."

"She's not a toy. She's a human being."

"No, she's mine. I chose her," Matt stated.

Danny shrugged, shaking his head. "She'll never be yours. No matter what you do to me or what your parents do to her, Skylar wants no part of you."

"Because you put stuff in her head," Matt burst out angrily. Then he took a deep breath, once more gaining control of himself. "I'm going to have fun watching these two torture you. They're very good at their jobs, and I've paid them very, very well to make sure they prolong your pain for days. Weeks, even."

Danny lifted his chin. "Fuck you."

Matt grinned and nodded to the men. A knife cut Danny's bonds as they grabbed him tightly. His arms were then yanked out to the sides and up, where his wrists were secured to metal shackles dangling from chains he hadn't noticed before.

Chapter 30

Skylar knew something was wrong the minute Cooper and Jace arrived. Through the office window, she spotted a racing green Jaguar F-type pull up behind them.

"That's Cash," Leslie said.

It was the anxious way the three got out of the vehicles and made their way to the door that alerted her to the fact that something wasn't right.

Skylar and Leslie got to their feet and walked from the office. They entered the kitchen the same time Cash was being introduced to Abby. He was tall, his long, black hair pulled together at the back of his head. Then his pale gray eyes slid to her.

She frowned at his intense look. Before she could find out anything, the door opened and Caleb, Brice, Clayton, and Shane, the ranch manager, strode inside.

Abby immediately went to Clayton, where they whispered to each other. It was the glance that Abby sent her that had Skylar on high-alert.

"What's going on?" Skylar demanded.

It was Cash who walked from the group and held out his hand to her. "You must be Skylar. I'm Cash."

She shook his hand. "I just learned from Leslie what you discovered about Matt and his previous girlfriends."

"You were lucky to get away."

"Am I really away from him?" she asked. It was rhetorical, but the way the entire room seemed to quiver with tension made her stomach clench with dread. "Someone please tell me why everyone arrived in such a hurry. Is Matt in town?"

"We aren't sure," Jace said.

Cash glanced at the floor. "To be perfectly blunt, the men I have watching him haven't seen Matt in three days. He went to work, we know that much, but sometime during the day, he left. His car is still parked there, so he must have taken another or left with someone."

Skylar slowly released a breath. It wasn't bad news, but it wasn't good either. "Which means, he could be back in town."

"It's a possibility," Clayton said.

Leslie pulled her keys from her purse. "I should get back to the office."

"I wouldn't suggest that," Cooper said. "We've been down that road before."

Brice's lips twisted. "I agree with Coop. Leslie, it would be better if you remained here for the time being."

Skylar fisted her hands at her sides. "Is Danny on his way? Or is he searching for Matt?"

The only one who would meet her gaze was Cash. His shoulders lifted as he took a deep breath. "We've just come from the sheriff's department. Danny left early. Three hours ago. We went to his house, but he wasn't there."

"Maybe he's on a call somewhere," Skylar said.

Jace shook his head. "The dispatcher tried to reach him. He's not answering his radio or his phone."

"What about GPS on his patrol car?" Abby asked.

Cash shook his head. "It's turned off."

"Then something has happened," Skylar said. "Danny would never turn it off."

Clayton said, "No, he wouldn't. We gathered here because we're going searching for him."

"All of you?" Leslie asked, her brows drawn together. "This could be a trap to get to Skylar."

Caleb shrugged. "It most likely is, which is why Shane and the other men working the ranch will remain. No one is allowed entry onto the ranch unless it's one of us."

Skylar's knees grew weak as she realized the implications. Matt had Danny. She knew it in her bones. Was it to get her away from the ranch? Or did Matt just want to hurt Danny for what he perceived as him coming between Matt and Skylar?

"We should never have gone to dinner," she said.

Cash caught her gaze. "That might have contributed to things, but trust me, Matt is the type who decided to target Danny the moment he realized the two of you had a past connection. It wouldn't matter if Danny was married to someone else. In Matt's eyes, Danny is responsible for you coming here and trying to get away from him."

"We need to get out there and look for Danny," Cooper urged.

Abby brought out a map of the county and laid it out on the dining table, but it was Caleb who suggested they broaden their search. Another map was produced, displaying the three surrounding counties, as well. All Skylar could do was stand there thinking about what Danny might be going through—all because of her.

"This isn't your fault," Leslie said.

Abby took her arm and led her to the stool at the island. "Leslie's right. This isn't your fault at all."

"I beg to differ. If I hadn't come here, this wouldn't be happening."

Leslie set her purse on the bar and took the stool next to Skylar. "If you hadn't come here, you'd probably be dead."

Abby pulled out some bottles of liquor and began pouring the shots into glasses, handing them to Skylar and Leslie while keeping one for herself. "God, Leslie's right again. When I think about you stopping anywhere else . . ."

Abby couldn't finish. She shuddered and tossed back the tequila she'd poured.

Skylar's hand shook as she took her shot of vanilla vodka. She winced as it burned going down her throat, but it was just what she needed. "I'll never forgive myself if Danny dies."

"Take a look in there," Leslie said as she jerked her chin to the dining room. "There are six men, all ex-military, and one who's also a damn good private investigator, looking for Danny. He'll be found."

"In time?" Skylar asked.

Abby shrugged. "All we can do is help the men and pray."

A buzz alerted them that someone was at the gate. Abby glanced at Clayton before she went to answer it. Skylar didn't recognize the voice that came through the speaker, but obviously, the others did.

"Ryan is the local police chief," Leslie told her. "He and Danny are close."

Abby poured more liquor into the shot glasses. "With the police, the sheriff's department, and that group in there looking for Danny, he won't be hidden for long."

Skylar grabbed the shot glass, but she didn't drink the liquor. "What if Matt took Danny somewhere else? What if they aren't in the area?"

"That's why Ryan's here," Jace said as he walked to the back door to greet not only Ryan but also a sheriff's deputy.

Skylar smiled at Deputy Wilson. He'd been the one to take her statement, and also the one who arrested Matt. With Ryan and Wilson joining the group, it was soon determined that Ryan needed to alert the surrounding area police departments, and even Houston. Deputy Wilson put in similar calls to the other sheriff's departments.

She had never been a part of anything like this before, and Skylar never imagined that a group could amass so quickly. This was because of Danny. Not just because he was sheriff, but because he had the ability to connect with people, and also because he was that good of a friend.

Skylar tried to listen to the men, but much of their conversation was too low for her to make out. And then they were gone. The house seemed quiet as she, Leslie, and Abby looked at each other.

Even the kids seemed to realize that something was going on. They remained occupied in their playroom. Leslie walked away to make a call to her firm to let them know what was going on.

"It's getting dark," Skylar said. "They won't be able to see much."

Abby grinned. "That's when my husband works the best. The darkness allows him to move unseen."

"This all seems so surreal. Like it's a dream, and I just need to wake up." Skylar shook her head.

"This isn't the first time my husband, brothers, or Cooper and Jace have been involved with dangerous people."

Leslie walked in and resumed her seat. "I sense a story, and I think we could use one to take our minds off things. Besides, I've only ever heard snippets of what happened with Caleb and Audrey. I know nothing about Brice and Naomi."

"Then I shall tell all," Abby said.

Skylar drank her shot and leaned her arms on the

island. "Start from the beginning. I want to know about you and Clayton."

For the next two hours, Abby shared the stories of how she and Clayton got together, as well as the villains both Brice and Naomi and Caleb and Audrey battled."

"Damn," Leslie said with a whistle.

Even Skylar was impressed. It gave her hope for Danny. "I had no idea any of that happened."

"Danny was a big part of all three stories," Abby said. "We consider him family."

"I wish I could be out there helping." Skylar sighed and looked out the window to see that night had fallen. "Danny is suffering, I know it. I also know just how vicious Matt can be with his punches."

Leslie shook her head and refilled Skylar's glass. "Don't think about that. Think about what you'll say to Danny when he walks through that door."

Skylar wished she could, but her mind was on other things. "What about the Gaudet family? Can we go after them? Surely, they know something about what Matt's doing? They were a part of things with the other girlfriends. Certainly, they're responsible for some of this."

"That's an idea," Leslie said, drumming her polished nails on the island. "If we can get any of those women to put things in writing, then there is a state prosecutor I know who could go straight for the family."

Abby thought about that for a moment. "What if you alert him or her that this is happening? Wouldn't it be their job to get the confessions from the women?"

"Yes," Leslie said with a grin. "Though it would be helpful if they were done beforehand. The women would want assurance that the Gaudets couldn't come after them."

"Which is what you're for," Skylar replied.

Abby grinned. "I think it's time the Gaudets come tumbling off that pedestal they've built for themselves."

"Let me make some calls," Leslie said as she took her phone and walked away.

Skylar swung her gaze to Abby. "I don't care if the Gaudets want to sue me. I don't even care that Matt cheated on me with Madeline Gross, or that she came here to vandalize Danny's vehicle. All I want is for Danny to be found, Matt to be caught, and for me and Danny to start our lives together."

"If Matt had that one girlfriend killed, then he's not doing this alone," Abby cautioned. "Clayton and the others know that, as well. It's why we all need to be careful and not let anyone onto the ranch. Matt could have hired anyone."

Skylar slowly spun the shot glass full of vanilla vodka. "It should never have come to this."

"Just think where we'd be if Cooper hadn't called in Cash to help."

"Based on what he drives, he must be doing well as a PI."

Abby nodded and braced her hands on the island. "I've only heard Cooper speak of Cash a few times. He's in very high demand because he gets results. I know he hires a few people to help out, but mostly, he does it all on his own."

"I'll be happy to pay his bill," she said.

Abby snorted and rolled her eyes. "I tried to pay him, but Cash told me he wouldn't take any money. He said this was for a friend, and he never charges friends."

Skylar looked down at her hands. "Danny never responded to my text today."

"I'm sure there was a reason."

"Matt was able to put a virus on my phone that allowed

him to see everything on the device. He's not that technical, so I don't think he did it himself." She met Abby's gaze. "But it was done. He has money. Lots of it. People like that can get in touch with others to do their dirty work."

Abby's brows snapped together. "Then I think it's time someone takes a look at Danny's phone records more closely."

Chapter 31

December 16th

What day was it? Danny had lost all track of time. He couldn't remember how many times he'd been knocked unconscious by the two men taking turns hitting him. They knew exactly where and how to strike him to inflict the most damage.

He couldn't feel his arms and hands any longer. The pain from being strung up had been excruciating. In fact, he thought that might be what did him in. Then, thankfully, the numbness finally set in. When—*if*—he was ever freed, the agony would be unbearable once the blood went back into his fingers.

Danny didn't lift his head. It took too much energy. One eye was swollen shut completely, and the other had a cut over it so that blood kept dripping into his eye. He must have blacked out again, but the last thing he remembered was the punch right to his cheekbone.

He was coming to hate the smell of the old barn. It made his stomach roil. Or that could be his sweat and the blood mixed with it. Hell, he didn't know.

The one thing he was sure of, however, was that Matt had no intention of letting him live. The torture was just a way for Matt to get back at him. Danny's mind drifted to Skylar as it had since he'd been taken.

As long as she stayed at the ranch, Clayton would watch over her. Danny knew that with certainty. And despite what Skylar might think about him and their budding relationship, Danny knew she wasn't a fool. She would be careful.

Though he had to wonder if anyone knew he was missing. Surely, at least his own deputies were looking for him. Then again, everyone knew it was his two days off. No one would think he was missing until those two days had passed.

Since the bastards who had used him as a punching bag could be heard laughing some distance away, they didn't seem too hurried to end his life. That was good since he had some time.

It was also bad because it meant that he had more beatings coming.

His stomach rumbled when he caught the smell of barbecue. His mouth was parched, and he was in desperate need of something to drink. And food. The smell of the barbecue made his mouth water.

Dimly, he heard what sounded like a helicopter flying over nearby. The fighter in him wanted to find some way to alert them to his presence. It was a joke. He knew they wouldn't see him, and if they did, they wouldn't have a clue what to think of him.

The realist in him comprehended that it was just a matter of hours before his life was snuffed out. Matt had worked everything perfectly, but the only way he could've done that was if he had known that Danny had scheduled two days off.

The sound of footsteps reached him. Danny cracked open his good eye and spotted Matt slowly coming his way. With his eye stinging from the blood, Danny closed it once more.

"You look like shit, sheriff," Matt said, a smile in his voice. "You aren't so big and bad now without your gun, are you? Hell, your shield means nothing if you don't have something to back it up. And you have nothing."

Danny concentrated hard and did his best to use his numb hands to flip Matt off.

"That's real mature," came Matt's reply.

Danny grinned, even as his busted lip split open again. "You would know."

"You know nothing about me." Matt was closer now, just inches from Danny. Anger colored his words. "I can give Skylar everything she wants. You can give her . . . what? Long hours by herself as she waits on you to come home from taking care of other people you don't even know?" Matt made a sound in the back of his throat. "That's no life for Skylar."

Danny couldn't argue with him because Matt was right. It hurt to hear it, but generally, the truth always did.

"Skylar will come to see that I'm the only thing for her. I'll make sure my family leaves her alone. We had several good months together. We will again," Matt stated.

Danny wished that were true, but he knew it wasn't. "Right. And then you'll go back to hitting her again."

"I won't!"

Matt's bellow echoed off the walls of the empty building. Danny just grinned in response.

That expression turned into a wince when Matt grabbed a fistful of Danny's hair and yanked his head back. "You'll die knowing that I took Skylar from you. It was so easy to make you think she didn't want you. One text was all it took." Matt laughed, the sound evil and cold. "Hijacking cell phones is pretty easy if you know the right people."

Danny wanted to kick himself. If only he'd gone to talk to Skylar, then none of this would be happening. But he hadn't wanted to invade her space if she really did want time. Reading that she didn't want to see him over text had been bad enough. He really hadn't wanted to hear it from her lips.

"Oh, if you could only see your face," Matt said with a chuckle. He shoved Danny's head forward as Matt released his hair and walked away. "It'll be that easy to get Skylar back."

"You'll never get Skylar back."

"Sure, I will. I'll make certain of it. All I have to do is threaten her parents, and she'll come running straight to me."

Danny lifted his head and opened his good eye. "You're the one who threatened her parents."

"No, that was my folks, but it gave me the idea. I saw how Skylar reacted. If I want to be the one who comes in and saves the day and her, then I need to make the situation a dire one. There's only one thing Skylar really cares about, and that's her parents."

"You're a cold bastard."

Matt just grinned. "Yes, I am. And it's given me quite a lot in my life."

"Money has done that."

"Skylar had no idea who I was, and she still wanted me."

Danny sneered, even though it caused him agony. "Yeah, she found out who you really were. Money or not, no man beats his woman."

"I can control it."

"Keep telling yourself that. No one believes it, especially Skylar."

"I'd say you'll find out how wrong you are, but you'll be dead. So, you'll have to take my word for it."

Danny held Matt's gaze, blinking away the blood that continued to drip into his eyes. There were so many things he wished he could do to Matt, but he was chained, preventing him from doing anything but wish.

"You'd kill me if you could," Matt said with a grin. "That's never going to happen, sheriff. Never."

"I've learned it isn't wise to tempt Karma by saying things like that."

"Karma?" Matt snorted loudly. "When you have as much money as I do, Karma stays away."

"Karma. Fate. Call it what you want. It always comes back around."

Matt laughed as he shook his head. "Not with me. Not with my family."

Danny didn't want to waste what little strength he had left by arguing. Matt wouldn't listen or understand anyway. It was like talking to a brick wall.

"Everything you're getting now is because you intervened when you shouldn't have," Matt continued. "Then you had the audacity to think you could step into my place as Skylar's man. No one is going to have her but me."

"She'll never go back to you."

Matt shrugged. "She'll have me or no one."

Danny knew exactly what those words meant. If Matt couldn't have Skylar, then Matt would make sure no one did. Danny jerked futilely at the chains holding him while Matt laughed as he walked away.

Danny looked up, squinting through his one good eye to see if there was some way he could get free. Even if he had to break his thumb, he was willing to do it. Because he had to get to Skylar before Matt could hurt her.

But when Danny lowered his gaze, the two men were

standing before him once more. He barely had time to prepare before the first punch landed in his kidney.

"I'm not leaving until I get an answer," Skylar told the deputy at the front desk.

The young man, who looked barely old enough to drink, shifted his gaze past her to where Jace stood.

Skylar leaned to the side to get the deputy's attention. "I'm the one talking to you, not Jace. Stop looking at him."

The deputy visibly swallowed. "Ma'am, I want to help you, I really do, but the thing is, I can't. You aren't related to Sheriff Oldman."

That was the last straw. What did being related have to do with anything when Danny was in trouble? Didn't everyone realize that? Before she could say anything, Deputy Wilson walked out.

"Skylar," he said as he approached, shooting her a quick smile. "Come with me."

"You found something, didn't you? Danny told me you were good," she said as she followed him so they could speak without being overheard.

A slight blush stained Deputy Wilson's cheeks before he cleared his throat. He glanced at the deputy behind the desk.

"Please tell me you know where Danny is," Skylar said when they were out of earshot of everyone.

Wilson flattened his lips as he shook his head. "I wish I could. We've tried to activate the GPS on the patrol car as well as the sheriff's phone, but both are disabled."

"That isn't an accident," Jace said.

"No, it isn't. Everyone is working overtime to locate the sheriff." Wilson took off his hat and ran a hand through his cropped, dirty blond hair. "Several deputies are out looking for Danny now, and the police are also working in conjunction with us, but I don't think the sheriff is around here."

"Neither do I," Skylar said.

Jace frowned as he crossed his arms over his chest and widened his stance. "If they turned off the GPS on his cruiser and phone, then they could have very well kept him in the area, but I agree with Skylar. With Danny being sheriff and so well known, I believe whoever took him brought him out of the county."

"Look, I'm going to be honest," Wilson said. "The sheriff knew Matt Gaudet was a bad apple from the get-go. He's had everyone on the lookout for anyone that fit Matt's description in case he came back into town. No one has seen him, not even the undercover deputies or police."

Skylar paused, letting that sink in. "You don't think this is Matt?"

"I'm not saying that. What I'm telling you is that Matt isn't in the area," Wilson said.

Jace caught her gaze. "In other words, Matt probably hired someone to take Danny."

Images of all kinds of horrors being visited upon Danny ran through her mind. "We've got to find him."

Wilson shook his head and put a hand on her arm when she tried to leave. He dropped it as soon as she halted. "No, ma'am. You need to get back to the East Ranch. This could all be a ploy to get you away from the ranch so someone can grab you."

"I know that," she began, then stopped, an idea forming.

Jace immediately shook his head rapidly. "No. I know what you're thinking, and I won't be a part of any of that. Danny would have my head."

"I'm doing it with or without you," she informed him.

Wilson scratched his chin. "What are y'all talking about?"

"She's going to use herself as bait," Jace said with a long sigh.

Skylar adjusted her purse in her hand. "If we want to find Danny, then we need to go to the source."

"I agree with Jace, Skylar," Wilson said hesitantly. "I can't see this going any way but wrong."

Chapter 32

"It's going to go wrong."

If Skylar heard that one more time, she was going to scream. This time, it came from Leslie.

Once Skylar had convinced Deputy Wilson and Jace to help her, Jace had put everyone on a group call so they could all be told what was going on.

"I don't know," Caleb said. "It could work."

Ryan quickly added, "With the right planning."

"Skylar needs to have a tracker on her," Cash said. "I have some. We just need to get it on her person so we know where she is at all times."

Wilson then said, "If you need a place to set up, there's room here at the station. Every deputy available will join in to help."

"The PD, as well," Ryan said.

Brice asked, "Are you sure, Skylar?"

"Absolutely," she stated. "Danny would do it for me. He'd do it for any of us. I'm not about to sit on the sidelines helplessly when I'm who Matt wants. If we want to find Danny before it's too late, then we need to do this."

Everyone but Clayton murmured agreement, including Abby.

Skylar waited a moment before she asked, "Clayton? You haven't said anything."

He blew out a loud breath before his voice traveled through the phone. "It's a tough situation. I know you want to save Danny, and we just might pull it off. But if something happens to you during it, Danny will never forgive us."

"Let's worry about that later," Cooper said.

Jace nodded as his gaze met hers. "Time isn't on our side. We have to put this plan together quickly."

"Stay at the station. I'm on my way," Cash said.

Skylar swallowed, thankful to her very soul that she had convinced everyone to help her undertake such a risky plan. She was terrified to be around Matt again, but she would do anything for Danny.

Anything.

And with the men Danny was friends with, if any group could pull this off, it was them. Skylar was merely standing there. Everyone else would have the difficult part.

She barely listened as the group began laying out plans. Skylar knew next to nothing about military operations, and she certainly didn't understand the jargon they used, but she didn't need to. All she had to do was trust that they had her back.

It wasn't long before Cash walked in with a black bag in hand. Wilson motioned him to follow, and the four of them went into the back of the building to a conference room that had several TV screens mounted to the wall.

With one click from a panel she hadn't seen, Wilson flicked on the screens. She was able to see the camera from the helicopter, as well as several patrol cars.

"We'll watch you on these," Wilson said.

Cash set the bag on the table and unzipped it. "Let's get you ready."

Danny spit out a mouthful of blood. He hurt everywhere. His legs could no longer hold him—one might actually be broken. But without his legs, he hung by his arms, which pulled at the already numb limbs, doubling his pain.

The two men beating him were talking among themselves since they likely believed he was unconscious. They were discussing the time, saying that they only had a few more hours before it was time to kill him. The fact that they were having fun beating the shit out of him shouldn't surprise Danny, but it did.

Danny had witnessed all sorts of things in his time working in law enforcement. He shouldn't be shocked anymore, but new things kept cropping up every year. No wonder so many cops were jaded. It was hard not to be in such a career.

"I need my souvenir."

That caught his attention.

"You take souvenirs?" The one with the beady eyes asked.

"Always."

There was a snort. "I just get more ink added. I don't need to carry anything around." After a short pause, he asked, "What do you take?"

"A pinky."

"What? You mean you have a box of pinky fingers at your place?"

Beady Eyes laughed. "It's way more than a box. You should've seen all those bastards I killed in Afghanistan."

Danny knew his chance would come when they tried to take the *souvenir*. They couldn't do it with his arms chained above him, which meant they'd have to loosen at least one arm. Now, if only his body would obey his mind and move like he needed it to.

"Let's get it done," the brute said with a sigh.

Beady Eyes rubbed his hands together in excitement. "First, I have to get my knife."

Danny remained limp, his mind going through exactly what he was going to do. His father always said to visualize what you wanted to do, and your body would follow. Danny really hoped it worked this time. So much depended on it.

Beady Eyes returned, and only then did the two of them come toward him. Danny kept his eyes closed, letting them believe he was unconscious. When one of them hit him in the ribs, he grunted because he had clenched his teeth together. That was the only thing that kept him from crying out in pain.

"What are you worried about?" Beady asked. "He's so far gone, he won't even know we've taken his finger or slit his throat."

"True."

Danny heard the chains rattle as they loosened them. The next thing he knew, he was falling. He landed hard upon the packed earth. The men were on him immediately, and he wasted no time in lashing out.

He wrapped his arm around the head of the one nearest him as he squinted through his good eye. The second Danny saw that the brute was near his feet, he quickly locked his ankles around the man's neck.

Danny tried to knock away the knife from Beady Eyes before it cut into his side, but he wasn't quick enough. Danny then kicked Brute in the face, knocking him on his ass as he tried to shake him off.

That gave Danny enough time to get his feet under him to stand up. He twisted, moving behind Beady Eyes, and using a combined move from what he'd learned as a policeman and something Clayton had shown him, gave a hard twist, breaking the man's neck.

The knife fell to the ground out of the dead man's hand. Danny reached for it, but Brute kicked it away before kneeing Danny in his cut side.

Danny grunted and used his arm to shield his injured side as he squared off against the big man.

"You won't get away."

Danny grinned. "I was never supposed to get this far, and yet I killed your friend."

Brute shrugged in concession. "Perhaps, but you won't do the same to me."

They circled each other. Danny realized that he was too injured to fight properly against someone so much taller and heavier than he was. The only way to win this was to use his weakness to his advantage and draw his opponent in.

Danny sidestepped and pretended to go down to one knee. As soon as he did, Brute rushed him. Danny dove to the side where the knife was and rolled. His fingers wrapped around it. Before he could use it, Brute viciously tossed him onto his back and kneeled on Danny's chest before pulling a gun.

"Mr. Gaudet wanted you to feel pain. I just want you dead," he said.

Danny struggled to breathe even as he brought up the knife and embedded it in the man's thigh. Brute howled in pain, giving Danny the opportunity to use his other hand to knock the gun away just as it fired.

The bullet missed him by a few inches and landed in the dirt near his head. He yanked the blade free and stabbed Brute again. Brute tried to grab Danny's hand, and he would've succeeded, but Danny had one thing on his mind—getting to Skylar.

He twisted and shoved, gaining enough force to throw

the man, who was already off-balance, to the ground. Danny immediately rose up and sank the knife into the man's heart, killing him.

Danny took a minute to get his breath. Then he grabbed the knife and the man's gun and got to his feet. He threw open the barn door and rushed outside to the black SUV. Danny got inside the vehicle and realized that the keys must be on one of the men.

He bit back a curse and jumped back out to search for them. They turned out to be on the second man. Danny ran back to the SUV and started the engine. He threw it into reverse and stomped on the gas, sending the vehicle careening backward before he turned the wheel. Then he put it in drive and sped away, churning up dust and rocks as he peeled out.

His heart was racing as he got his bearings and realized where he was. He turned the truck toward the north and gunned it. If he had a phone, he would've called someone, but neither man had one on them, and he didn't see one in the SUV.

Danny had only gone about ten miles before he saw the lights flashing in his rearview mirror and heard the sirens. He pulled over while gripping the wheel. He didn't have time for this, and he could only hope that whoever the policeman was, he would believe everything that Danny had to say.

Rolling down his window, Danny waited as the cop got out of his patrol car and headed his way. The man took one look at him, and his jaw went slack.

"Sir, are you all right?" he asked.

With a sigh, Danny said, "You're probably not going to believe this, but I'm Danny Oldman—"

"Yes, sir, sheriff. I recognized you when I walked up," he said. "Everyone has been out looking for you. Hop in my car. I'll get us back to Baxter County."

Danny shut off the engine and followed the officer to his car. Seconds later, they were racing toward Skylar. The officer used his radio to call in the fact that he had found Danny and that they were headed toward the East Ranch.

"May I borrow your phone?" Danny asked.

The officer handed it over, and Danny called Clayton, but it went to voicemail. He tried to remember Caleb's, Brice's, or anyone else's number, but he couldn't. That's what he got for putting everything in his phone and forgetting about it.

"What do you need, sheriff?" the officer asked.

Danny explained, and within minutes, the officer had relayed the information to dispatch. They said they'd get in touch with Caleb and have him call.

Less than five minutes later, the officer's phone rang. Sure enough, it was Caleb.

"Danny, is that really you?"

Danny smiled at the sound of Caleb's voice. "It's me."

"Are you okay?"

"I've been better," Danny answered. "Look, Matt is on his way to find Skylar."

Caleb made a sound, interrupting him. "Yeah, we figured that's exactly what he would do. Skylar then had the idea to use herself as bait."

"She what?" Danny bellowed before he closed his eyes. "Please tell me you dissuaded her from it."

"Right. As if we could. She was intent on getting to you, and she knew using herself was the only way to do it. We knew it as well, so instead of letting her do it alone, we helped her. Cash is tracking her."

Danny opened his good eye and tried to see the road before him. "Where is she?"

"There's something you need to know. Cash found evidence that Matt has been beating women since his

years in high school. As a matter of fact, he had one of his
college girlfriends killed."

"That's what he intends with Skylar. He said if he
couldn't have her, then no one could."

Caleb snorted loudly. "That's not going to happen."

"He's got it all planned, Caleb."

"Not against us, he doesn't."

Danny wanted to believe him, but he wasn't so sure.
Matt might be a spoiled rich kid, but when it came to his
women, he got creative. And with his money, he brought
in outside resources.

"He hired ex-military to take me," Danny explained.

The officer glanced at him and twisted his lips. "Sir, if
you don't mind me saying so, we should be taking you to
a hospital."

"Shit, Danny, are you that bad?" Caleb said.

Danny gripped the phone. "Tell me where the hell
Skylar is."

Chapter 33

It was probably the worst idea of her life.

It was also one of the best.

Well, if she succeeded in finding Danny, it would be.

Skylar couldn't stop shaking. There were dozens of eyes on her, but that didn't make her feel any better. Not when she would be coming face to face with a man she hoped never to see again. Someone who hadn't hesitated to have one of his girlfriends killed when she didn't want him anymore.

It didn't take a rocket scientist to figure out that Matt would do the same to her if given the chance. Thankfully, he would never get that close to her. There were sheriff's deputies and undercover police all around her, not to mention all her friends waiting nearby to rush in if anything got out of hand.

And with Matt involved, it was guaranteed to get out of hand.

Skylar parked her car. It stood out like a sore thumb, which would get Matt's attention. She tried to act as if she did this every day. As if going to the grocery store with a tracker on to potentially meet the man who had abused her and kidnapped her current lover happened all the time. What a crazy life she led.

But she wouldn't change a single thing.

She had found herself back in her hometown—as crazy as that seemed. It wasn't just Danny and her calling she'd discovered, but also a group of friends that she knew she could trust with her very life.

Skylar took a deep breath and got out of the car. When she shut the door, her gaze caught on the new window, a window that Matt had broken days earlier to pull her out of the car. But Danny had been there that night to save her. Now it was her turn to save him.

She walked into the grocery store and grabbed a buggy. She didn't really see any of the items on the shelves. All she could do was continue looking at everything out of the corner of her eye for some sign of Matt.

Twenty minutes later, she had a few items that she brought to the checkout. Though when she looked at the chocolate, aspirin, and tampons, she bit back a laugh when she saw what she had haphazardly put into her cart.

With the groceries paid for, she walked back to her car and put everything in the trunk. She'd missed her car, but even now, she wondered if Danny's people had gotten all the trackers out of it. Then she realized that it would be better if they hadn't because then Matt would be able to find her.

And the sooner he found her, the quicker they could get to Danny.

"Please don't let him be hurt," Skylar whispered a quick prayer.

Then she drove to a nearby liquor store. The first thing she saw when she walked in was a woman handing out samples. Skylar didn't even care what it was. She needed some liquid courage, and she didn't much care what kind.

"Thank you," she said as she took the little plastic cup and downed the shot.

She put the back of her hand to her mouth and closed her eyes as the alcohol burned a path to her stomach. It took a few seconds, but her shaking calmed somewhat. She had to be composed and unruffled. Otherwise, Matt would notice.

Skylar walked up and down the aisles. She chose a few bottles of wine and then got the vanilla vodka she'd had at Abby's the other night. She added some Sprite, as well.

The minutes ticked by slowly. There were few people in the large store, and with the shelving rising up high around her, it almost felt as if she were closed in. A prime spot for Matt to approach her, which was why Cooper had suggested the location.

Skylar didn't know how long she had been in the store, but her buggy was quickly filled with various bottles of liquor. She was looking over the different scotches when someone bumped into her.

"Excuse me," she said and tried to move out of the way.

Then she felt something press into her side that made her immediately think gun. She stilled, one hand on the cart as she faced the shelving.

"Don't say a word," the voice ordered behind her.

It wasn't Matt. Damn. She'd really hoped that he would make an appearance so the authorities could swoop in and arrest him. But Matt wasn't that stupid. He knew they would be looking for him, and then there was the restraining order.

The man gave her a push to the side. "Come with me."

She released the buggy and grabbed her purse before letting him direct her down the long aisle. There wasn't another soul near them, but she wasn't worried. She had the tracker on so Cash and the others would know where she was at all times.

"Who are you?" she asked.

The man didn't say anything, and when she tried to turn to see him, he gave her shoulder a rough push.

"All right, all right," she replied testily. "Just tell me where you're taking me."

"You'll find out soon enough."

She realized that she was being a bit too compliant, so she dug in her heels and refused to move.

He pressed the weapon deeper into her side. "Look, lady, I have no problem at all pulling this trigger. I know I'll get away."

"There are cameras in the store. They would see you."

He laughed, sending chills down her spine.

"Now, let's try this again," he said close to her ear.

Skylar turned her head away because his breath stank of cigarettes. She tried not to gag but didn't quite manage it.

"Move your fine ass. You really don't want me to get angry."

She shivered at the icy tone that told her he wouldn't hesitate to end her life. Skylar continued walking. The way he stood, it would look like he had his arm at her back to anyone looking.

It wasn't long before she realized that he was taking her to the back of the store. He walked them through the Employees Only door and handed a guy who was playing a game on his phone a wad of cash. The employee didn't even look up at her.

Skylar then found herself meandering through boxes of liquor until they reached the exit. She was then shoved into a van, the man climbing in behind her.

Her gaze slid to the driver, but before she could see who it was, something covered her eyes. She tried to pull it off, but someone gathered her hands together and zip tied them.

Coldness settled over her. Was this what that poor girl had suffered before she was killed? Were these the same men who had done the deed for Matt? Skylar shivered at the thought.

She didn't try to talk to them because she knew they wouldn't tell her anything. Instead, she tried to determine how many people were in the van and in what direction they were going.

"Cop," someone muttered.

Skylar had mixed emotions about the police sighting. A part of her wanted to be free of this nightmare before she had to face Matt.

The other part—the one that couldn't stop thinking about Danny and the life they could have together—refused to let her do anything but let the men take her to Matt.

They drove for a long time before they finally pulled over, and the van came to a stop. She heard the driver put the vehicle in park, and then the engine shut off. No one said anything as they started moving around inside.

Next, she heard the doors open and then close. Still, no one said anything to her.

Skylar wasn't sure what to do. They had bound her wrists, but they were in front of her. She raised them and took off the material covering her eyes.

She blinked against the bright light coming in and then jerked back when she saw Matt sitting next to her, turned toward her with one arm along the back of the seat.

"Hey, baby," he said with a smile. "I've missed you."

He leaned in for a kiss, but she dodged it. The anger that sparked in his blue eyes made her flinch away, and she expected to be hit.

He held up his hands. "I'm a new man, babe. You opened my eyes and made me see what I'd become. Thank you for showing me how badly I treated you. But things will be different now, I promise. You can come home, and we can get back to our lives."

She and her friends had discussed the option of letting Matt believe that she would be his once more versus trying to make him see that she was moving on with her life. There were pros and cons to both options, and it came down to what was easier for her to do, as well as what would gain them information on Danny.

"No," Skylar said.

Matt's smile stayed in place as he placed his thumb and forefinger on a lock of her hair, letting his fingers trail down it. "You have the most beautiful hair. That's what first made me spot you. It's like gold. Then I saw your smile. Damn, baby, but you have a smile that could light up the world."

At one time, his tender words would've made her smile and give him compliments as well, but she was past that. His mask had come off, and she had seen the monster underneath.

"We were good together," Matt said, holding her gaze. "You can't deny that."

"I'm not denying it. But you changed."

He lifted one shoulder nonchalantly. "I'm sorry about that. It won't happen again."

"Yes, it will. It's just the way you are."

"Baby," he said, his lips tightening as he fought his anger. "I'm trying here. The least you can do is meet me halfway."

Skylar shook her head. "It's over, Matt. I don't know why you can't accept that."

"Why?"

"Because I refuse to live the rest of my life being

beaten by you each time you get in a rage." It felt good to say all the things she'd wanted to say before. Freeing, even.

She knew she was poking the bear, but she couldn't stop once she'd begun. No matter what happened, she was going to get Matt and the poison he'd filled her life with out of her system once and for all.

She shook her head in disgust as she shifted away from him, angling her body toward him so she could be prepared for anything. "How can you expect anyone to want to be with you when you treat them like shit? You hit me, Matt. Repeatedly. And you were careful about where you landed those punches so no one would see the evidence. Which means, you knew *exactly* what you were doing. And you enjoyed it."

He sat back, a small smile on his face. "I do enjoy it."

Skylar was shocked that he'd admitted it.

"I'm in control," he continued. "Always. I get to decide what you do, when you do it, and how you do it."

"The hell you do," she retorted.

He merely smiled. "You'll come to learn that it's easier just to agree with me. While I like the independent streak in you, I'm going to love breaking you of it even more."

"Break me?" she asked, brows raised. "You won't get the chance."

Matt threw back his head and laughed. "Oh, baby. Your naiveté amuses me."

"What does that mean?"

"That if you think the sheriff is going to come to your rescue again, you're sadly mistaken. He's dead."

It was like the ground had dropped out from under her. Matt kept talking, but her ears were ringing as she tried to grasp what she'd just heard. Danny was . . . dead? No. That couldn't be. She wouldn't accept it.

"Wow. If you could only see your face."

She blinked, aware that he was studying her with what looked like curiosity. She wanted to lash out at him, to hit him and scream, but the coldness that had seeped into her soul froze her body in place.

Matt cocked his head to the side. "You really fell for him, didn't you?"

"I love Danny."

"Sucks for you, but you'll be just fine with me. I'll shower you with jewels and give you magnificent places to live. Not to mention all the travel we'll do on my private jet. With all of that, the few beatings I give you should be tolerable."

Skylar heard everything he said, but it was like she wasn't in her body but instead looking down at the situation, utterly detached. "There is nothing in the world that could make being beaten *tolerable*, you dick."

"Oh, ho," he said with a chuckle. "Resorting to name-calling now. I have to say, Skylar, we'll have to work on that, because that was pretty lame."

"Where's Danny?" she demanded.

Matt's smile grew. "I'll take you to him. But only if you agree to be mine."

Skylar didn't have a choice. She would do anything for Danny. "Is he really dead?"

Matt held out his hand and patiently waited for her to make a decision.

Chapter 34

"What the fuck do you mean she's with Matt?" Danny demanded as he stared at his friends.

Thanks to the police officer, he'd gotten back to his county in record time, but it wasn't soon enough to stop Skylar before she went through with her plan.

"We tried," Ryan said. "One of my undercover detectives was on his way to her when he saw the man take her."

Danny glared at him, anger churning in him like a hurricane. "And you thought it was fine to go through with the plan?"

"Yes," Caleb replied.

Danny swung his gaze to the youngest Harper. Several retorts almost fell from his lips, but he managed to hold them back.

"Look, Danny, I know you're upset," Clayton said. "But there's no need. Cash is tracking her."

Cash nodded and turned his cell phone so Danny could see. "I know exactly where she is."

"Let us get to her while you let someone see to your injuries," Brice said.

Danny had already waved off Marina and Karl, the

paramedics that Caleb had called in after their conversation. "I'm fine."

"You're far from fine," Jace stated with a hard look.

Danny didn't argue because he was saving his strength. The fact was, he hurt. Badly. He didn't want the others to know because they might try and keep him from getting to Skylar, and that simply wasn't going to happen.

He finished chugging his second bottle of water and looked around at his friends. The only one who hadn't said anything was Wilson. The deputy had been staring at a map the entire time.

"Wilson? What is it?" Danny asked.

The deputy looked up, his frown deepening. "Sheriff, I don't mean to alarm you, but if Cash's tracker is right—"

"It's right," Cash interjected.

"Then Skylar isn't far from the Misk farm."

Clayton shrugged. "Why is that important?"

Danny couldn't remember how he knew the Misk name, but he realized it meant something. He searched his brain before he finally comprehended what it was. "Shit."

"I'll call the chopper," Ryan said as he turned away.

Danny reached out and grabbed him. "No. You'll spook Matt. We know what he plans. Let's not make him run. There's no telling what he'll do to Skylar."

"What's going on?" Jace asked as he looked between them.

Ryan was the one to answer. "The Misk farm has been turned into a subdivision where people keep their personal planes and helicopters without having to pay hangar fees at the airport."

"Shit. I forgot about that," Brice said.

Danny was done talking. He started toward Clayton's truck when his friend caught up with him.

"Going somewhere?" Clayton asked.

"To get my woman."

"Mind if I tag along since you're getting into my truck?"

Danny had opened the door and was about to step in when he looked at Clayton. His good eye was open only a slit, but that wasn't going to stop him from going after Matt.

"Danny, I'm not going to stop you, but you can barely see. At least let me drive so you get there in one piece," Clayton said.

There came a time when a man had to realize when to take help. This was one of those. Danny nodded and made his way to the passenger side, but Ryan was already in the seat.

"You're riding in the back," Ryan said and hooked his thumb over his shoulder.

Danny didn't want to waste time arguing. It wasn't until he was in the truck with it started and moving that he realized that Karl Vega, the paramedic, was in the back with him.

Karl grinned. "We've got a little time. Let me see to the worst of your injuries."

"I'm fine," Danny retorted.

"Dude, you're the opposite of fine," Ryan said.

Danny sat back and closed his eyes as Karl began tending to him. All Danny could think about was what Matt might be doing to Skylar.

No, it wasn't Matt that he worried about. It was the people Matt had hired. Especially since it wasn't Matt who had gone into the liquor store to get Skylar. That meant those men—because there was always more than one—were around waiting to be given orders.

"You ready for this?" Clayton asked Danny.

Danny opened his eye. "You mean am I ready to possibly have to kill someone? Yeah. I've already taken two lives today."

"You didn't have a choice," Ryan said. "They were going to kill you."

It didn't matter. A life was a life, and Danny would have to deal with that. But that was later. This was now. He looked at the road they traveled. His face and body were bruised and battered and his leg hurt like the devil. It was probably broken, but he'd deal with that once Skylar was safe. However, his hands worked fine. His arms, well, that was another matter entirely, but he would ignore the shooting pains that continued up and down his extremities. He hadn't felt anything when he was fighting the two men at the barn. He hadn't felt anything when he ran to the SUV or when he was driving.

It wasn't until the trip back when he was able to relax a little that he was slammed with the pain that made him sick to his stomach.

"There's going to be more ex-military there," Danny warned Clayton and Ryan.

The two exchanged a look before Ryan grinned and said, "I sure hope so. I'm ready to kick some ass, and those bastards seem to especially need it."

"We're going to have to park some ways off," Clayton said.

Danny had already thought of that. "Y'all get out. I'll drive straight to where Skylar is."

Ryan turned around in his seat. "Is that wise?"

"Yeah," Clayton said as he looked at Danny in the rearview mirror.

A few minutes later, Clayton pulled the truck to a stop on the side of the road. Clayton, Ryan, and Karl got out of the truck, and Danny got behind the wheel.

"Good luck," Clayton said.

Danny grinned. "No matter what happens, get to Skylar."

"We've got your back."

The door closed, and Danny drove off. He looked in the rearview mirror and saw the men hurry off the road. Danny had no idea where the others were, but he knew they were surrounding the area. He probably should've waited a few minutes before leaving so they could discuss where everyone was going, but he had only been thinking about Skylar.

The great thing about having the friends he did was that they knew exactly what to do—and he trusted that they would do it.

Suddenly, a ringing came through the speakers. Danny looked at the screen in the dash and saw that a call was coming in. He answered it, not realizing that Clayton had left his phone in the truck.

"It's Cash, Danny," the PI said. "Clayton told me what you were doing, so I thought I'd bring you right up to where Skylar is."

"Thanks."

He gave the PI his location, then followed Cash's directions as he drove toward Skylar.

"I see a van stopped in the middle of a dirt road up ahead."

"That's got to be them," Cash said. "Good luck."

Danny ended the call and slowed the vehicle as he approached the van. He stopped the truck and put it into park just as a man stepped out from the front of the vehicle. There were more, Danny was sure of it. No doubt they were in the trees up ahead, which meant he would have to keep a lookout there. With only one eye working, that wasn't going to be easy.

He turned off the engine and opened the door before palming the handgun next to him. The minute the man saw him, he reached behind him to grab a weapon. Danny lifted his pistol and shot him through the space between the door and the truck.

The man jerked from the impact of the bullet dead center of his chest and fell back. Danny headed straight for the van. He saw it rock from side to side and tried to run, but his leg gave out.

He fell to one knee and heard the ping of a bullet slamming into the side of the van. Danny turned his head in the direction where the shot had come from and saw Ryan appear out of the trees with his rifle aimed. He pulled the trigger just as a man rose up to take another shot at Danny.

Danny got to his feet and pulled open the door of the van. For a moment, he couldn't move as he spotted Skylar slamming the heel of her palm into Matt's nose. Blood spurted everywhere.

"You bitch!" Gaudet shouted and tried to reach for her.

Danny grabbed her arm and gave a tug, but she fought him. "Skylar."

She swung her head around at the sound of her name. The relief on her face made his heart race. She was so intent on him that she never saw Matt reach for her. Danny tried to get her out, but Matt was too quick. He had his arm around Skylar's neck and her back against his chest as he hid behind her.

"Well, sheriff, I didn't expect you to make it out of that barn alive," Matt said. "How did you manage it?"

"You hired idiots."

Matt made a sound at the back of his throat. "We both know that isn't true."

"Let her go, Gaudet," Danny ordered and raised his gun, pointing it at Matt's head. The problem was that he couldn't get a clean shot.

And Matt knew it.

The bastard smiled at Danny. "You won't pull the trigger because you don't want Skylar harmed."

"Do it," she told Danny.

He ignored her, keeping his attention on Matt. "You won't get away from this place."

Matt laughed. "If you think I only brought two other men, you're mistaken."

At that moment, two more shots were fired. Then a pause, and another gunfire exchange on the opposite side of the field. Danny raised his brows. "I'm thinking those men you hired won't be helping you now. In fact, you're surrounded, Matt. You not only violated the restraining order, you kidnapped me and Skylar."

"Technically, I didn't take either of you," Matt retorted.

"You can try to explain all of that to a judge."

Matt shook his head. "That's not going to happen. My family won't let it. Besides, I'm leaving, and Skylar is coming with me."

"I'm not going anywhere," she said and tried to get free.

Matt merely tightened his hold.

Every time Danny shifted to get a better angle to shoot, Matt moved, as well. They were at an impasse, and Matt knew it. Danny couldn't fire his weapon without hitting Skylar in the process.

Finally, he looked at her. She smiled at him and gave him the slightest nod of her head. It was her way of telling him to do what he had to do to end this.

Danny sighted down the barrel of the gun. The bullet would go into Skylar's outer arm. It would hurt like hell, but it would be enough to spin Matt away to give Danny a better shot.

"Lower your weapon, sheriff," Matt said.

Danny did just that to throw Matt off. As soon as Matt smiled, Danny lifted his weapon and fired. The bullet went through the upper part of Skylar's biceps and hit Matt in the neck.

Just as he expected, it caused Matt to spin back, which

let Skylar dive down to the floor of the van. Danny kept
his pistol aimed at Matt even when Matt looked at him.
He didn't have a weapon, so Danny could lower his, but
he didn't take the chance.

Skylar crawled out of the van and straight to Danny.
Only then did he lower his gun and wrap his other arm
around her. He closed his eye and sighed. It felt so good
to have her against him once more.

"I thought you were dead," she whispered.

"Danny!"

The moment he heard his name shouted, he looked
at the van and saw Matt had a gun in his hand. Without
hesitation, Danny fired two shots.

Chapter 35

The pain meds took effect quickly. Even then, Danny didn't stop holding Skylar. Her arm had been seen to by Karl and his partner, Marina, who had driven the ambulance to them.

It wasn't until they were at the hospital that Danny was given treatment. The doctors and nurses kept trying to get him to loosen his hold on Skylar's hand, but he refused to. When they finally finished with him, she crawled into the bed next to him.

"I've never been so scared in my life," she said.

Danny kissed the top of her head. "Me, either. I envisioned all sorts of things happening to you."

"Me?" she said in shock. "I was thinking about you. And look at you. You've got several busted ribs, lacerations all over, and a concussion. And your leg is broken. How the hell were you even walking on it?"

"I had to get to you. I didn't feel anything."

"I realized before all of this that I had fallen in love with you, Danny Oldman. The idea of losing you, of having you taken from me . . . I felt empty."

He forced open his good eye and turned his head to

her. She lifted hers so their eyes met. He smiled then, careful not to split his lip again. "Sweetheart, I've loved you for so long."

"This is forever for me. You understand that, don't you?"

"It's forever for me, too."

She carefully lowered her head back to his chest. "We're going to have a great life."

"There will be ups and downs," he cautioned.

"Yes, there will be because that's life. But we'll have each other."

He took a deep breath, then winced when his ribs rebelled.

"I'll always be here for you," she said. "I'll support you in anything you do."

"Same for me. I'll respect you and love you with everything I have."

He felt her smile against him. "I'll drive you nuts with my neatness, but I'll make it up to you by doting on you."

"I'll most likely drive you nuts with forgetting dates. I'm horrible at remembering birthdays and such, but I'll make it up to you by treating you like the queen you are to me every day of our lives."

Skylar chuckled. "I like the sound of that."

"You realize we just said vows to each other."

"Yes, sheriff, I certainly do. We'll do it again when you aren't so doped up on pain meds."

He grinned because he knew he would never forget this moment for the rest of his life.

"I love you, Skylar."

"I love you, Danny."

Jace spotted Ryan standing outside the door to Danny's hospital room as he walked up. Ryan's lips twisted as he jerked his chin toward the narrow window of the door.

"I don't think we should bother them."

Jace reached him and glanced through the window. He saw Danny and Skylar snuggled together on the bed, talking. "I agree. They should be left alone."

Ryan ran a hand down his face and moved away from the door a step. "I'm glad they're both okay. We could've lost Danny."

"Yeah. I think it was closer than we realize. He hasn't told any of us what happened in that barn."

Ryan briefly raised his brows. "I saw it. I was out there with the mayor and some of Danny's deputies since it was a crime scene. Based on his injuries, he suffered greatly."

Jace glanced at Danny and Skylar again before he too backed away from the door. "It was Skylar that got Danny out of that situation."

"I do believe you're right. I knew love could do great things, but this is a first for me."

Jace grunted as he thought about the entire situation. "Did you need to talk to Danny?"

"Just wanted to let him know that he's been cleared in Matt's death. With all of us as witnesses, along with Skylar's account, the shooting was justified."

"Meaning Danny won't lose his job."

Ryan nodded. "No one in their right mind would run against him next election."

Jace chuckled, nodding. "No, they shouldn't."

"You need him for anything?" Ryan asked.

"Naw. Just coming to check on him, but I can see that should wait."

Ryan was silent for a moment. "Want to get a drink? If I go back home, my sister will be over and try to set me up on another blind date. I'm not in the mood to deal with that."

Jace laughed and nodded. "I'm all for a drink, chief, and definitely agree on the no blind date thing."

"If my sister ever approaches you about setting you up with one of her friends, run," Ryan cautioned as they walked out of the hospital together.

Epilogue

Midnight Christmas morning

"Merry Christmas, baby."

Skylar smiled as Danny's arms came around her to pull her close. She opened her eyes and realized that candles had been lit all over, and the Christmas tree was on in the next room, shedding light into the hall. And in Danny's hands was a small box, wrapped in white paper with a red bow.

She turned over and sat up. "Did you do all of this?"

He couldn't stop grinning. "I thought you were going to wake up, but the wine really puts you out."

"Yeah," she said with a chuckle and held the box in her hands.

She looked up from it and around the room. They had been in the house for a week now, and the first thing they had done was paint the master bedroom a soft dove gray. There were still boxes of her things as well as Danny's to be opened and gone through, but without a doubt, this place was their home.

Even Gray now called it home as he grazed in a pasture behind the house. No doubt he was the first of many horses for them. How she couldn't wait.

"Aren't you going to open it?" Danny urged.

Her head swung to him. His wounds were healing, but they were still a reminder of everything they had nearly lost, and all they had gained together.

She put her hand on his cheek and smiled. "I love you so much."

"I love you too, sweetheart."

Skylar swallowed and pulled the end of the ribbon to loosen the bow. Then she tore off the paper and found a white velvet box in her hand. She opened it to reveal a single orange, pear-shaped diamond in a rose gold band.

"I've lived too much of my life alone and dreaming of you," Danny said. "This is probably entirely too soon, but it's the only thing I can think about. I want you as my wife, Skylar. Will you marry me?"

Tears clouded her vision as she looked up at him. "Yes. Yes!" she repeated and threw her arms around him.

They held each other, basking in the joy of the season and their love.

Also by DONNA GRANT